In the Field

IN THE
FIELD

CLAIRE TACON

For Brianna and Mike,
With much love and
admiration. Thanks so
much for all your support with
writing and other endeavors.

Claire

BIBLIOASIS

Library and Archives Canada Cataloguing in Publication

Tacon, Claire, 1979–
     In the field / Claire Tacon.

ISBN 978-1-926845-26-5

     I. Title.

PS8639.A23162   2011   C813'.6   C2011-903426-3

This is a work of fiction. Names, characters, businesses, organizations, places, events and incidents either are the product of the author's imagination or are used fictitiously. Any resemblance to actual persons, living or dead, events, or locales is entirely coincidental.

 Canada Council   Conseil des Arts   ONTARIO ARTS COUNCIL
for the Arts   du Canada   CONSEIL DES ARTS DE L'ONTARIO

  Canadian   Patrimoine
       Heritage   canadien

Biblioasis acknowledges the ongoing financial support of the Government of Canada through The Canada Council for the Arts, Canadian Heritage, the Canada Book Fund; and the Government of Ontario through the Ontario Arts Council.

PRINTED AND BOUND IN CANADA

for Julio

The character of a soil is profoundly influenced by its parent material. Some primary materials resist change and retain their characteristics, even as particles. Others react with water, oxygen and other minerals to form secondary materials, such as silicate clay. Due to these reactions and the ongoing weathering process, younger soils will reflect more characteristics of the parent material than an older soil.

1

I LEAVE LATE. Twenty blocks in fifteen minutes. At every crossing, I check my watch, worried the lights will be off in the auditorium and I'll make a racket with the pushdoor. It's the last day of school. It's not going to start on time.

There aren't any other parents outside the squat brick Montessori which has been leaching our savings for the past eight years. Watch check. Five minutes. Inside, kids are buzzing through the halls. The little ones are already lined up outside their classrooms, fidgeting with the trimmings on their costumes. Fallen clusters of sequins and tissue paper decorate the vinyl tile. A few older kids are still emptying out their lockers, scooping a year's worth of paper into the recycling bin. Along the corridor, the locker doors hang open, the hall a decimated beehive.

The cafetorium's at the far end of the school. There's a small proscenium stage curtained off at the far wall and the cafeteria tables have been converted into seating, the middle panels tilted up as backrests. I spot Richard right away, his long legs spilling out into the aisle. His trousers ride up his bent knees, showing off matching charcoal socks. The other men are wearing runners or thin cotton socks that droop into their loafers. Even with the humidity, Richard stays crisp as lettuce.

He doesn't rise when I reach him, but lets me struggle to squeeze through the narrow gap between his shins and the bench in front. When I'm halfway across he grabs my waist so I topple against him, onto his lap. That's when he kisses me, playful in a way I haven't seen in ages. I slide into the gap between him and his father.

"Quit terrorizing your wife," Terrence teases, standing to greet me. As soon as we pull apart, he reaches into his breast pocket and pulls out two newspaper clippings. "Ellie, these are for *you*." The emphasis is for Richard's benefit. His father's habit of passing along articles drove him crazy growing up. I find the gesture sweet, like chess by correspondence. One is a cartoon—an archaeologist excavating his teenager's messy room—and the other is a column on the founder of the human genome project.

"After all those years running these things," Terrence says, "I never thought I'd live long enough to see my grandson at one."

"You getting nostalgic?" I ask.

"Ellie, these bones will die happy if they never have to sit on these benches again."

"You want me to sew you a cushion?"

"Good idea. A person could make a fortune hawking them outside."

"Have you seen Stephen yet?" Richard asks.

"No."

"Five dollars the tie didn't make it through the dance." Richard finds my hand and laces his fingers between mine. He glances at his watch but doesn't press me for an explanation.

There's no good excuse for why I'm twenty minutes late to our son's grade eight graduation—except that it was the first day in several months that I had the house entirely to myself. That and yesterday marked the last hurrah of my botched academic career at Guelph University's Land Resource Science Department.

"I've got good news," Richard whispers.

I start to ask but he shakes his head, later.

Earlier in the week, a few of my colleagues threw me a farewell lunch. We ate Thai food out of Styrofoam containers in the student lounge and compared birth stories because one of them is due next month. As the department secretary detailed her episiotomy, I struggled to pick up a water chestnut. Half an hour later, they presented me with a card and a mug full of jelly-beans. The rest of the faculty was too embarrassed to show up.

The lights fade and I catch a glimpse of Richard. He's still smiling, pleased as punch about something. Good, I think, we can use some of that.

The grade ones file out first in a haphazard array of costumes. They're performing a cultural heritage skit that looks like a budget version of *It's a Small World*. Our youngest, Luke, is wearing one of Terrence's old Mas costumes with a feather and sequin headband. He parades out next to a red-headed boy who's mortified in his Scottish Highland getup, an altered uniform from a local catholic school. One by one, the kids step forward and say a few words about where a relative came from. When it's his turn, Luke talks about his grandfather emmigrating from Trinidad. "We have Carnival there," he says. He shows off a few Caribana dance shakes. The adults burst out laughing and Luke blushes, retreating back into the line, next to England and Korea.

"What a ham," Terrence whispers.

The grade two theme is the environment. It's a bit forced when one girl stumbles her way through a mouthful about reducing our personal carbon footprint. It reeks of school propaganda—proof the extra tuition is turning our children into well-rounded socially conscious beings.

Luke joins us at intermission, still in costume, and we shift over so that he can sit next to his grandfather.

"I've got something to show you." Richard reaches into his messenger bag. He holds his fist over Luke's open palms then quickly retracts it.

Luke claps his hands over Richard's, laughing and wrestling for the present inside.

Richard deposits a plum sized rock in our son's hands.

Luke's face scrunches, so exactly like his father when he's perplexed.

"This was sent over from another university today. It might be the oldest rock in the world." Richard is a senior researcher in the geochronology lab at the University of Toronto. I can understand why he's so excited—his work is mostly with mining applications, but the holy grail of geochrono is finding material old enough, unchanged enough, to offer insight into the planet's formation.

Luke raises the rock to eye level, appraising it like an auctioneer with a rare china figurine. For a minute he's completely absorbed by Richard's description of where they found it, how it was formed, how many billions of years old it could be.

Then Luke wants bake sale.

He passes off the rock to me and heads to the PTA tables in the hallway. We trail after our son, ready to slap down a few dollars for cookies. The rock is heavier than it looked, cool to the touch, except on the side where Luke was holding it.

"Are they bringing you in on it?" I ask.

"Early stages. But probably not. Maybe a small mention for the lab or something."

He'll probably be first-author when they publish.

"What was the outlying like?"

"Are you asking flora or fauna?" Richard sucks air through his front teeth, chiding. "Soil scientists are all the same. You're given a monumental geological specimen and all you care about is the dirt above it."

Richard's ribbing me. It's my pet peeve—using the word dirt to describe soil.

"Soil is the building block upon which all life is sustained," I parrot from my Soil 101 lecture notes. "It's a textile factory, recycling depot and construction supply in one."

Our battle for Earth Science supremacy is postponed by our arrival at the baked goods. Our Rice Krispie squares have sold out and I reclaim my glass casserole from the parent volunteer. I feel an irrational surge of pride over this small accomplishment, noting that Kerri Donaldson's chocolate chip cookies have barely been touched. She's the PTA fundraising chair and mother of Sabrina, a girl who is likely perfectly nice, but strikes me as a carbon copy of her mother, fake as Cool Whip. Kerri waves to us, hovering over her own baking.

"Last year for the kids."

"We've still got Luke for another seven."

"Oh, of course," she says, blushing, apologising more than necessary. Kerri's always acted over-friendly around Richard. We think it's because he's black and she doesn't want to seem racist. She's cornered me a few times to tell me how great she thinks it is to have "mixed" kids at the school.

"Any summer plans?"

"Sabrina's going to more camps than I can name." Kerri rhymes them off anyway.

"We're visiting my mother for a week or two in August."

"Maritimes, right? New Brunswick?"

"Nova Scotia, an hour out of Halifax."

There are more parents behind us now, waiting to buy snacks. We lay down a fiver for the cupcake Luke's already eating and a few of Kerri's cookies.

"So is this geriatric rock your good news?" I ask.

Richard ignores the question and bites into the chocolate chip cookie. He grimaces. "Carob."

I pocket it along with the rest, hoping Stephen will be so hungry he won't notice.

They've got all the grade eights sitting on stage for the graduation ceremony, most of them visibly bored. The girls look fifteen years older than the boys, sucked into small, strappy dresses, their eyes thick with eyeliner and clumping mascara.

They can't quite manoeuvre in their high heels. When their names are called, they wobble across the stage like cadets struggling to find their sea legs. In contrast, the boys slouch their way over to the presenters, their sneakers showing under suit trousers. Stephen wanted to wear his runners too. Richard insisted on dress shoes.

After the diplomas are handed out, the principal says a few words and then it's on to the awards. Stephen does well in school, but he gets mostly high Bs and low As, so I doubt he'll get an academic prize. As they roll through the subjects, Kerri's daughter keeps getting called up. The principal, a thin man with hair plastered to his forehead, pretends to be surprised each time he calls out her name. *Sabrina Donaldson.*

"I hope her parents brought a truck," Terrence whispers.

We'd both like our son to excel more in science, considering what we do for a living, but Stephen's more interested in sports. I keep my fingers crossed as they go through the team awards. Stephen's been on almost all of the junior high teams, but he lives and breathes soccer. He'll be disappointed if he doesn't get anything. So far, he's been taking everything in stride, cheering as his friends go up to get their trophies. Even when someone else gets the soccer MVP, his smile doesn't look forced. The last award is the Fair Play Prize, *given to the athlete who has distinguished him or herself in all aspects of the game.*

Richard leans over. "He's got it in the bag."

The kid next to Stephen nudges him with his shoulder and nods to the podium. Stephen shrugs it off, but I can tell he's invested, that he's waiting to hear his name too.

The principal fumbles a little bit with the mic. "Sabrina Donaldson."

It's petty, but none of us clap.

It's a quiet walk over to the roti shop, all of us trying to sidle up to Stephen to tell him he should have won, that the game was fixed, you don't want to peak in grade eight anyway.

"Just wait until next year," Terrence says. "Harbord Collegiate's not going to know what hit it."

Richard's more forthright. "Doesn't change a damn thing that's really important."

He used those exact words when I told him about Guelph.

As soon as we open the door to the roti shop, Batula's voice greets us, a kettle rising to boil. "Look what's dragged in to plague us. Shoo! Go away!" she says, her breasts shaking against the counter as she waves Terrence off. "Them little ones can stay, but that old riff-raff's got to go."

Terrence grips the shirt material around his heart and slumps at the waist, playing wounded. He and Batula both grew up in Port of Spain and they've worked out that their grandmothers were cousins by marriage. Besides that, her daughters all went through high school when Terrence was principal and he's the godfather of one of her grandchildren. If you count all the rotis I had when I was pregnant, then our boys have been eating here since before they were born.

Terrence doesn't usually have much of an accent, but he butters it on with Batula. "I don't see any old riff-raff."

"No, yuh not old," she says, a wicked glimmer in her eye. "You ancient."

"Child, I got to jump over the counter and make my own damn roti?"

"Come out looking like what the dog chewed yesterday."

The other cook hunches over, laughing.

Batula's hand is already behind the counter, pulling out samosas. She hands one to Stephen. "You look like you could use a little sustenance." She grabs one for Luke too, but stops short before giving it to him, doing a double take with his costume. "I see your plan now, you're just going to come down here and break my heart!"

Luke starts showing off his Carnival dance moves again and Batula claps out a beat, saying, "If you whine like dat, trouble sure to ketch yuh . . . somebody woman going to be hornin' she man."

Luke shakes harder, his feathered shoulder pads a few jerks away from detaching. He belts out the chorus from "Booboo Man," imitating Lord Melody's accent from Terrence's old calypso records.

Richard and I stand to the side, odd ones out. With their olive-tan skin and loosely curled molasses hair, the boys look more like their Indo-Trini grandfather than either of us. I'm pale as potato. Richard's closer to obsidian, often gets mistaken for Nigerian. He was adopted as an infant and doesn't know much about his biological parents.

Stephen bumps his hip against his brother's and laughs along with Batula. It's nice to see, because lately he's been embarrassed by his little brother's public displays.

"The usual?" Batula calls out our order to the cooks. "One butter chicken medium, two korma mild, one goat medium."

Stephen leans tentatively against the counter. "Medium for one korma, please."

"Big man going into high school now?" Batula teases, looking over for our approval before changing the order.

"Are you sure?" I ask Stephen.

"I had some of yours last time, remember."

As I recall he had a few bites and then had to get a Coke to wash it down. Tonight I don't feel like being the word of caution. "Sure, one medium spicy korma."

Richard gives our son a high five. "Bascom men have stomachs of steel."

Batula laughs again. She pats her stomach and points at Richard's hint of a potbelly. "Steel on the inside—outside more like korma."

We take the food back to Terrence's, an older condo overlooking Kensington market. Terrence pops open some bottles of Carib and proposes a toast to his grandsons. He, Richard and

I clink glasses and the boys tap their cans of iced tea against each other. They stare at their grandfather, Stephen's hands already on the cutlery, waiting for permission to start. The rule in our family is that no one eats until the oldest person touches their food.

Richard interrupts just as his father reaches for his fork. "There's another matter of business."

Stephen groans. Terrence looks back and forth at us as if he's expecting me to announce another pregnancy.

"Your mother will be teaching in September after all."

"Back at Guelph?"

"No, at U of T with me." My husband hands me an envelope. "It's just a sessional position, but the official word came down today."

Terrence leads a round of congratulations. I'm too stunned to form the obvious questions.

When the applause dies down, Luke turns to me, winning as Oliver Twist. "Is it okay if we eat now please?"

Stephen put him up to it.

Once the food's out, it's a competition to see who can haul the most dough and curry into his mouth in the shortest amount of time.

Richard asks Stephen about the dance.

"Great. I showed off my sweet moves." Sweet is his new ironic word.

"Do you have slow dances at these things?" Terrence asks.

Stephen answers too quickly, no.

"What about with Amanda?" Luke mimes putting his arms around a woman's shoulders and makes squelching kissy noises. In response, Stephen opens his mouth with partially chewed roti.

Better to head this off right away. "How's the medium?"

Stephen rubs his stomach and puts on a Buddha grin. "Now that you're working again, does this mean we can get an Xbox?"

"It's a job. Not a lobotomy."

We've never minded if the boys play video games—as long as it's at friends' houses where we don't have to argue about off switches.

Conversation jumps to the FIFA World Cup and tomorrow's quarter-final between Germany and Argentina. I fade out as Richard, Terrence and Stephen rhyme off player names and debate the odds of either team proceeding. It's gibberish to me—Ricardo Cruz, Podolski, Klose.

It was very touch-and-go as to whether the university could lay me off. The funding shortfall came down in the first semester of my tenure-track appointment and they first asked for volunteers to switch, temporarily, to other departments. Then our chair formed a committee to eliminate two of three recent hires. I'd already slogged five years as a sessional instructor. Between the low pay, long commute and constant comparisons of my career to Richard's, those years were like the protracted birth of a twenty-pound fetus. Now the university administration was back sniffing, asking if I felt like fooling around.

The union grieved but, in the end, the test of "financial exigency" was proved and my contract terminated. Even if I'd agreed to a transfer, they'd cut back in all the areas of my expertise. By the time the situation was resolved, it was too late to put out applications for the fall.

Richard must have pulled strings because I wouldn't be an easy sell—I'm behind on publications and my focus is agricultural applications instead of pure science.

He shouldn't have done it without consulting me. Still, I open the letter, relieved to have a job offer so soon, even just one or two sections of Intro to Soil Science.

The white of the envelope matches the rings where the table's teal paint is chipped. This was Terrence's first piece of furniture in Canada and as its use changed over the years, so did its colour. Since his wife's death, it's remained the same algae green that she picked out.

I skim through the text, then catch on the course code. My husband did pull strings. Three sections of Geology 101.

Richard registers my shocked expression, discreetly shakes his head. This isn't the place.

Luke is going through a phase where he picks out all the peas from his roti and lines them up along the seam of the aluminium tray. Stephen reaches across the table fork-first to stab them, his elbow narrowly missing his drink. Both of them should know better but I don't want to reprimand them again. At least they're learning about symbiosis.

"Was that your friend in the kilt?" Stephen asks, corralling more of Luke's veggie discards. "I bet he was pissed off with his parents."

Terrence crosses his arms, straightens his spine and leans into the table towards his grandsons. In the fifteen years since he's retired, Terrence hasn't been able to shake his principal's repository of gestures guaranteed to put adolescent cheekiness on ice. "There's nothing wrong with a kilt. Next year you could wear the Nova Scotia tartan."

"They wear kilts there?"

Terrence explains the origin of the province's name.

Richard allows his father the didactic segue but it still cracks him up. "Never saw anyone in kilts when we went out. Ripped jeans and trucker hats, plenty."

Stephen leans back in his chair, snickering as I glower.

"Come on, Ellie, you told me half the people you grew up with were hicks."

"Some kids did Highland dancing."

"Did you?"

"No."

"Case closed."

"Did you ever dance in Carnival?"

"What's your point?"

I shouldn't be so riled up. When we first got together, I used to entertain Richard with all the half-brained antics my friends got up to—barrelling down gravel roads then jacking the wheel and jerking the emergency brake to spin donuts, bashing in the pumpkin heads of the Kentville scarecrow displays at Halloween, hiding under blankets in the back of pickup trucks so the cops wouldn't pull us over on the highway.

"Did I ever tell you that I went to Halifax on a teacher's conference? Beautiful province."

"Thank you, Terrence."

"I'm sorry I called you a hick." Richard wraps his fingers around mine. "But when we first started dating you were still drinking instant coffee with creamer." He starts laughing again, so hard he has to pull his hand back and cover his stomach.

I'm fuming now, but it's the boys' night so I don't let it show. "How's the spice?"

Stephen burps and grins, sniffing the air in mock disgust.

By the time the boys are in bed, I'm pretty wound up. I strip next to the hamper, sliding my socks off with my big toe, then collapsing on the bed in my bra and underwear—an old pair from a Costco bulk purchase with sagging elastic. The only good thing about job hunting is that I'll need new clothes.

Richard takes off his shirt and smells the armpits, evaluating whether he can wear it again. "Well?"

"It's rocks for jocks."

He's down to his boxers now. Richard's still got the muscular frame that he had when we met, but he's stopped running and swimming in the past five years. The skin over top has gotten looser, like he's very slowly starting to melt. "It's a foot in the door."

"It's a dead end."

He joins me on the bed and nudges me into him so my head rests on the pad of his chest. Richard is 6'1" and I'm 5'2", so when I lie like this, my feet only touch his ankles. When we first got together, we measured my entire body against his arm-span. My head and heels met the bends of his elbows.

We joked that we should have been ice skating pairs.

"Don't you think it'd be fun to be back on the same campus?"

"When you were my age, you'd had tenure for two years." I slide on top of him and prop myself up on my elbow so we can make eye contact.

"I thought you'd be happy about this. If it's not what you want...."

I bite my lip and consider not mentioning it, but then I do. "I keep wondering if I'd applied to that job at Western." It was five years ago, long past the statute of limitations on marital complaints. Luke was so young. We decided it wasn't feasible.

"You didn't even like the hour commute."

I know, I know.

At thirty-nine, I don't have time to pour four more years into adjunct work, especially in a different field. "It's been twenty years since I set foot in a geology classroom. When am I going to apply for jobs if I'm stuck doing prep?"

"I've probably got a syllabus and lecture notes."

"I'm not asking for a cheat sheet."

I push over to my side of the bed and grab my Sudoku book from the nightstand. Richard waits a few moments to see if I'll start the discussion again then retrieves the new issue of *Discover* from the stack of magazines on the floor. I scratch a few numbers into the boxes but can't concentrate. After ten minutes I realize that I've made an error somewhere and toss the book back in the drawer in frustration. The cover catches the side and falls to the floor. I bang the drawer back in place.

Richard keeps reading.

I feel foolish for throwing a tantrum.

He glances over out of the corner of his eye. "Are we friends again?"

"Yes."

"Good, because I need you to take a look at this." He's got an ingrown hair on his back hip that the waistband of his boxers has been irritating. It's inflamed with a yellow head, the swelling about the size of a pencil eraser. He reaches around to scratch it, but I hold his hand back.

"Hold on." I grab the peroxide and a Q-Tip from the bathroom, along with a hot facecloth. It drains easily, and the hair springs out as the disinfectant bubbles over the wound. "Surgery complete."

"This wasn't meant to start a fight."

"It's been a long week."

"All I'm asking is that you think about it." Richard turns out the light and we settle in under the sheets. As we're cuddling, Richard gets an erection, just from the proximity. We kiss for a bit, and he pulls me in tight against him.

"What time do you have to get up tomorrow?"

"Six-thirty. If you want to sleep in, go ahead."

"No, I should file my Guelph stuff, maybe put out some feelers."

He brushes his lips against my earlobe. "I'll see if I can steal you some chocolate croissants from the breakfast meeting."

I laugh and push myself back on top of him.

"What are you trying to do to me?" he asks, running his hands down my sides and squeezing my ass.

We both turn, as if on cue, to the alarm clock, with its bleating red LED numbers. 11:12.

"Better not," he says and I slide off. "Maybe tomorrow night after we drop the boys off?"

We kiss a bit more but without any fervour. It's been this way a lot since Luke was born. My period came almost a week late last month but I knew there was no possibility that I could be pregnant.

In the end, I masturbate quietly, trying not to wake Richard with the shaking.

Around three in the morning, Stephen knocks on our door. The spice has given him a stomach ache. He still shares a room with Luke so I find some TUMs for him and we go downstairs to wait for it to pass. He puts on an old Disney movie that he used to like and sprawls across my lap so I can rub his belly to get the gas moving.

His face and arms are already tanned from soccer and against his paler belly they look like the two parts of an acorn. As I massage his stomach I can feel how his shape's changed this year, how he's starting to build muscles on his skinny frame. Before, he was getting older in regular, manageable increments. Now, it's only at moments like these that he still seems like a little kid. Sometimes I want to prop him in front of a camera like a plant in the hands of a time-lapse photographer just to see if I can capture the transformation.

Next fall will be new beginnings for both of us. For him, it's high school, it's progress—another move towards a natural conclusion. I find it hard to imagine myself just down the road from his classroom, clicking through a PowerPoint presentation for a few hundred first year geology students. I don't know whether to be furious with Richard or grateful.

My husband is one of the only professors who is at the university Monday to Friday, eight-thirty to five-fifteen. When he's not in class, he's consulting with grad students, applying for grants, serving on one committee or another. He's brought in more money over the past decade than three of the other professors combined. He's also chaired the department for two of those years and served as graduate advisor for an additional four.

I find myself falling well short of Richard's pace. I've always considered myself a hard worker, but by the end of the day I'm beat. Not by the teaching but by the drudgery of admin duties—the interminable departmental meetings about scheduling, the number of forms required to requisition a handful of stationery, the ceaseless stream of email from the listserv.

In our early years together, Richard talked a lot about the pressures of growing up black in a white city. Added to the

grab bag of racism at school, there was the separate negotia-
tion of being adopted into an extended Indo-Trinidadian
family. Back in T&T, most of his relatives had had serious mis-
givings about anyone who looked like him. Everywhere he
went outside of his immediate family was a racial minefield.
A lot of people crumble under those circumstances, but to
Richard it was a thrown gauntlet to not only equal but excel.

We used to dream that we'd be some kind of research power
couple. We'd lie in bed, post-coital, and map out our joint
domination of the field—he'd develop environmentally sound
methods for mineral extraction and I'd spread the gospel of
agroecology. In the past fifteen years, I've struggled to keep
up my end of the bargain. It's not hard to read the sessional
appointment as Richard tipping his hand. It drives me crazy
that he thinks I need some kind of leg-up.

Richard leaves for campus at seven thirty in the morning when
I'm still exhausted from being up with Stephen. There's no time
for discussion. What there is is plenty of time during the day
for me to stew, especially after dropping the boys off for their
sleepovers. By three, pretty much everything is pissing me off—
the smudges on the stairwell walls that we've been meaning to
paint over for years, the three-day old dishes that Stephen still
hasn't loaded into the washer, the drink rings on the coffee
table from Richard's scotch glass.

He gets in at half-past four, earlier than I expect. Like yesterday, he's ebullient. As soon as he's in the door, he wraps his
hands around my waist and tries to work his hands down into
my jean pockets, like a teenager at a dance. I wriggle away after
the compulsory peck.

If this were any other weekend that we found ourselves
without the offspring for the evening, we'd open a bottle of
red, maybe fool around, then watch a movie in our underwear.
Richard's already primed for this outcome. He drops his work
things by the newel post and picks out a bottle from the rack in

the hall closet. I swoop in to whisk the pile away to the upstairs office.

He waves me off the mission, *leave them.*

"I just tidied."

He raises an eyebrow but lets it slide. He brings over two of our nice goblets and pours almost to the lip. He motions for me to sit down then fishes around in his briefcase, almost spilling his wine over the papers he extracts.

It's the contract.

"Cheers." He holds his glass up, his eyes all expectation. He's sincere, so sincere that I second-guess my bristling.

I lick Shiraz off my lips and try to make the question sound casual. "So why did you keep all this a secret?"

"Are you upset that I did?"

"A little."

He settles into the loveseat and tells me that he's not the only one excited to have me in the department. "I ran into Leila and she's looking forward to catching up."

I haven't seen Leila Johnston since I stopped going to Richard's departmental Christmas parties. She's married to the Dean of Arts. When we first met she gave me a limp handshake and said, "You're the one at Guelph, no?" Her face pinched in a condescending smile, as though she could still smell the manure on my shoes.

"You're not excited at all are you?"

"I wanted time to think things through."

"You don't want to be out of the game."

Am I supposed to bring my catcher's mitt?

"Do you want me to put out feelers for a spousal appointment?" There it is again. The leg-up. He looks over at me the way he does with Luke when he's on his last attempt to placate.

"I'm not looking for a hand-out." I testily retreat to the kitchen. The pots clank satisfyingly against the wire tines as I load them into the dishwasher. *If I hadn't taken those years off with the boys.* It's easy to draft a laundry list of complaints—the commute, being stuck in Toronto because Richard has tenure, years of being the fallback when Richard's meetings run late. Reaching down, I misjudge the distance and knock one plate against another, nearly breaking it.

Richard strolls in and hands me his wine glass as I'm filling the detergent compartment.

"It's crystal. We wash it by hand."

He winces, exaggerating the recoil from my snap.

I hold out my hand to take the stem.

"Don't worry, I'll do it." Richard slouches against the countertop and reaches over to stroke my arm. "You're a better teacher than Steeves. It's not your fault there was a major funding shortfall."

The mention of his name starts me boiling. Steeves was the one recent hire who wasn't laid off. His end-of-year evaluations were the lowest in the department but he's developing software to analyse GM crop yields, which means he's fist-deep in industry pockets.

"But if you're serious about tenure," Richard continues, "don't kid yourself about reconsidering your research."

"What's that supposed to mean?"

"There are projects you tackle before you get tenure and some you save for after. There's no money in shit on a field." Richard tries to win me over with my own joke. I've spent the past two years examining which method of applying poultry manure results in optimum nitrogen fixation. "Take the courses. It'll buy you time to think."

I jerk the dishwasher lock and the machine lurches into action. Perhaps Richard could give me an itemized list of projects to tackle in the geology department while I'm sharing an office and teaching frosh. "You had no right to apply for them without asking me."

Richard cows his head and rubs the vein of salt and pepper around his crown. "My intentions were benign. You needed a job. The position came up."

"Do they know you didn't ask me?"

"I didn't think it would play out this way. Trust me, I'm sorry."

My back is pressed against the cabinetry with the same kinetic expectation as a swimmer on the blocks, every muscle primed to lunge. It's not that I don't trust the apology—it's a bona fide concession. It's the rationale for his secrecy that's cutting. Either he didn't want to get my hopes up because he wasn't convinced they'd give me the sections or he knew I wouldn't apply but thought it was the best offer I'd get. "I could have had a lot more options if you'd been willing to move."

"Where?"

"Halifax."

He waves away the suggestion. "What about the boys?"

"Toronto isn't the only school district in the country. I went to a rural school. I got a PhD."

"Along with how many of your classmates?" Richard's knuckles clench the lip of the countertop then suddenly release, his hands falling limply to his thighs. "You'll have two weeks this summer to convince me that Canning is a sophisticated metropolitan area."

"Whenever something comes up with your work—"

"Don't break out the women's lib." Richard's speech gets quieter as his fury mounts, the words super-articulated but barely audible—a signal to wake the fuck up and pay attention. "I'm not some chauvinist asshole."

"You make me feel like a failure."

"I'm not going to apologize to make you feel better. I've worked too damn hard for that."

I stalk down to the basement and get busy organizing the remains of my Guelph office. There's an entire box full of soil— twenty-four varieties collected in yoghurt containers, each identified by strips of punch label. *Silty Clay Loam, Humic Podzol, Grey Luvisol.* I shove them into the crawl space among the seventy-eight others I've accumulated, next to the boxes of old dishes, baby clothes and diplomas—things our family has outgrown but failed to shed.

Richard's kidding himself if he thinks he can finish the basement this summer with so much junk down here. I cull a garbage bag full of paper recycling from some of my older Guelph files—assignments that never got picked up, departmental memos. Some are over four years old and I don't know why I kept them in the first place. The growl of the shredder filters out the television sounds from upstairs. Richard's watching some crappy talent search. After an hour, I've got two bags ready for Goodwill and another pile of shredding. It hasn't made a dent. Cleaning this place out could take the whole summer.

The last thing I want is for September to arrive and still have no direction. Between making Luke's costume, taking Stephen shopping for dress pants and the usual errands, the past week was completely eaten up. If things stay the way they are, any chance for reflection's going to be strangled by the minutiae of our life.

Financially, the only option would be for me to drive out early to Nova Scotia. It's not my first choice, but a few weeks hunkered down at my mother's would at least give me time to think. Besides, it would be nice to have some time with her. We haven't been alone in a room together since Stephen was born.

Let Richard cope on his own with the boys.

The TV shuts off upstairs. A few moments later, my husband's seated on the top step, the kitchen light glowing around his silhouette. He drums out a weak percussion on his knees, waiting for me to stop.

"Just for the record, I don't think you're a failure."

It's enough to start the tears. I angle myself away from him, blinking.

He ducks as he comes down, almost grazing the support beams with the top of his head. He doesn't try to hold me, just grabs the bags I've filled and carries them upstairs.

I find him at the kitchen table with the crossword and a scotch.

"I was thinking about going out to Nova Scotia early."

"Ellie, I don't want us to keep fighting."

"I need to clear my head."

He collects his pen and paper, downing the last of his drink. "Bed."

"I'll be up in a minute."

"Take your time."

When I slip under the sheets, I think he's asleep but he twists over to spoon.

"I'm sorry." Richard props his head up on one arm and turns me around so that we're facing. He caresses the small of my back as he repeats his apology. "You really don't want to take them?"

"Let's not bring it up again."

"Would it really be so terrible if you never got tenure? Some people build perfectly respectable careers as permanent part-time. We can make do financially."

"Permanent part-time? You wouldn't settle for that."

"If I had to."

"No research lab, no grad students to churn out publications, no senior level courses?"

This is his embarrassment talking. Fifteen years in the department building his reputation and now he's mortified to admit he didn't ask me.

I'm cross-legged now, feeling ridiculous fighting in my underwear and sports bra. It's too damn hot in our house for pajamas. We've been saving for forced air but it's out of our means. Another reason why permanent part-time isn't going to cut it. "What do you think about me going to my mother's?"

"When?"

"Mid-July."

"After my Banff conference?"

"When do you get back?"

"The sixteenth, but then I have the BBC article due."

"Stephen can look after Luke. Or you can ask your father."

"He already does enough child care."

"Can you postpone the article?" I know his response as soon as I ask. Richard's been working for years to get an article in a popular science magazine. For one thing, geo-chronology doesn't generate a lot of mainstream interest and for another, he's more comfortable writing for an academic audience. *BBC Science* is a big deal. "Fine, I'll take the kids with me."

"Stephen won't like it. He's got soccer."

"Then they can stay here."

Richard's frustration translates on his face as a thatch of lines in the corners of his eyes. "Maybe it will be good for your mother to have more time with them."

We both huff off to separate edges of the bed. I shift through sleeping positions, vigorous as a yoga instructor. Mostly I want to provoke him so we can finally get through the argument and make up. We never fight for more than a few hours before sitting down and figuring things out. All it would take is him agreeing to give up the courses, maybe give me the place to myself for a weekend. I'd rather spend the bulk of the summer here with him and our sons. By quarter past one, he's already snoring. It kills me that he can sleep.

I sigh, loudly enough to startle him awake. He flails over, fleetingly concerned.

"I'd like to leave next week."

He slides his hand under his pillow and curls away from me. "Is this your way of sending me to my room for misbehaving?"

2

*R*ICHARD STANDS in front of the pantry, surrounded by an outer ring of cereal boxes and an inner oval of cranberry cocktail Tetra Paks. When it was just the two of us, the kitchen was enormous. Now we're running out of storage. Every time we open a cupboard door, the shelves threaten to spill their produce over the tile floor. It annoys Richard to no end that he has to empty the whole shelf to find his brand of cereal.

"Maybe when you're away I'll finally put a rolling basket in here."

He brandishes the box of wheat squares in the air.

I don't know what to make of his nonchalance.

Richard carefully steps over the cardboard fortress and serves up his breakfast on the island. He eats standing, flanked by stools. "You should get the car serviced."

"I'll drop it off before I pick up the boys."

"Are you going to take it to our guy?"

"Canadian Tire."

"I'd feel better if you waited for an appointment at the dealership." Richard doesn't trust anything walk-in.

"We're just checking the blood pressure, not doing a full physical."

When I was seven, my father told me that God put dealerships on this earth for the sole purpose of gouging suckers. You either work on your car yourself, or you make friends with a mechanic.

"If they can sneak it in over the weekend, fine."

"Are you planning to leave this week?"

I run my finger along a gouge in the butcher block. "I was thinking Tuesday."

"Fine," Richard says, pulverizing the wheat pellet into the milk. "It'll give me a chance to polish my conference paper."

My mother retired from the Grocery Co-op last year when she turned sixty-two so I don't have to worry about her getting the time off. It's ten when I call, her time, but she sounds distracted, like she just woke up. She's never been natural on the phone. When I first moved to Toronto, the long distance rates were so exorbitant that she'd set her oven timer before each call and hang up exactly fifteen minutes later.

"I was thinking of bringing out the boys a bit earlier."

"Let me get the calendar." My mother shuffles off before I can tell her how soon I was hoping to arrive. The phone clacks down on the counter and I can hear a radio in the background. The volume is up high—a woman is talking to a man with a cracked voice, giving him the licence plate of a car that's on the shoulder of Highway 101, by the Greenwich exit. My mother's listening to her police scanner again.

"Okay," she says, loudly flipping through the pages. "When were you thinking?"

"Wednesday or Thursday."

"This week?"

"Richard's away in Alberta the week after. I thought it would be nice for the boys and me to have a longer visit with you."

"It's awfully sudden." She takes a minute before continuing. "Is there a way you can get here from the airport?"

My mother's hated the 101, the asphalt tendon that connects the Valley to Halifax, her whole adult life. She's part of a
large percentage of the population that's convinced it's a death
trap because it isn't completely divided. It's true that there are
a lot of accidents on certain stretches, but it's a cakewalk after
rush hour on the 401.

"We're driving from Ontario."

"What do the boys eat these days?"

"Don't worry about that, we'll go shopping once we're out
there."

"They're reporting a break-in in New Minas," she says
breathily, as though she doesn't want the neighbours to hear.
"Can you call back?"

"I'll call you from the road when we reach Amherst."

"You always call on Sundays."

Sunday's eleven-thirty phone call is our family's most awkward weekly event. A rehashing of the week's activities inter-
spersed with banal news items—grocery store specials, weather
forecasts, updates on the backyard garden. The boys line up for
a quick hello, and answer a question or two about school.
Richard makes an appearance and then it's a final goodbye from
me. I'm hoping it will be easier for the boys after they get to
know her better over the summer.

"Do you want us to bring you anything?"

"What's that?" The volume's gone up on the scanner and
she's lost to the developing police crisis.

I tell her I'm looking forward to seeing her.

She's already hung up.

We hit the big box stores on the way home from the boys' sleep-
overs. It's such a rare event that Stephen's already excited when
I park in front of Future Shop. It'll be a twenty-plus-hour drive
to Nova Scotia. Without Richard, I'm going to need all the electronic help I can muster.

The boys tear off and I catch up with them at a display of handhelds. Luke's standing next to his brother, waiting for his turn with the demo unit. He's not quite tall enough to see the screen in Stephen's hands and soon abandons his post to crouch in front of the games vitrine.

My eldest is completely absorbed, stabbing the console with a stylus in time to a cheesy '70s song. This is the point of the game.

"How much is it?"

Stephen hits pause. "For real?"

"Can your brother play it too?"

Sensing victory, Stephen hands his brother the game. It's a move so calculatingly generous that even Luke hesitates before accepting. They look up at me in a pantomime of longing. At least it's not a puppy.

"You both did very well at school."

The nearest employee, kid in his late teens, slouches over and unlocks the storage compartment. He explains that we're going to want the Rumble Pak add-on that makes the controller shake whenever there's a crash. Stephen nods his head vigorously. There's a sale on that shaves off the taxes, which is a small mercy. A quick swipe of plastic and we're down five hundred dollars but are two systems, four games and a Rumble Pak richer.

I make the announcement after the boys are buckled into the backseat. "Your father and I have decided that the three of us are going to drive out early to see your grandmother."

"I thought we were already going there on vacation." Stephen wedges his knees against the front seat. "Is this because Dad called you a hick?"

"No."

"Is he coming too?"

"Not until after his conference."

Stephen refuses to make eye contact. "I can't go, I've got soccer."

"Nova Scotia is the soccer capital of Atlantic Canada."
There's a big sign to this effect at the highway exit ramp. Stephen
isn't biting.

"Nova Scotia is boring."

"You had a great time last visit."

"I was Luke's age then. I mean, I used to like the baby coaster
at Wonderland. Then I grew up."

Luke strains against the seatbelt to shove his brother. "I'm
not a baby."

"I didn't call you a baby. I said it was a baby coaster." Stephen
shoves back. "Don't be a baby."

"I can walk right back in there and return the games."

In the five minutes we've been sitting in the car it's gotten
uncomfortably hot. Stephen leans his head against the window, sulking. I consider lowering the power window to tease
him but decide not to push it. Instead, I distractedly reverse
out of the parking spot, narrowly missing the adjacent vehicle's
bumper.

At home, we're greeted by the burnt smell of microwaved popcorn and staccato outbursts in a Welsh accent. Richard and Terrence are in the living room watching the soccer game. They're
both perched on the lip of the couch, disputing a call along with
the commentator. Stephen marches straight over and informs
his father that he wants to stay put. Richard tries to shift Stephen
to the side so that he can still see the screen. Stephen doesn't
budge. Luke hovers close to me, sensing tension. I don't want to
fight in front of Terrence and the kids.

"I'm teaching, buddy. No one would be around to take care
of you."

"I'm old enough to be left alone. Legally, I'm old enough."
The problem with a Montessori education is that it encour-
ages debate. We don't always feel like running our family like a
democracy.

"Your mother and I have decided."

I give Richard credit for toeing the line.

"I'm finally on a good team and this is what you do?"

"This isn't a punishment, Stephen," I say.

He and Richard both jerk their heads to face me.

"Why can't I stay with Grampy?"

Terrence makes room for Stephen on the couch. "Of course you can stay with me." He wraps his arm around his grandson and Stephen gives into the physical affection in a way he won't with me anymore. "But I get to see you all the time. I've got to spread you around a bit. How long's it been since you've seen your grandmother?"

Stephen slumps in resignation.

Luke asks if he can go play his games now. Richard raises his eyebrows as I hand over the electronics bag. I disappear into the kitchen on the pretence of grabbing some nacho chips.

Richard follows me and pours salsa into a bowl, smirking. "I never thought you'd go in for bribes."

"What did your father say?"

"He thinks you've had a rough time of it this past year and it will be good to have some perspective."

"Do you agree with him?"

"I want to know how much that plastic bag cost." His laugh has an edge to it. It's not hard to hear the kernel of rebuke.

Too quickly, it's Tuesday morning. We leave after the commuter rush and by then a thin drizzle has spread across the city. It's early but the day already feels stale and vaguely disappointing. The humidity makes the car interior sticky before we even get going. There's none of the excitement of an expedition that should be accompanying a trip halfway across the country.

Richard sees us off in the driveway. There's a false calm between us, even though we still haven't discussed the argument. We've made the tacit decision to set the fight aside, like gristle in a cloth napkin, something unpleasant to be dealt with later. Now that the shock of the fight's ebbed, compassion's setting in.

It's going to be a difficult conversation with Prescott and I wish there was a way to spare Richard the awkwardness.

Whatever this is, it's not worth parting in anger. I pull Richard in for a full kiss, press all my limbs against him. When we drift apart, he scans my face, trying to divine what this means. It's not a blank slate. It's the remnants of a fear that settled in when I lost my father at twelve. Losing my father so young imprinted in me the threat that what you love can be snatched away in an instant.

"I know you," my husband finally says. "A week out there and you'll go stir-crazy."

New Brunswick is a ten-hour corridor of trees and blacktop. By the time we reach the Nova Scotia border, Stephen's so bored, he's even participating in Luke's spot-the-licence game. We briefly try singing *Down by the Bay* but it quickly devolves into rhymes with "dumb-ass." Luke cracks up each time Stephen belts one out: crumb-ass, thumb-ass, gum-ass, dumb-bum-mum-ass.

Even if the boys aren't, I'm starting to get excited about the summer's possibilities. It's been over five years since I've been back and almost two decades since I've spent any amount of time here. I'm looking forward to showing the boys my old haunts.

The sun is setting as we drive through Windsor and muscle memory twists my neck towards the ocean at the right juncture to catch the mudflats. Tide's out and it's a sliver of coastline that whizzes past. Only forty minutes until home.

Once, on a tour of his school's music room, Terrence picked up a violin and played it next to a cello. As he sounded the E string, the A on the cello vibrated because they share an overtone. It's why people fall in love, he said, because even though one is a violin and the other is a cello they sense their sameness.

This demonstration of sympathetic resonance came early on in my marriage, when I wasn't sure if Terrence minded that his son had married a white woman. I took it as confirmation that it didn't bother him, just as it hadn't mattered to him and Evelyn that they'd adopted a son with African features, even though it shocked their Indo-Caribbean family back in Trinidad.

Tonight, Terrence's words play in my head again as I strain to catch a last glimpse of the water. Something about seeing the carved channels of slick red clay gets me humming.

I get off the highway early to drive through Grand Pré and down the Wolfville main drag. It's a Tuesday night and the street's dead. I half-expected there'd be a line by the Pulpit, Wolfville's notorious off-campus bar, but the place doesn't look open. Only a handful of students stroll along the sidewalk towards Traders Restaurant. I don't recognize a lot of the stores along Main Street, even from the last time we were here. Everything's quainter, as if Wolfville's polishing itself into the kind of boutique small town that sells to weekend urbanites. Thankfully, the facelift hasn't yet spawned signs with extraneous lettering like "shoppe" and "olde."

Canning is still the same. You could shoot a corset drama here and only need to edit out the power lines.

It's well dark when I pull into my mother's drive. I let the boys sleep for a few more minutes, and look at the house, a lone light on in the kitchen. Nothing's really changed since my father's death almost thirty years ago. My mother's repainted the house, but always in the same robin's egg blue Dad chose. I think about what's waiting inside—the mismatched furniture and crocheted throw pillows that my mother collected in the seventies, that she's kept looking new with meticulous cleaning. The hideous olive and mustard backsplash that Dad laid behind the stove using a box of tiles he found at the dump. I was nervous bringing Richard out here the first time, having him see where I grew up. It felt like showing up to a tapas party with mini-donuts. This time, I worry it's Stephen who'll think the place is corny.

I hoist Luke onto my hip and Stephen groggily follows behind. My mother's left the place unlocked. There's only the one lamp on and it's hard to see our way around. I find her dozing in the armchair, a word-search book in her lap. She's wearing the sheep-print flannelette housecoat that the boys gave her a few years ago. The fabric pools around her hips. We must have misjudged the size.

It takes her a minute to get her bearings. "You're here."

"I didn't think we'd get in so late."

I motion for Stephen. He stands in front of his grand-mother, unsure of what to do. She gets up to give him a proper hug. "Look at how big you are. I thought you were Richard at first."

Luke's still asleep.

"It's fine, we can visit in the morning."

I almost trip on something on the stairs, but regain my balance. I undress Luke down to his briefs and T-shirt and tuck him in.

Stephen wants to know if he has to brush his teeth.

"Don't bother. Do you want to call your father?"

Stephen flops on the bed.

"I'll let him know we got in."

My old room is a time capsule from 1979. It bears all the marks of my life before and after the death of my father. He painted the floorboards brown, even though the wood underneath would have been a nicer neutral. He also chose the massive circular rug under the bed—bid on it at a church rummage sale. It looks like a fabric mosquito coil, green and brown tubes twisted round and round. The sheets on the bed, however, were bought when I was in grade nine—pale beige with sprays of yellow flowers and curlicue green stems—my widowed mother's taste.

The twin-sized bed has a crocheted ladybug blanket over the comforter. Whenever Richard's come out before, we've put the boys in this room and slept on a double futon in the spare room. Once, Stephen had fallen asleep on our bed and it was so late that we decided to share the single bed instead of disturbing him. We were younger then and it was an adventure, hanging onto each other so we wouldn't fall off in the night. I wonder if that's how it would be if Richard were here now, if we'd have any contact that giddy.

I open the drawer of the nightstand and pull out an old paperback from university. On the flyleaf I've written my name, the residence address and course number. I may as well have been going off to summer camp and ironed my name into my underwear. There's a dormer window on the East side, facing out to Dad's old tool shed. In the last summer before university, I used to open the window and straddle the sill to smoke up, a towel under the door so my mother wouldn't catch me. As I work my toes through the blanket's crochet holes, I can summon the twin feelings of expectation and suffocation that I felt living here. I guess I've gotten as far away as I can, living downtown, teaching at Guelph, instead of working at the Co-op grocery like my mother or the Michelin plant like Dad.

There's lots I remember about my father—his mannerisms, how much fun he was to tag along with, the way he'd whistle himself out of a bad mood, even his swears. What I can't do is reliably picture his face. Sometimes it happens in dreams or when a memory flashes, but it's nothing that will hold still and let me examine it.

Back in Toronto, I've got two framed photos of him. The first is from a beach bonfire and he's got an arm around a string bikini version of my mother, a can of beer in his other hand. The second is Dad holding me as a baby—I'm bundled into his coveralls and he's looking straight into the camera. That's the picture that comes to mind the most, even though I could have no real memory of it. It terrifies me, this idea that my own memories of my father have already been lost, rerecorded like VHS—the memories paved over by photographic artefacts.

In the morning, I see why I tripped on the stairs—my mother's been using them as a filing cabinet, storing mail, newspapers and flyers on alternating steps. The bottoms of the stacks already tea-dyed.

My mother's hunched over the stove, slicing a quarter cup of butter into a cast iron skillet big enough to brain a bear. To her side, the pancake batter waits in an oversized measuring cup with a chipped spout. It's a benchmark scene from my childhood, replayed every Christmas, birthday, first day of school. As steady an indicator of our family's progress as my height charted against the door frame.

She's still in the housecoat from yesterday, the too-long sleeves hanging dangerously close to the burner.

"You going to come say hello?"

She sweeps the butter across the heat as I hug her. An unwieldy sideways embrace, her shoulder aligned to my sternum.

"Did you sleep?"

The grease has splattered over the backsplash so I grab a J-cloth from the sink. When I reach for the faucet, I find it's filthy. Along the basin, the caulking's gone black with mildew and there's a thick, furry smudge between the sink and the wall. Bits of dried food pock the countertop.

I should have given her more notice.

"Can I make you some coffee?" I ask.

"I'm cutting back," she says. "Makes my heart race too much." Last time we were here she couldn't start her day without two full mugs. "There's some orange juice in the fridge. I got cranberry cocktail for the boys. Do they still like that?"

I grab three glasses from the cupboard. There are still lip stains on one and I discreetly wipe the rim with the hem of my shirt.

"Did you go to bingo on Monday?"

"Haven't been in years." It's hard to make out her words because she's facing the stove, which is against the other wall, in between the door and window. Most kitchens work the stove into the cabinetry but Dad didn't want to pay for a fume hood. "It's like your father always said, if all the little old ladies who play the lotto every week just saved their money...."

"I thought bingo was more of a social thing."

"Hand me a plate." The stack of pancakes has grown too high for the one she has in the oven. I retrieve a plate from the cupboard, willing myself to not look. She deposits the pancake and motions for me to open the oven door.

There's an old linoleum table at the far end of the kitchen and I give it a wipe before grabbing placemats from the hutch drawer. Mercifully, the placemats are all clean and the cutlery looks fine. I polish the forks with a tea towel anyway.

When I'm fetching the napkins, however, I find mouse turds in the back of the drawer. There's a small hole in the back panel, no bigger than a quarter, scratch marks around the edges.

"Have a seat, Ellie."

"I'll just set the table."

"Don't think I don't know what you're up to."

Upstairs, someone flushes the toilet. Stephen comes down a few minutes later and my mother wraps him up in a big hug before he's even in the kitchen. "You're so big. Ellie, he's so big. What do they feed you in Ontario?"

Stephen tries his best to not squirm away, unsure how to respond. He's only met his grandmother a handful of times.

"I miss you boys so much."

I answer for him. "We miss you too."

My mother scoots Stephen into a chair and fusses pouring his juice. "I've saved the last of the batter for our special pancakes." The bubble in her voice flattens at the end as she appraises this grown version of her grandson. "Maybe you're too old for them."

He shakes his head politely, encouraging her as she pours three blobs to form a decapitated Mickey Mouse.

. "Is Luke up too?"

Stephen checks that his grandmother's back is turned and points upstairs, mouths *wet the bed*. I blink out my understanding. He mimes projectile vomiting.

Luke is naked from the waist down, his bum on the very edge of the double bed. He's been rubbing his eyes but isn't crying anymore, thanks to Stephen. As much as he teases his younger brother, he can also be very tender with him.

It doesn't take long to clean up, but in the brief time it takes to shower Luke, I can see that the bathroom's in worse shape than the kitchen. The ceiling paint has buckled and started to shed onto the floor. When Luke pulls the toilet seat up to pee, the underside is flecked with splotches of dried urine. There are spots of mould in the bowl itself and a layer of dust on the visible toiletries. It's nothing that would be amiss in a college dorm, but completely out of character for a woman who once kept our under-sink cupboards clean enough for surgery.

I curb my impulse to explore further because Luke's nervous enough already. He hasn't seen his grandmother since he was two, after which she's only existed for him as a disembodied voice on our weekly phone calls and as a signature on cards and presents.

Downstairs, Stephen's steadily chewing his way through the juvenile pancakes. My mother's busying herself over the stove, just as unsure of what to say.

"Another giant," she says as soon as she sees Luke.

He doesn't move from my side.

My mother crouches down. "Knee-high to a grasshopper you were, last time I saw you. Now you're almost as big as your brother."

Luke loves that.

"Do you remember me?" She leads him over to the fridge. "Recognize anyone?"

The fridge is plastered in photos of the boys. There's a wallet size of Stephen from each grade running parallel to the handle. Next to it is a smaller column for Luke. There's even a picture of Richard and me at our wedding and a 5 x 7 of Luke's entire grade one class that I forgot we sent. Luke relaxes after he's seen the pictures, as if they're proof that she actually belongs to him.

"Why don't you tell your Grandma about the assembly?"

Stephen takes his time, as if the whole process is painful. "We had graduation last week."

"Did you win any awards? Ellie was always winning this or that in school."

"The principal had favourites," I explain. "Stephen did very well on his report card though. Straight As and one A plus."

He sighs out a correction. "Mostly A minuses."

"That's still an A," my mother chirps. "No shortage of brains in this family."

"I had an A plus too," Luke says, eager to participate now that Stephen's broken his silence. Between demonstrating his reading skills with the syrup label blurb and recounting his dance performance, Luke safely steers us through breakfast.

*   *   *

The toilet bowl is sweating. Along with the water faucet, our glasses of Coke, the gap where the seal has failed on the fridge, anything fortunate enough to be cooler than the thirty-one degree kiln outside. The condensation pools where it falls, unable to evaporate in the humidity. We prop open the front and back doors, inviting a cross-breeze that never arrives. The boys are bored.

It's as good a time as any for a swim. My mother stays behind to have a lie down.

Parking is a length of gravel in front of the old White Rock community centre, a squat yellow and brown bungalow. The boys are skeptical when we leave the car and wander back through a grass corridor towards the woods. They haven't swum much in fresh water because Richard isn't fond of setting foot in anything he can't see clear through to the bottom.

Stephen hacks his arms against the grass like a machete. "Are there leeches?"

"I've never gotten one here."

"What are leeches?" Luke asks.

"They're big worms that swim up and suck your blood." Stephen wriggles his finger up behind his brother's ear.

"No they aren't."

"Yes they are."

Luke slaps his brother away. "Are they real?"

"Leeches are completely harmless."

We reach the wooded area and make our way along a rock and clay path towards the water's edge, the soil dried and yellowed in the heat. A bunch of logs are chained together across the river, perfect for diving. On the other side is the electrical dam.

"You'd better be careful that a leech doesn't swim up your shorts," Stephen taunts.

"Make him stop it."

"Stop it, Stephen."

"It'll bite off your wiener."

"Stephen."

Next to the water there's another warning sign, a stylized depiction of a swimmer being sucked into the turbine. Growing up, we came here all the time, but I still hesitate. The sign's probably liability insurance for Nova Scotia Power, but there's a chance someone did drown here. Stephen's a good swimmer, but Luke's so young we shouldn't risk it. "I'm sorry, boys, we'll have to go to the beach at Lumsden's instead."

I don't want to draw their attention to the sign. Between this and the leeches, Luke'll never want to go swimming again.

"This is dumb," Stephen says. "When are we signing up for soccer?"

I don't bother to reprimand him, just lead back up the path and get in the now-boiling car. At Lumsden's, it's only a quick dip before the sky clouds over, rains.

Dinner is pork and beans. The pork being sliced wieners and the beans being canned. The boys love it. As I scoop the food onto my fork, what comes to mind are the thick mucous trails left behind by mating slugs.

The boys do the dishes. At home they don't have many chores because we have a dishwasher and a cleaning lady who comes twice a month, but they don't protest when I ask Stephen to wash and Luke to dry. It's nice to see them working together.

That's what I tell Richard when he calls. I've taken the cordless outside for privacy but have to flatten myself against the slat board siding to keep it dry.

"Stephen seemed grumpy about it."

"He did a good job anyway."

As Richard speaks, I curve my neck to cradle the phone as if it were his chest my face was pressed against. At this point, I just want us to make up.

"Your mother sounds happy to see them."

"We're having a nice time. How's the fort?"

"Hot. Too hot to cook. It's my third night of Thai food."

"Eggplant?"

"Chicken panang with pumpkin."

"Your dad come over?"

"Last night."

"You know, he was smart, getting out of the house and moving to the condo." I lower my voice so no one will overhear. "I think this place is starting to get away from my mother. There was an open box of crackers in a drawer and the mice got into it."

"Doesn't sound that bad."

"It's not." A pickup tears out of the neighbour's drive. "It's not. It's just not like her."

"So help her clean."

Richard's tone makes me wonder if he talked to Prescott today.

"Is it true that she doesn't have a TV?"

"She doesn't have cable."

"So no FIFA?"

"Unless it comes on CBC or ATV."

"Did you get a chance to check out the soccer leagues?"

"It's the first day."

"The sooner the better."

"Well, if we're cleaning tomorrow we probably won't get to it until the end of the week."

"Sign-up deadlines are usually in May."

"I'd rather the boys didn't get hanta virus before the cheque clears on the league registration."

"Hanta virus comes from deer mice."

The fake-look-wood on the alarm clock clashes with the oak-stained pine nightstand. I've been staring at it for the past twenty minutes, watching the plastic numbers flip through from one nineteen to twenty to two. I'm not getting to sleep anytime soon, so I might as well get up, get started.

Because the tub is brown, the filth doesn't show as acutely. When I rub the finger pads of the rubber gloves around the enamel, thick grey grime collects in the ridges. The accumulation of sloughed skin and soap looks obscene against the relentless yellow of the gloves. A few squirts of Tilex and the place reeks of ammonia. Normally, I'd clean with vinegar or baking soda, but the filth has passed the scope of eco-friendly cleaners. I prop the window open with an old can of hairspray.

The grout has turned black on the tile backsplash and I spray wildly with the cleaner, working it in with an old toothbrush. The toothbrush digs deep grooves into the putty and when I rinse it off, a couple of tiles fall and clank in the tub. I freeze, terrified it's woken my mother or the boys. Stupidly, I crouch behind the shower curtain, as if that could conceal or excuse this.

The black mould has spread so far that the underside of the tile looks like it's covered in lichen. There must be a leak—who knows what condition the wall is in.

After my father died, house cleaning became my mother's and my weekend ritual, everything scheduled by hour. Saturday mornings: tidying, laundry, ironing. Afternoons: yard work and vacuuming for her, homework for me. Sunday mornings I'd do the bathroom; she'd scrub every surface in the kitchen. We'd both dust the rest of the house, liberally spraying Pledge on squares cut out of Dad's long johns. The afternoons were reserved for "special tasks" like the monthly emptying of the fridge and defrosting of the freezer box.

We'd finish by four and would sit down for an early supper, usually fried bologna served on toasted white bread and held in place by a smear of highlighter-yellow mustard. Sometimes I'd be relieved early and could go ride my bike to a friend's. I remember coming back early one day and seeing my mother hunched over the tub that I'd cleaned that very morning, using an old toothbrush to bleach the grout.

"You can't go soft on mildew," she'd said. It wasn't criticism, just dedication. She looked up at me, smiling. "You need the toilet?"

Looking at the moulding wall, I'm relieved Richard isn't here to witness the house's decay, this lapse in my mother's competence.

3

HREE DAYS IN and the rain hasn't let up, so I've been rooting through the basement for any surviving diversions from my childhood. We're steadily dog-earing an old deck of cards with rounds of Go Fish and Cheat, and we've played so many games of Trouble that the Pop-O-Matic bubble cracks and we have to drive into town for dice.

When it first came up, I didn't think that coming out here would be any different from visiting Terrence. We might as well be on the moon. There's no computer, which for Stephen is something out of the Stone Age. Luke's adapted better to the slower pace out here, but Stephen's annoyed that he hasn't been able to check his MySpace or log into IM. He reminds me several times a day that people are trying to get in touch with him. Twice, I've broken down and let him use the cell to text his friends, despite exorbitant roaming charges.

There's also the problem of the TV. Yesterday was the FIFA final and Stephen's stopped finding the lack of technology funny.

We've got to find him a soccer league quickly.

It's what I propose first thing Monday morning. Within fifteen minutes, he's showered, dressed and ready for breakfast. The cereal is down his throat before it has time to settle in the bowl.

"You know I need to sign up for the under-fifteen, right?"

"Wasn't it the under-fourteen?"

"Back home, it's a crappy team. The coach put me in the better one." His reproach hangs in the air.

"Maybe it won't be a crappy team out here." I swing open the fridge door to replace the milk carton. There's a flash of red and purple next to the lettuce. The tongue of a shoe is pressed against the underside of the glass shelf. Luke's sneakers are wedged in the crisper, next to the greens. The leather's cold as the ketchup bottle. They've been in the fridge all night.

My first thought is Stephen. He's by the sink, rinsing the orange pulp out of his glass. Oblivious. I hold up the sneakers.

He glances at the shoes, surprised as I am.

"I'll go ask your brother."

I trudge upstairs to give Luke a talking-to, wondering if I should keep it quiet from my mother. It's part parental embarrassment, part not wanting to hurt her feelings. For Luke to act up like this is a shock, especially since he's been steadily warming to his grandmother. In fact, he's been demonstrative, leading her by the hand into the living room to show off his somersaults or to play "I spy." If anything, he's tiring her out—she's been napping for a few hours each afternoon.

Luke's fishing through the suitcase for a T-shirt. I wait for him to finish getting dressed, then hand the shoes over to him and ask if there's anything he wants to tell me.

It's easy to tell when he's lying. He isn't. When I think back, he fell asleep on the couch last night, watching the Sunday Night movie on CBC. He still had his sneakers on and my mother took them off as I carried him upstairs.

There used to be a shelving unit where the fridge is now. After doing yardwork or puttering in his shed, Dad preferred to come into the house through the kitchen. He'd stack his boots in the cubbyholes next to the door and hang his coat over the corner. It was a sore point between them—the dirt inevitably tracked in. One day they had a blowout fight and he tore the unit down, repurposed the lumber into the hall bench that's still in the front entrance. He started bringing home rejects from the tire plant and jimmied them into a giant welcome mat that ran four feet down the hall. Once a week, he'd haul it outside and hose it off or rub it clean in the snow. It was one of the only things my mother got rid of when he died.

It's possible she was tired and got confused. A colleague of mine walked into the kitchen one Thanksgiving to find her mother-in-law drinking tea out of a gravy boat. It could just as easily have been me. Still, I knock on her door to check on her. She's brushing her hair, watching her reflection in the bedside vanity. The swing of her arm is laboured.

"Stiff this morning?"

"What?"

I touch her shoulder and she shakes her arms like chicken wings to get me away.

"I'll be down soon." She's rarely this cranky. I don't ask her about the shoes because it's so preposterous.

Downstairs, Stephen's giving Luke the silent treatment, thinking his brother's in trouble.

"I don't know who did it," I say before they start squabbling. "Maybe I was sleepwalking. Maybe your grandmother did it by accident."

Luke takes his sneakers straight over to her when she comes down. "Good joke, Grandma."

"What is it, dear?"

"The shoes in the fridge."

"Good idea, stop them from smelling." She has no idea what he's talking about, but Luke thinks she's hilarious.

Stephen discreetly circles his index finger around his ear, *crazy*.

Still, it wouldn't hurt to make a doctor's appointment.

At the New Minas rec centre, there's a spread of six soccer fields interrupted by a few outbuildings. Two are just school portables but there's a larger, brick Lego block one field over with boarded up windows that doubles as a snack bar. Through a screen door at the back, we can see there's a meeting in progress. A group of eight people are moving neon photocopies around a giant white board. We linger, unsure about entering, until a blonde in a fleece vest notices us and props herself between the door frame, concealing the progress behind her. "Are you here about the tournament?"

"Just trying to get my son into a soccer league."

She narrows her eyes a bit. "Leagues started in spring. They put the notices through the schools."

"We're just back for the summer, staying with my mother. Maybe there's a league we could fit him in?"

Nothing about her expression softens. "How old's he?"

"Thirteen."

"Under fourteen's our biggest league." She turns back into the room. "Rick!"

"Ya-llow." Rick joins us at the door opening, a stack of cue cards in his hand.

The woman in the vest makes just enough room for him to squeeze one shoulder through to shake my hand. "These people want to join the soccer league."

"Too late in the season for that. We're already organizing the August tournament."

Stephen interjects. "In the city I play in the under-fifteen."

"You live in Halifax?"

"No, Toronto."

"Not gonna happen. You can try Kelsey Johnson. We call her Doc Soccer in these parts. She's up at the main office."

They stare as we walk away. I realize for the first time since arriving that everyone here is white.

Stephen and I trudge up the trail towards the next building. There's no shade on the path and I'm sweating through my shirt.

"If I can't get into a league—"

"Let's not worry about that until we know."

"—I'm going to be pissed."

Doc Soccer is easily identified by the three lanyards around her neck, each with its own whistle and a jersey with the slogan "New Minas is the soccer capital of Atlantic Canada." Her hair's chopped into severe salt and pepper bangs, clipper number four on the sides. She still has the tanned, lean physique of an adolescent rower.

"We're all booked up," she says, not bothering to look up from the letter she's opening. "Tryouts are in the spring, so it wouldn't be fair to the other kids."

"What if he could be a kind of swing player, for when the other kids are away? I'm willing to pay the full registration fee."

Doc Soccer puts her hand on her hip, creasing the letter. "We've never done that before."

"Can I leave our name and number in case a spot comes up?" The words are soaked with desperation.

The Doc glances at the receptionist. "Leave it if you want. We can't make any promises."

"Thanks for your time." I nudge Stephen.

"Thanks," he mumbles.

The best thing to do would be to call Richard. It'd mean serious pride swallowing, but he'd be able to suggest another tack—a pick-up league, maybe. At the very least, he'd be able to console our son. Stephen's so angry that he catches his head against the door frame as he slams into the car and refuses to acknowledge the injury.

Richard, however, is on a plane to Calgary. He won't be in Banff for another seven hours.

"I'm still going to work something out."

Stephen doesn't respond. There's a quarter-sized swelling over his temple. A good mother would have let him stay in Toronto.

A trip into Halifax is the only way to salvage the rest of the day. The whole drive in, my mother grips her armrest, nervous about the highway.

I scan the radio for channels, hoping music will relax her. As I'm fiddling with the speaker balance, a row of three transport trucks approaches us and my mother gasps as they pass. "They shouldn't be allowed to drive at the same time as regular vehicles." She's recovered her verve since this morning's strangeness.

I ask if she's been feeling more tired lately, hoping to ease into a medical discussion.

"No more than usual."

"Have you had a checkup?"

"Ellie, you don't fix something that isn't broken."

There's a slow car in front of us and plenty of room to pull out and pass but my mother clucks her disapproval when I overtake the vehicle. "If this is about the cleaning, you didn't give me much warning."

It's been years since I've been in Halifax, but the geography comes back as we pull into downtown. I catch myself taking the right turn without thinking, the city remapping itself like a language I'd half-forgotten.

Parking is in an overpriced lot down by the water. We stroll along the boardwalk, the boys running ahead to check out the ships and peer over the edge into the harbour. The water is murky with floating debris. I shepherd the boys past a fist of algae-covered condoms. Stephen smirks, but Luke's too absorbed by the boats to notice. We grab some BeaverTails and rest at the giant wave sculpture. There's already a handful of kids trying to mount the crest, which looks as much like a tongue as a wave. Most only make it to the halfway point before losing momentum and sliding down. There are warning signs, of course, but no one pays attention.

At least Stephen asks for permission. It's a six-foot drop onto concrete if you overshoot the top, but judging by the other kids, Luke won't make it up. "Be careful," I say. "Watch your brother."

Let them burn off some of their cabin fever.

"Did you get him on the team?" my mother asks.

I shake my head.

"You should call Jason McInnes."

It's like the quick drop of an elevator. Hearing that name brings me right back to seventeen. Jason's the younger brother of Bernie McInnes, my best friend from high school. We haven't stayed in touch since my first year of university.

"Jason's running the autobody in Canning."

I can't make the connection with soccer.

"The shop sponsors some of the teams." My mother never knew about the rift with Bernie and must think this'll give me leverage. It was a painful split—a dog you don't just leave sleeping. A rabid dog. Old Yeller better out of its misery.

Stephen backs up several meters before sprinting up the wave. He falters near the top, but digs in with his toes, scrambling to right himself. He makes it to the crest and waves for me to snap a picture. It's a nice shot, Stephen holding his arms up in victory, the mast of a tall ship behind him. Luke still can't reach his brother. Stephen plants himself at the top and lets his legs hang down so that Luke can grab on. It makes me nervous, but as soon as I take another picture, they slide back down and join us. I hope this means I'm forgiven. Either way, I'm going to have to throw myself on Doc Soc's mercy.

My father died in September, the third week of school, and it sparked a brief rise in my popularity. I'd had friends before that, but I'd always been on the periphery. When Dad died, I became that girl, the one all on her own with her mother. I got invited to birthdays, to people's houses for dinner—my whole first term was flooded with social interaction—but I didn't really make friends. I'd go to events but always felt like I was in a fish tank, on display and inaudible through the water and plate glass. Over the Christmas holidays, people lost interest and there were new things to talk about when we got back to school in January.

It was only Bernie McInnes who stuck with me. In grade eleven, Bernie would grow to be one of the tallest boys in the class, but in grade eight he was a squirt. His folks were farmers on the far side of the school's catchment area. It took twenty minutes to drive between our houses, but his folks would often pick me up or drop me off so we could spend time together. His mom lost a parent young too and I think she made a project out of me.

Bernie had about a million cousins and the house was always full. I remember loving going to Bernie's for dinner—the chaos of it—boys wrestling each other against the cupboards, the dog barking under the table and Bernie's dad snapping at it but feeding it scraps. Someone always spilled something, someone got told to shut up and someone would fart discreetly at the table and wait until someone smelled it before claiming the stink as their own. Bernie's mom would wrinkle her face in disgust and say, "You're all pigs, the lot of you. Eileen Lucan, I'm glad you're here—you're about the only dime in the dung heap." At home, dinner was me, my mother and the radio, all failing to fill the quiet that had set in.

Bernie was never going to leave the valley. The first time I came back after Stephen was born, I wondered if I'd run into him at the farmer's market or out walking along Main. I think if I saw Bernie now, it would be like looking straight back to myself at fifteen, all those years I've spent evolving instantly erased. Beneath that, however, there's the deeper fear that Bernie's changed. That I've changed. That if we did meet on the street, we'd pass without recognition.

* * *

"There's nothing wrong, Ellie." My mother's voice a stage whisper that fills the narrow doctor's waiting room. She repositions her hip, cramping herself against the vinyl backrest, trying to get comfortable. It's futile. These chairs came off the line before ergonomics were invented. "If I were feeling unwell today, then fine. This is just silly."

It's tempting to remind her that she's the one who made the appointment. After our Halifax excursion she was too exhausted to get up until past lunch. This morning, however, she's blaming it on our choice of restaurant—a novelty Tex-Mex outfit, where even the salad came on a deep-fried tortilla.

"It could just be a vitamin deficiency," I say, hoping it sounds non-invasive.

"Oh, they'll find something." My mother relaunches her invective. "You look hard enough, you find anything. Fools down Bridgetown found the Virgin Mary on a scallop."

The medical centre has been converted from one of Kentville's Victorian estates—wedding cakes of houses sliced into office space and student apartments. Upstairs, there's a dental practice and the whirr of drills overlays the classical music playing from a radio on the receptionist's desk. The phone rings frequently, a full old-fashioned tremolo, and the receptionist answers loudly, muffling my mother's complaints.

There are only two other patients—a teenager with rainbow streaks in her hair and a woman about my age with a six-month old baby. She gets called in first and tries to squeeze the baby back into the stroller but gives up as it starts to fuss.

The girl tells her to leave the gear. She'll watch it. The woman drops the diaper bag and I wonder which of us she's supposed to protect it from.

I ask my mother if she wants to go shopping after this.

She clutches her purse tight against her stomach. "Ellie, I don't need your help with the shopping."

"I didn't mean that. It might be nice. We can go to the mall and grab a coffee."

The girl glances over. "There's a sidewalk sale today."

My mother nods at her curtly.

"I work at the record store across from the Northern Reflections. They've got fifty percent off."

"Thanks."

"Sometimes people do their Christmas shopping at the sidewalk sale." She scratches at a scab on her knee, right below her leggings. "Lots of stores put out their stuff. Even from way back in storage, just to see if it sells. Last year I got my Christmas cards 80% off."

This rouses my mother into conversation. "Ellie doesn't send Christmas cards."

"*Last* year I didn't send them out. I got caught up with exams."

My mother harrumphs. "Two years, Ellie." She keeps a record in her address book of each card she receives, a different colour ink for each year. She bumps everyone who's missed three consecutive Christmases.

"I post-date them," the girl says. "I start around Halloween."

"Very sensible. Ellie loves email. Doesn't send letters or cards, but always tells me how backward I am because I don't have email."

The phone rings, but this time the receptionist conducts the call at half-volume. "No, we don't do that here. You'll have to go into Halifax or try the hospital."

The girl catches my eye and mouths the word "abortion."

The physician's younger than I expect, with an auburn bob and toned muscles that wouldn't be out of place in a Yorkville Pilates studio. Back home, I bristled at that class of woman. Uniformed in lululemon racerbacks and New Balance runners, in perpetual training for half-marathons. But here her polish relaxes me. Next to the receptionist's ancient toffee-coloured set curls, Dr. Archibald seems like a beacon of modernity.

My mother emerges after barely ten minutes. She's beaming as she struts out of the office, not waiting for me to replace the magazine I was reading. I catch up to her by the car. Once we're inside she says, "I think I'd like to go to the mall after all."

"Well?"

"Well what?"

"How did it go?"

She's triumphant. "Perfectly. A good clean bill of health. Maybe a touch of high blood pressure."

"Don't you need to do any blood work?"

She shuffles to buckle herself in. "Dr. Archibald doesn't think there's any need to worry."

"You did have a physical, didn't you?"

"Just start the car and we'll talk about it later."

I start the engine and roll down the window for some air.

"Why don't you turn on the a/c if you're stuffy?"

"Because it's better for the environment this way."

She looks at me pointedly. "Then why buy a car with it?"

"Richard wanted this model."

She rolls her window down and stares at the passing houses. "Very sensible."

At the County Fair Mall, my mother decides on a pretzel for lunch. "One of the ones with all that cinnamon and sugar." We eat on a bench in front of the pretzel store as I try to balance my coffee on the wood slats and restrain myself from interrogating her. The mall is quiet, but there's a small congregation of senior citizens on the various benches closer to the Zellers.

My mother licks the sugar off her fingers and gestures towards the sidewalk-sale displays. "Maybe we can find some clothes for the boys."

Not likely. Stephen's gotten particular about his attire—if it doesn't have a team crest and isn't several sizes too big, he's not interested.

"So what did the doctor say?"

"You know, Ellie, I don't have to tell you anything." The corner of her mouth tilts up into a half-smile. "Dr. Archibald says that everything seems normal and that I probably got a bit overworked. She thinks it's good that you're here."

"What about the high blood pressure?"

"People get nervous at the doctor. I'm supposed to go down to the Wolfville Shoppers and put my arm in the blow-up contraption a few times a week."

I lower my voice. "Did you get a Pap smear?"

"I haven't been active in that way for almost thirty years. I'm not going to ask the doctor to hook me up to the stirrups."

My mother crumples up her wrapper and dabs her mouth with the napkin, finished with both her snack and the conversation.

"Why don't you wander down and look for things for Stephen? I'll catch up in a minute."

She's not fooled. "You're going to call the doctor."

"I just want to check on the boys."

My mother waits for me to back down.

I start to dial the house line, angling the cell so she can see the number.

"I'll be over at the Northern Reflections."

I hustle to the nearest entrance, waiting for Stephen to pick up. As the phone rings, I stare at the candy dispensers with their myriad trinkets and plastic capsules, shocked that they take toonies. I can remember when it was nickels. Stephen's annoyed that I'm checking up—we've only been gone an hour and a half. He's fine. Luke's fine. It takes twenty-three seconds.

Just in case she's still watching, I dial facing the parking lot. The receptionist picks up on the second ring.

"Dr. Archibald, please."

"She's with a patient now. I'll have to take a message."

"This is Ellie Bascom. My mother, Lynne Lucan, was just in. I have a question about her prescription. I can hold."

"You don't want to leave a message?"

"We're going out of town for a few days. It's a quick question about the dose."

"Hold on."

Dr. Archibald doesn't bother with pleasantries. "Yes."

"This is Ellie Bascom, my mother was just in."

"I know."

"I'm just calling because she was supposed to be going in for a physical and she didn't have a Pap or any blood work taken."

"I'm not at liberty to discuss your mother's medical history with you."

"Don't you think that after the exhaustion she's been experiencing, it would be good for her to have a full workup?"

"We had her down for a consultation." Dr. Archibald sighs, her interest already lost. She's flipping through papers.

"Look, we found a pair of shoes in the fridge."

"You are staying at your mother's place for the summer, right?"

"Right."

"With your two sons."

"Yes."

"If I were staying at my mother's house and a pair of shoes turned up in the fridge, I'd blame the six-year-old."

I glance towards the mall. My mother is ten yards away and quickly closing the distance, her scowl clearing the way like a cattle guard.

"I think she's run off her feet and needs a rest."

I whisper quickly, "I've been cleaning for a week."

"Mrs. Bascom, I am not a mediator. If your mother has concerns about her health, she's welcome at the clinic. Please don't lie to my receptionist again."

My mother isn't gentle when she opens the door and the arc almost clips my foot. "You called the doctor."

I flip the phone shut and strain to hide my seething. "I called Stephen."

"And?"

"I think I'm going to take the boys to Grand Pré tomorrow."

"That's nice, I haven't been there in years."

"I thought you might like the day off to rest. I don't want you run off your feet."

After the boys go to bed, the house noises settle in for the night like parrots under a blanket. It's impossible to get used to this quiet. The only sounds are the metronome of the alarm clock and the periodic whine of the refrigerator motor. There's no streetlight, no porch light, none of the perpetual orange glow polluting the city. It's a moment tailor-made for reflection, which is what I should be doing; contemplating the fight, my future in academia, all the other explanations I gave Richard. Instead, it's like a Valentine's dinner where everything points to the inevitable coitus, from the three-course menu to the lingerie, but no one's in the mood.

It's only seven in Alberta and a slim chance that Richard will pick up. When the hotel receptionist connects me to the room, I huddle against the far wall, my hand cupped over the mouthpiece, ready to leave a message.

The phone clatters off the receiver and Richard's hello is so startled that I lose my train of thought. "You're there."

"Just woke up."

"How long have you been sleeping?"

"Since five. It was supposed to be a power nap." His voice cracks, sending him into a coughing fit.

"Did you pick up a bug on the plane?"

He mumbles a denial while swallowing water, his gulp amplified.

"How's the conference going?"

"No complaints."

"You present tomorrow, right?"

"Ten a.m. sharp. But they've also got me pinch-hitting on a panel. Someone's brother died."

"That's awful."

"Car accident—died instantly. The rumour is plywood blew off the back of a pickup and crashed through the windshield."

It's easy to picture the impact, the plywood guillotine. The story temporarily unites us in the shared, shameful frisson bad news gives to those lucky enough to not be involved.

"I think I screwed-up with my mother." I describe the visit to the doctor and the subsequent disaster. It feels good confiding in him. Before the job squabble, Richard never failed to comfort me simply by listening.

Halfway through detailing the tiff at the mall, however, I only get the vaguest notion that he's paying attention. There are rhythmic clicks on the other end. I pause for a moment and the noises come to a halt a split-second later. "Are you typing?"

"If you're sorry, tell her you're sorry." A comparison to the earlier tragedy hangs in his response. Richard splutters into another coughing fit. His throat never gets like that except when he's sick or hungover.

When I ask, he laughs out a mea culpa, the embarrassment pure show.

"Open bar."

I didn't realize it would be so raucous.

"I was out with Rashid and Ewan—they sent me the rock. I'm meeting them again for dinner. I should have showered by now actually."

"Another hard night?" I know the rebuke isn't entirely fair but I'm irritated that he's out enjoying himself while I'm struggling with my mother and the boys. I'm the one who wanted time to myself.

"Tonight's wild game fondue." His voice sharpens into a hard edge, daring me to push the point. "At least it'll be a better base."

"Just don't spill any drinks on your laptop. I won't be there to help you make another slide show." PowerPoint's about the only area of academia where my expertise surpasses Richard's.

"Any word on a soccer league?"

For the first time since the fight, we sign off with "I love you" but we both say it so cold that it's worse than the omission.

*   *   *

Breakfast is donuts and hot chocolate out on the dykes. The tide's out, and as we eat, the hardest thing is restraining Stephen from running down the mudflats. I understand the impulse— summers when I was younger, we'd throw on our bathing suits and hurl ourselves down the ridges. If you launched yourself properly, you could get a decent run, way longer than the Slip 'n Slides they advertised on TV. We had to stop after a kid sliced his thigh and needed a blood transfusion at the Kentville hospital. At speed, a shell is basically a razor.

I pitch a rock in to show Stephen that the surface isn't as solid as it looks. As soon as the stone lands, it disappears under a skim of water drawn from the surrounding clay. It's just the three of us this morning. The humidity's finally lifted and for the first time since being here it feels like there's space to breathe. Even the boys are impressed by the scenery, the colours saturated by today's cloud cover. Until now, I hadn't realized this is something I've wanted them to see.

Farther down, the sandpipers are needling their beaks into the beach, fishing for shrimp. Luke's fascinated by them, the way their flight looks like a rising dust cloud. He asks how they know which one to follow. Most of the bird migration he's seen has been in the "V" pattern of geese and ducks. Having never studied ornithology, I'm as baffled as he is.

Stephen's less mystified by the fauna and wants to know why we have to go to the Grand Pré heritage site.

"You two like the ROM."

"Does this place have a bat cave?"

Spit flies out of my mouth as I laugh. I'm not sure why I'm forcing the edutainment on them either.

When we went to Grand Pré on school field trips, all there was to see were the gardens and stone church. Now there's a huge interpretation centre and an admission fee. As we wander into the multimedia room, Stephen almost knocks over a stanchion because his backpack is bulging with his hoodie and soccer ball. I told him it's not the kind of place for playing, but the ball's become a mix of security blanket and rebellion.

There's a busload of German tourists already in the theatre, their guide vigorously ushering them into the front two rows. The room is built like a ship, with buttressed wooden planks that curve towards the front screen. The stage is bare except for a lantern and stack of barrels.

We just get our headsets on as the lights dim.

The screen lights up with a woman screaming in pain as she gives birth in the hold of a ship. It isn't graphic, but the actress milks the agony and Luke grabs onto me, terrified. The scene brightens and pictures of the valley are projected throughout the theatre. People pop up on screens at the side and comment on the action—a genial farmer dressed in spotless period attire, an arrogant British General and a full-hipped Acadian mother each put their two cents in. It's way too cheesy. Stephen lowers his chin and looks over at me, halfway to barfing. He has to bite his fist to stop himself from laughing as a MicMac warrior explains in stilted English that MicMac side only with MicMac.

He lifts up Luke's headphone and whispers, "Lukemac sides only with Lukemac." Then he burps in his brother's ear. Lukemac makes a big show of wiping the belch off.

Stephen gets a bit more excited when the war scenes begin with gunshots and munitions explosions. The British are setting fire to the Acadian homes. They show a map of the Diaspora and I point out Trinidad when we see the Caribbean countries that have Acadian descendants. Not that it's likely that Richard's parents had any Acadian ancestors, but it's nice to think about a possible connection. Then we're back to the woman with the school children. She reminds me of Mrs. Harrison, our fifth grade teacher—same pat speech about this history belonging to all of us. Even then, I had doubts about its relevance to my life. Some of the kids in the class, the ones who lived closer to Port Williams in nicer estate homes, did have French names and made a big deal of it during the unit on Acadia. They might have been Acadian or they might have moved here from Quebec, but for that month it was as if their own blood had been sprayed over the dykes.

The focus of the exhibit hall is a plaster-cast Acadian stooped over a life-size dyke. The boys are pretty interested in the mechanics of the drainage structure, especially since there are several hands-on activities. I try to demonstrate the concept of valves using my arm vein, pressing down to stop the blood flow, drawing the blood away then releasing. It proves too popular an experiment. The boys lose interest in the sod clumps and take turns prodding each other's arms.

I shepherd them over to the rest of the exhibits, but they basically restate the film script. Stephen stands in front of each one, performing his impressions of the various pop-up characters. At the display for le Gran Dérangement, he plugs his nose and gives his best falsetto. "What will become of us? We all have a great derangement."

"What's a derangement?" Luke asks.

"It means you're crazy."

I'm impressed with Stephen's vocabulary, but am worried his voice is carrying over to the Parks Canada guides.

"Be careful, Lukemac, you'll be the next derangement."

"Will not."

"You will—you're a great derangement."

"Is that why the woman was screaming at the beginning?"
Luke asks.

Stephen starts to laugh—he's already been through sex-ed
at school—and says, "Yeah, that's exactly why. Mom had a big
derangement when she had you too."

Enough history for one day. I steer them over to the exit to
the gardens. "The woman was having a baby, but she didn't
want to have the baby on the ship."

"Was she crazy?"

"No."

"Why was she screaming?"

"Sometimes giving birth can hurt."

"Did it hurt when you had me?"

"Yes, but it was worth it afterwards." Good textbook answer.

"Mom was having a bigger derangement than that woman,"
Stephen says, "She screamed for two hours."

"You weren't there."

"Dad told me."

"Your father is exaggerating."

"What's that?" Luke asks.

"It means that he was lying," Stephen answers.

"That's not what I'm saying."

"That's what the word means. It means you're not telling
the truth."

"It means you're making something seem bigger than it
was, like saying you've caught a fish as big as a house."

"Or that Luke was as big as a car when he was born and
that's why you had the derangement."

"Stephen!"

"Can I play soccer?"

"Fine."

The bus tour is exiting the church at the end of the garden
walkway, so I hang back with Luke and point out some of the
flowers on the path. Luke likes to take pictures with my camera

and I let him, hovering to make sure he's not going to drop it. Stephen is on the other side of the flowerbeds practicing knee kicks.

There's a statue of Evangeline in the middle of the park and I hoist Luke onto my shoulders so he can touch the bronze. He's getting too heavy for me now—it'll probably only be another few years that I can pick him up at all and then he'll shoot up like Stephen and Richard and I'll be the shortest person in the family again. Luke and I take a few more flower pictures and I surreptitiously pinch off a small rosebud and put it in a Ziploc in my purse to press later. As I'm zipping up my satchel, I hear a Parks Canada employee behind me calling out, "Miss, miss!"

She's in her late forties, a face like butter left out in the heat. Her shorts bunch up over her waist, perspiration marks under the armpits of her taupe blouse. She probably saw me clip the vegetation and I'm going to be ejected from a public park in front of my children. "Miss." She pants a bit from the exertion.

She points to Stephen. "Does he belong to you?"

We're the only people in the park.

"Is he yours?"

I haven't been asked that kind of question in a long time. She squints at me as if she thinks she already knows something about the kind of person I am.

"That's my son."

She still doesn't address Stephen directly. "He can't do that here."

Stephen's stopped his knee kicks and is holding his soccer ball in front of his stomach, eyes downcast.

"He might ruin the flowers," she says. "This is a national heritage site. We can't allow any kind of recreation sports."

"I'm sorry. We didn't know. Stephen, can you put your ball back in your backpack?"

"I'll have to ask you to check it at the front."

"We're almost finished," I say, keeping my voice steady and low, like I'm approaching a dog. "I'll make sure it doesn't happen again."

She appraises me, unsure of how far she can exert her Parks Canada authority. Finally, she scowls at Stephen and retreats to the air-conditioned centre.

Stephen slinks beside me and I apologize. "I didn't know about the rules."

We climb the steps up to the church and I hold the door open for the boys to go in first. There's another guide at the front of the room, a summer student this time. She tells Stephen that he'll have to carry his backpack. Mostly the place just has paintings on the walls, but there are a few display cases. In solidarity, I slide my backpack off too and carry it.

Stephen reads one of the signs then goes back to the guide. "So this isn't the real church, right?"

"The first one burned down. This was built to commemorate it in 1923. It was purchased in 1965 as a heritage site."

"Does anyone pray here anymore?"

She shakes her head.

Stephen starts to walk away but turns back. "Is it right on top of the old one?"

The guide's voice takes on the singsong rhythm of a teacher trying to curb further questions. "No, it's a little farther down."

"What if they hadn't built the church?"

"What do you mean?"

"Like what if you had put a McDonald's here. Would it still be a heritage site?"

The corners of the guide's smile are getting twitchy and she glances at me to see if I want to interject.

"If all the houses got burned down, why aren't those heritage sites too? I mean everywhere's a historical site, isn't it?"

It's a good question but the guide doesn't choose to answer it. Instead, she feeds us a weak explanation, something about some places being more special than others.

There's a meadow with a duck pond to the left of the church and a ditch we can probably climb to get back to the parking lot. None of us want to go through the building again. When we reach the field's edge, however, there's a row of shrubs woven together to make a fence. There's enough of a gap that I suggest we just crawl through. It's a scramble up a slight embankment before we hit the train tracks and even then there's a fence barring us from reaching the parking lot. They don't want anyone appreciating their heritage without paying admission.

We're close enough that I just give up and walk the tracks towards the road. There are signs warning people against it, but I used to do it all the time when I lived here. In the parking lot, the Germans are sitting on lawn chairs, enjoying croissant sandwiches.

"Mom," Stephen says. "This place is giving me the grand derangement."

Me too.

On the drive home Stephen asks if I've heard from Parks and Rec. We both know I haven't called. He just shakes his head as I apologize and stares out the window, his feet wedged against the dashboard.

At the house, Stephen bangs up the stairs, straight to his room. When I check on him an hour later, there's a suitcase on the floor, his clothes jammed into it. He's crying, his face pressed against the cell, his biceps tensed. He refuses to make eye contact but his bravado makes him look so vulnerable, all soft flesh like a shucked clam. The first impulse is to scoop him up, comfort him. He holds the phone out for me to take it, keeping as much distance from me as possible.

"Richard?"

No, it's Terrence.

"Stephen called to ask if he could borrow the money to come home."

"What did you say?" It's a mixture of embarrassment and relief talking to Terrence. He's always seemed less like a father-in-law and more like a long lost friend. When I was pregnant, he came by the house a few times a week, bringing an article to read or fried plantain for me to eat. He'd tease that it was his job to fatten up the baby. He always wanted to see my belly, liked to rub his hands in a smooth sweep across the bulge. Richard was adopted, so this was new for Terrence. He launched into being a grandfather with the fervour of a first-time parent. At this point, I'm prepared to take any advice he offers.

"I told him he needs to stick it out longer."

"I should have called the Parks people again today."

"Ellie, he's a thirteen-year-old boy. The whole world doesn't understand him." Terrence isn't ruffled. "It's nice for your mom to have them for a while."

I want to ask if he thinks the trip was a good idea, but can't get the words out.

Terrence guesses at my silence. "You having a good time out there?"

"It's different than I expected."

"Always is."

When I hang up, I take Terrence's suggestion and drive the boys into Wolfville to check their email at the public library. Stephen still isn't speaking to me. He hasn't had a lot of privacy since he's been here, and chatting with his friends or writing his dad might help.

The boys bolt to the only two computer workstations and I log into my own account standing at the express computer. It's mostly spam, but there are several email threads from U of T Geology. Richard must have forwarded his work email to mine by accident. A message comes in from him when I refresh the page after deleting the previous emails. It's sent from his Black-Berry and written like a telegram.

Dad called. I've sent Stephen an email. Are you doing okay? Conference going well. Good news about the BBC article. Possible collaboration on the oldest rock project. Still foetal.

Look, if you're ready to come home, just come.

If you're ready to come home. It's what we tell the boys when we send them to their rooms. If you're ready to come down now. If you're ready to behave.

Leaving now is an apology that I'm not prepared to make.

I can't call Jason McInnes to get Stephen on the team without talking to Bernie first. So after the boys have gone to bed, I finally ask my mother where he's living.

"Last I heard he was still up at his uncle's old place off Ridge Road. I seen his Dad from time to time. Always says hello."

She takes her cup upstairs at quarter to ten. It might not be too late to drive over—Bernie never slept much anyway. The rain starts as soon as I get in the car. I drive the back roads, over the Port Williams bridge and out past the university, up the hill to Ridge Road. It's like driving down a tunnel of yellow headlight, the rain obscuring the boundaries of the road.

The driveway always came up fast and I'm not sure that I'll be able to recognize it on the first pass. I round the last corner, back over the top of the mountain to the lee of Gaspereau. At the first driveway, I cut the headlights and turn through the cover of the maples, using the fog lights until I can be sure I'm at the right place. Sure enough, the house is there, a stark wood frame two-level.

There are no lights on inside and no vehicles around, no tools or toys scattered about the yard like there used to be. When Bernie's uncle lived here, there was a steady rotation of mutts, none of them lasting very long. There was always something wrong with them—a sliced lip from a fight, three legs, an eye sewn shut. There was a boxer named Butterscotch whose ears had been lost to frostbite and I can still make out the depression near the hedge where she used to sleep.

There's traffic on the back road so I kill the fog lights. People around here are nosy. Someone's bound to come poking in, wanting to know what I'm doing. It's pitch-black now, and I'm barely able to make out the charcoal lines of the house.

Whatever I was expecting to happen isn't. There's no guarantee that Bernie still lives here. He could have flipped the property years ago. Best thing would be to call Doc Soccer first thing in the morning and beg.

For a few beats, I hear the music—CCR's *Bad Moon Rising* on full blast—before the rear-view floods with light. A truck's turned into the drive and I'm temporarily blinded. A large engine drones through a weak muffler. The driver's not going to see me. There's no time to start the car.

I brace for the crash as the truck brakes squeal. There's the crack of impact, a hollow metal and plastic crunch. The car lurches forward and I realize I shouldn't have gripped the wheel, the air bag's going to break my arms.

It never inflates. The car rocks back slightly. The chemical hum of adrenaline is dripping down my neck, through my arms and trunk, but I'm all right. I'm all right.

The door flies open. "What the fuck do you think you're doing?" A man towers over the car. All I can see are his thick steel-toe boots, his face hidden by the glare.

I stare up, blinking, unable to speak.

"Jesus Christ. Ellie?" Bernie hauls me out of the car and runs his hand over my forehead and along my chin, checking for injury.

I'm so shaken, I start to cry.

"Oh, fuck, are you hurt?" He's got his hand on my shoulder, gripping hard to guard against me collapsing. "What the hell are you doing out here?"

The words come out in half sucks through tears. "I didn't think you were home."

"You scared the shit out of us."

There's a line of pale faces peering out of the pickup's window. Someone turns the music off. "Just go on and pull in by the house," Bernie says.

I can't get back in the car yet, so Bernie hops in and manoeuvres it down beside the house. He then pulls the truck up directly behind and leaves his lights on so we can see the damage. He hollers out the window, "She'll be all right. Glad we got the brakes in order."

He cuts the engine and steps out of the cab. Three figures pour out from the passenger door. When they hit the light, I see it's a woman—mid-thirties—and two kids. Bernie calls to them across the hood. "Come on over, Linda, come on and meet Ellie."

Linda ambles over, arms wrapped around her waist. She waits for an explanation.

"Ellie here was my best friend in high school." He rubs his hands up and down my arms, like he's drying me off. He shakes his head, then nudges me in Linda's direction.

"Pleased to meet you." I hold out my hand. She takes it weakly, retracts hers quickly.

Bernie points to the kids. "This one's Max and this is Lisa."

"Pleased to meet you."

The girl's blonde like her mother, skin transparent as a newt. I guess she's about Luke's age. The boy's older, probably a year past Stephen, but he takes more after his father—brown curly hair and a slight pudge to his cheeks, just like Bernie at that age. Neither of them looks at me directly. I wipe my face dry and try to compose myself. The kids are probably terrified enough.

"Well, come in," Bernie says. We file up to the porch and he flicks on a light and leads us into the kitchen. Linda sets her purse on the table and I realize I'd misjudged both her age and hair colour. She's probably only 27, 28 and the blonde is all peroxide. Linda reaches up and massages her neck, a pinched expression on her face. She's pretty but has the tanned, furrowed look some small-town girls get.

"I'm really sorry." I struggle to navigate the situation. "I should have left the lights on."

The girl huddles on her mother's side of the table. The boy stays by the door.

"Truck's got a grill at the front," Bernie says. "Just gave us a start, that's all." He holds out a chair for me and I sit down at the wooden harvest table that's replaced the old line of card tables his uncle used. Bernie putters away at the sink, filling up the kettle and setting it on the stove.

"You've really fixed up the place." I smile at Linda, trying to look as benign as possible.

"Oh, Bernie done all that."

Bernie swings round and corrects her. "No, she's the one who made it homey. I got the outside into shape, but she painted it and put up the decorations." He points to an ivy wallpaper border near the ceiling—small pink flowers curl around the vines. The cabinetry's been painted a matching cream, the middle stencilled with the same ivy motif.

"Did you do the painting yourself?"

Linda nods, still stony.

Bernie presses her. "Tell her, Lindie. Tell her how you did it."

She glares at him. "I got one of those books. Then I got some stencils at the V&S."

"Linda's got a real talent with arts and crafty stuff."

"I can see that." I'm still smiling stupidly.

"How y'all know Bernie again?"

"Cornwallis."

She taps her front tooth with her nail. "Hadn't heard of you."

Bernie comes up behind me and puts his hands on the back of my chair. "Ellie and me went right through together from grade seven."

"Right." Linda drapes her arms on her daughter's shoulders. She tilts her head towards the hall. "Bern, I'm gonna take the

kids up to bed." She's halfway out through the doorway when
she turns back to face me. "If I don't see you before you leave,
nice to meet you."

Bernie follows Linda into the hall. I start to stand, but he
raises his finger, hold on a second. Whatever Bernie's saying to
her, he's whispering, but she makes no effort to quiet her voice.

"She normally lurk in people's drives?"

I slump back into the seat and look around the rest of the
room, trying not to eavesdrop. Linda's gone to town with the
tole paint. There are miniature wooden figures everywhere—
kitschy angels, brightly coloured hearts and a home sweet home
sign. None of it looks much like Bernie, except for a pile of agricultural magazines in the wicker basket by the phone hutch. His
dad used to keep the same ones in a receptacle by the toilet.

Bernie returns, deflated. "Might be a bit late for a cup of tea
now. Are you okay to drive?"

"Oh, sure, yes." I make a hasty retreat to the door. "I'm
really, really sorry for stopping by like this. I didn't know if you
still lived here."

He sees me into the vehicle. "You in town long?"

"For the summer."

"Where are you staying at?"

"My mother's."

"Come by sometime in daylight hours." He grins and taps
on the hood.

"Please apologize to your wife again for me."

"Oh, don't worry about Linda," he says, chuckling and shaking his head. "She'll warm up to you. Next time she'll be right
happy to see you."

I reverse extra carefully around the truck, mortified.

Bernie stands there waving. Same old, same old.

4

GOT ACCEPTED to Acadia on early admission, full scholarship. School wouldn't finish until June, but by February it felt like I'd already bought my ticket out.

The first weekend of March break there was a massive snowfall and a group of guys from my class organized a ski trip at Martock. Bernie was roped into driving them. Normally they'd never invite me, but Bernie sensed that I wanted to come, so he picked me up first and we all crammed into his dad's half-ton.

I sat next to Bernie, my legs on either side of the gearbox. Chuck—Cornwallis' resident stud and Supertramp enthusiast—was next to me, with his girlfriend Charla. The three other boys were crammed in the back with Bernie's brother Jason. None of them other than Bernie and Jason had paid much attention to me before, but if they were surprised by my presence, they didn't comment. Charla's annoyance, however, took up all the remaining space in the cab.

"Bernie," she said. "Jennie Murphy was supposed to come with us."

"No room."

When he wasn't looking, Charla slid a finger in her mouth and pulled out a wad of grape gum, which she pressed against the underside of the dashboard at the exact spot my knee hit on every bump.

I was wearing my old snow pants from grade eight. I hadn't grown much and they still fit. The bright pink my mother had thought was so cute had faded to a pale flesh tone. With my oversized wool sweater, I still looked like a little kid.

Charla was wearing a new ski suit, teal with white piping, and a fluffy cream scarf and matching toque. Her dad was the manager of one of Wolfville's banks and she went to Kings Edgehill, a girls' boarding school in Windsor. She was slumming with Chuck.

As soon as we got to the ski hill, the two of them split to get lift tickets. My mom had given me money to rent equipment, on account of my grades and the scholarship, but hadn't realized there was also an admission fee. Bernie'd thought of that though, and reached into the pickup and handed me a pair of skis. "Got them from the dump." Bernie worked weekends at the waste transfer station.

I didn't know how to ski, but neither did Bernie. One of the other guys showed us how to snowplow and by the end of the day, we could make it down the whole run without falling. Charla and Chuck left the slopes early to screw in the chalet bathroom. They met up with us as the run closed, looking flushed and sheepish. Charla made a point of wiping her mouth with the back of her hand.

"That's fucking foul," Jason said.

"I offered to bring my friends."

"I don't want my dick to fall off."

Chuck glared but didn't jump to Charla's defence.

We drove to the Pulpit bar in Wolfville, because it was the only place we knew we'd all get in. It was close to Charla's house and we stopped on the way so she could sneak out some of her dad's liquor. She and Chuck went in and after half an hour they made it back out with bottles of gin, vodka and rank banana liqueur. She'd spent most of the time changing into tight butter-yellow pants and a blouse that laced and gaped, revealing the trim of her bra cups. She had a jean jacket over top and must have been freezing, but she bounced into the truck as though she couldn't feel the cold. Her eye shadow glittered in the overhead light.

I dabbed my lips with Chap Stick.

The bottles didn't last long with so many people, but there was enough for a buzz by the time we got to the 'Pit. Inside, it was mostly university students enjoying "Beat the Clock." Beer started off at fifty cents and went up by a quarter every half hour. Charla recognized some people and sauntered off, leaving the rest of us in our winter gear. It was too hot in my snow pants, and I looked ridiculous, so I took them off, along with my sweater and tossed them in the booth. I had on my jeans and an old tank top, really just a cotton camisole, something to keep the sweater from scratching. I wasn't wearing a bra either, because I didn't have to—I didn't grow into my current B cup until I was in university.

With Charla gone, the boys warmed up to me, kept bringing me over to the bar and buying me beer, teasing me about falling so much on the hill. One of them, I forget which one, asked me to dance when *Fly Like an Eagle* came on. It wasn't really a fast song, it wasn't really a slow song and we spun in a slow circle and gyrated a bit. By the end, he had his hands on my hips and was grinding me into his crotch, slurring along to Steve Miller. Bernie stayed perched on the barstool, plowing his way through pints of Moosehead. It was only quarter to eleven but I was already feeling pretty flushed. After the song ended I squirmed away and went to sit with him.

"Having a good time?" he asked.

"Yeah." I was. I was having a great time.

I leaned my head on his shoulder and he pulled my hair back from my face. "Just tell me when you want to get going."

We sat like that for a while, the rest of the bar sliding in and out of my vision, like the slow turns of a giant kaleidoscope.

Then Chuck came over and pretended to do a double take. "You sure look different without your snowsuit, Ellie."

Bernie asked him where Charla was.

We could see her across the room, sitting on some Acadia jock's lap.

"You want to dance?" Chuck asked.

Bernie set down his pint glass. "We're heading out."

It wasn't until I stood up that the full force of my inebriation hit. I stumbled over to the washroom and pushed open the door, then puked into the first cubicle. I missed the bowl a bit, so I had to go to the next one to pee. I rinsed my mouth over the sink and dried my face, rubbing with the coarse paper towel until it turned beetroot.

Looking at myself in the fluorescent lighting, my skin's olive tinge bleached out, I saw that I'd grown curvier around the hips. My jeans were tighter than I'd imagined and my tank top rose above them, showing off a flat, light brown stomach. I could see that yes, one day, some guy would want me.

As I looked at my shirt, I realized that the cotton was thinner than I remembered. You could make out the fleshy maroon of my areolas, two quarter-sized mounds.

Three girls, university students, burst in. As they walked into the stalls, carefully avoiding the one I'd soiled, they looked over at me and giggled. The taller one muttered something under her breath. She didn't have to repeat it; I knew from the contempt on her face what she was thinking. *Townie.*

*   *   *

Bernie calls at six in the morning, before any of us are awake, and offers to fix the car. The McInnes autoshop is in Canning, a few minutes' drive from the house. I'm not sure I want to take him up on the offer, but when I haul myself out to look at the car, it's worse than I thought—the bumper's on a distinct diagonal, the left corner crumpled.

My mother catches me inspecting the damage. Still in her nightgown, she squints at the vehicle, her breasts propped up by crossed arms. She exhales through the gap in her front teeth and the whistle sends me straight back to seventeen, embarrassed and waiting to be grounded.

"I got rear-ended."

She arches her left eyebrow, expecting me to flesh out the details. "Did you get the license plate?"

"It was dark." Everything about last night feels preposterous now.

"You let them get away?"

Facing the heat of my mother's disapproval, the truth peels away, easy as paint. "It was just at the stop sign on the corner. They sped off in a truck."

"A blue truck?"

She stares at me, dumbfounded, as if she can't believe she raised a daughter with such a lack of street smarts. "You should have called George." George is the RCMP officer who lives a few houses away. "What if the kids had been in the car?"

"I'll bring it down to the garage after breakfast. Give me a chance to ask Jason about the team."

"Were they young?" my mother persists. "There's the Penley teens two roads over. They've got a truck. Licence BYJ 649, like the lotto. Comes over the scanner all the time. Drag racing." She launches a series of tut-tutts. "I think we should still call George and file a report."

"We don't need to get him involved." I climb into the driver's seat, desperate to diffuse this. The sooner I drive over to Canning, the less time I have to dig myself in deeper.

"It's a hit and run."

"It's a fender bender."

I drown my mother's protests with the car engine.

Jason strolls out to meet the car, wiping his hands on blue twill pants. His girth has doubled since I've last seen him—his gut a lip of stretched cotton over his belt. He looks me up and down when I get out of the car and crushes me into a hug, as if he can't quite believe I've reappeared. "Eileen Lucan. Been a dog's age." Jason's still got the kind of face that gets you acquitted of murder when you're guilty as sin—big eyes, double dimples and a fist-sized cowlick.

Bernie wanders over, the straight man to his brother's imp.

"You been in town a week?" Jason asks.

"Just over."

"Already in a scrap." He chuckles, looking back and forth between his brother and me. "Just got word that you were hit by a drunk driver last night."

Bernie's eyebrows shoot up in surprise.

"Your mom put the call in. Any minute now, George'll be knocking on the Penleys' door."

"Does everyone out here have a police scanner?"

"In my business, it's market research." He laughs again, the dimples in his cheeks deep as pencil gouges. "Won't do the little shits any harm, having a chat with the law."

Bernie shifts from foot to foot, waiting for a chance to jump into the banter. Jason notices his brother's twitchiness. "Thought you were heading over to the farm."

Bernie nods and takes a few steps towards the truck. He pauses and fiddles with his keychain, dangling it on the knuckle of his index finger. "Feel like checking out the old place with me, Ellie?"

I shrug, not really wanting to draw out the process, but not wanting to seem ungrateful.

"Jason," Bernie lays on his older brother voice. "You don't mind banging that old tin into place, do you?"

"Yeah, yeah." Jason cups his hands like a catcher's mitt and I toss him the keys.

Bernie's truck is raised up on oversized tires and it takes a moment for me to judge where to grab on and hoist myself in. It's like riding a bus, the seats high as the other cars' hoods. If he hadn't braked when he did, the car would have been a write-off.

"Your brother got children now too?" I can't quite picture Bernie's kid brother hitched and breeding.

"He's got a daughter, but he and the mom split. Shacked up with someone else in Berwick. Jason sees her every couple of weekends."

"Sorry to hear that."

"My niece is cute and all but the mom's crazy. Remember Shelley V.? It's her cousin."

Shelley was hard to forget. When she caught her junior high sweetheart cheating, she threatened to castrate him with an exacto knife. By grade twelve she had the name of a classmate's uncle tattooed on her left hip.

"I heard you married some professor out in Toronto."

"Who'd you hear it from?"

"News travels. I used to see your mom at the co-op sometimes."

This is the moment when I should apologize for not keeping in touch. Instead I roll my window down and hang my arm out. "How are your folks?"

Bernie grins, as if no time has passed and he's surprised at the banality of my question.

The farm's visible from the bridge over the 101, but it's a long drive through the field access road to reach the buildings. A trail of dust follows the truck and obscures the objects in the side mirror. They're growing corn to the left and alfalfa to the right. Bernie barely keeps his hands on the wheel as he gestures to the bordering acreage they've purchased. The whole op's expanded—there's a second barn and an addition to the original, along with a covered manure shed. The only item untouched is the old shack where his grandfather used to live. We used to play in it as kids, but the place terrified me. It was full of weird bits of scrap metal and old-time vanilla extract bottles, remnants of his tinkering and alcoholism. It's just as depressing in its decay—the tarpaper roof peeling and the whitewash grey as old Y fronts.

"Keep meaning to tear that down," Bernie says.

I look away, not wanting to embarrass him. "Remember when you invited me over to help out with the chickens?"

"Sure."

It was back in grade nine or ten, when Bernie took me to help with the thanksgiving slaughter. The farm hadn't been such a big operation then, and most of the birds still met their maker with the twist of a neck, instead of the electric wands they use now.

"You know I'm studying poultry farms?"

"Oh yeah?"

"Just the manure." I try to describe it as non-technically as possible. "I'm researching the different levels of nitrogen absorption between slurry and litter and its application with no-till farming."

Bernie shakes his head. "You need a degree to spread shit on a field?"

In the chicken coop, Bernie plows straight through the crowd of birds to reach the feeding troughs. He's wearing his big Wellingtons but I'm in suede sneakers and the chickens are attracted to the plum colour. As soon as I lift one foot off the ground, the birds swarm under, jumping and clucking over the laces.

Bernie catches me like that, with one foot up and just starts howling. I manage to find a foothold and try to hover my feet an inch off the floor in a kind of slide-walk. Straw and excrement collects all along the front of my sneakers. I end up kicking a chicken's rear. Bernie doubles over laughing as I stand there flustered.

"Just don't move," he says and lumbers over. He hoists me on his back in a fireman's hold and carries me across the room, planting me down next to the sliding doors. "Thought you had experience on chicken farms."

He walks the perimeter of the barn, making sure the automated feeder is working. There must be thousands of chickens in here and you can't see floor space because they take up the whole area. It looks like a roiling mass of popcorn, white bundles popping up around the room. I discreetly wipe the shit off my shoes using the door frame as a scraper.

Looking at Bernie across the barn, he doesn't look so different from himself at seventeen or eighteen. His hair's grown out a bit and the ends curl off in loose corkscrews but he's got the same ropey beanpole physique. Mostly he seems more relaxed, like he's given himself permission to take up space. He notices me looking at him and waves. "Almost done." He's found a dead bird by the wall.

Bernie loops back around, the dead chicken rigid in his hand, and unlatches the door to the original barn, where we find the turkeys. Only half of the pens are full, the rest of the birds are grazing in the attached corral. "You study turkey shit too or just chickens?"

"Just chickens."

"And here I thought you were a big city girl now."

When we step into the light again, an old Dodge K-car has come down the drive. The dust hangs in the air like a jet stream.

"Dad's here," Bernie says. "Come on and say hi."

I check my watch. Quarter to twelve—the boys should be making lunch by now.

The sun is behind him as Bernie's dad walks towards us. I can't make out his features, just the general slope of his silhouette. Bernie's jumping next to me, flagging his Dad down, and I'm beginning to feel like some prize fish that he's caught and can't wait to show off.

When his dad reaches us, Bernie shifts from side to side. "Look who we've got here."

His father hasn't aged much either. He's always been a smaller man, with ash-brown hair and quick, ferrety eyes. The lines in his face have deepened, stained a dark nicotine. The skin around his mouth is puckered from smoking. He doesn't say anything at first, so I hold out my hand, recoiling from the unexpected high pitch of my voice. I sound like I'm fifteen.

"I heard from Jason you were in town," he says, kicking at the ground and studying his fingers. "You been in to see the chickens?"

"How have you been, Mr. McInnes?"

"You can just call me Clarence now, I guess." He pulls out a pack of smokes from his back pocket and hands one over to Bernie. "Don't suppose you want one?"

I shake my head.

Clarence McInnes has always been a man of few words. When I'd visit after school he'd usually be out on the roads or working in the barn. The few times he was home, he'd sit quiet in the living room with a TV tray in front of him as his wife, Irene, served him coffee. *Wheel of Fortune* was always on the television. Irene encouraged him to watch it—she'd comment on the contestants, point out Vanna White's dresses and guess wildly at the puzzles. He just sat there, kind of beat looking, like it didn't matter to him if the TV were on at all.

"Been a problem up at the Brooks," he says between puffs. "One of the inspectors has been around looking at the drugs." He spits on the ground as he says this. "Told them you'd go by later." Clarence takes a final drag from his cigarette, puts out the butt against his boot heel and flicks it away. He claps his hands against his thighs and asks Bernie if he's finally ready to get to work.

"Already been through," Bernie says. He gestures to the clump of feathers by the barn door. "I'll incinerate it later."

"Thought you were going to give me a hand today."

"I'm in the shop today."

"Fixing cars with dented bumpers?" If I'm the prize catch, Clarence's ready to toss me back into the lake.

"We should probably head back. I'm supposed to find my son a soccer league today."

"You signing him up for peewee?" Bernie asks.

"No, the other one. He's in the under-fourteen."

"Max is in that."

His dad coughs to interrupt. "Linda's been ringing our place for you, Bernie. Wants you to call her at the store." He reaches into his overalls pocket and pulls out a cellphone.

Clarence faces me as Bernie dials. "You met Linda yet?"

"Last night. She seems like a very nice woman."

"You got that right." He doesn't make further effort at conversation until Bernie flips the phone off. "Come over later and give me a hand anyway."

"Nice to see you, Clarence."

He tips his cap by way of goodbye and rambles off to the barn.

Bernie and I get in the truck without saying anything. He checks the rear-view mirror, as though he's afraid someone's in the pickup listening in. "You know how rumours are around here. He thinks you've become some kind of inspector. We've been getting a lot of grief from inspectors."

"I'm a soil scientist."

"That sounds an awful lot like inspector to someone like Dad."

The manic spark's gone out of Bernie. We drive back through New Minas so he can stop into the Superstore to visit Linda. New Minas has always been a squat town—commercial gristle between Wolfville and Kentville's heritage homes—and the arrival of big box stores has only entrenched this. It's a bleak view of the store's loading dock as I wait for Bernie's return, the dumpster piled high with plastic wrap and expired produce.

My mother always thought Bernie was sweet on me but I think she just wanted me to get sweet on him. He spent enough time at our place that she'd come to see him as the son she'd never had. Mom had always wanted a whole passel of kids, but Dad got testicular cancer shortly after they'd had me and that was that. Financially, it was probably easier that way—just one kid to support through the relapse and after he died. Siblings would have been company for her, though. One of us would have stuck around and raised a family within driving distance.

It wasn't Bernie I was interested in. After that March break ski trip, I was allowed into new circles that included Chuck and his friends. Chuck had this great shag cut and dirty blond hair and was muscled from working on the farm. Bernie was Bernie, lanky and curly-haired, sweet and awkward.

We all went to a kegger in the bush one night in late June, up at Three Pools. Bernie'd gone home early to look after some business with his folks. He didn't want to leave me there, but I'd brought my sleeping bag and figured I'd camp out. The weed and Miller Lite made me brave and when some people decided to go skinny-dipping, I figured, what the hell. I peeled out of my clothes and slipped in near the side, where I didn't think so many people would see. Chuck swam over next to me and pushed my head under the water. I swatted him off but he grabbed my hand and held it in his. He slid his thumb up and down my palm and asked if I wanted to go to the top pool.

We were the only ones up there and he didn't waste any time. I hadn't really kissed anyone before and it took some time to get used to, especially since I was trying to tread water at the same time. The second time I kicked his shin, he manoeuvred me over to a rock and leaned me back against it. I was glad to be drunk, hoping it meant he wouldn't notice how awkward it was.

After a while, Chuck reached below the water and started pushing his fingers up and inside me. He kept bobbing his cock against my thigh as he did it. In the dark, in the water, it felt like Jacques Cousteau gone wrong—his fingers like lobster pincers inside me, the eel on my leg. None of it really turned me on, but I thought this was what sex must be like. I didn't say no. I wasn't saving it for anything.

The rock left thin red scrapes on my back. If I hadn't been trashed I might have cried, but I wasn't feeling very much, so I just bit my lips and tried to get into the rhythm of it. What I remember most was the algae smell of the water, the campfire smoke in Chuck's hair as it curtained my face and the sound of the water slapping on the rocks. It didn't take long. Chuck had the sense to withdraw.

We lay by the rocks for a while, not touching. I've just been screwed, I thought, and didn't know how I should feel about it. Chuck pulled me against his side and kissed my forehead. "I've been waiting to lay you for a long time, Ellie." I'm embarrassed to admit it made me feel special.

When we got back to the party, the clutch of people still around the campfire catcalled as we got dried off. One of Chuck's friends high-fived him. The girl on his lap gave me a sideways smile. She was a few grades younger but already had a reputation. At the time it felt like she was saying, "See. You're no better than me." I'd spent all of high school keeping my head down, getting good grades, avoiding the kind of trouble girls like her got in.

Classes had already ended so I was spared hallway rumours. It meant that I could spend the summer insulated, hanging out with people who couldn't judge me because they'd done worse. None of them would be following me to Acadia. The only person I'd have to fess up to was Bernie.

When he gets back in the cab, Bernie spares me by bringing up the soccer team straightway. "You going to put your boy on the Canning league?"

"I have to call. Last week they told us it might be too late."

"Jason's the team sponsor. He'll talk to the coach if you want."

"Really?"

"Sure," he says, as if it's no big thing. "It'd be good. That way Linda can meet you properly and your boys can meet Max and Lisa."

"Max really looks like you."

"He does?" Bernie gives me a strange look. "They're good kids."

I settle up with Jason in the auto-shop office, an old storage closet that's been converted into the accounts department. Jason fiddles through some papers and pulls out a receipt book. "Most of my customers just give cash."

I've only got plastic but he waves off my apology. "Don't worry, just means I have to find the clicker." He locates an old credit card press and hands me the triplicate to sign.

Bernie opens the door, which makes a tight fit. He runs his thumb over the top of a receipt spike. "Jason, Ellie wants to get her son on the soccer team."

"I just pay for the uniforms."

"Well, that's a start," Bernie says. "You got any shirts out in the back?"

Jason looks at his brother and suppresses a grin.

Bernie turns back to me. "Just bring him by practice on Wednesday, we'll sort it out on the field."

*   *   *

It's after eleven when my mother emerges the next morning, looking tired and pale. I bustle around her, laying out an English muffin and fruit salad, asking how she slept. She picks at a few segments of grapefruit. There's a thud as Stephen's soccer ball collides with the outside wall and my mother jumps at the sound.

"The boys."

My mother's attention's already lost. She opens and closes her right hand like a baby asking for a dropped toy.

"Do you need anything?"

She points at the bear-shaped honey bottle. Once I deliver it, however, she goes back to the fruit. I start to squeeze out some honey over her toast but she bats me away and it dribbles on the tablecloth. As I dab it clean with a J-cloth, I point to Stephen out the window. "He's already gearing up for the team."

"You should ask Bernie about that."

I tilt my head, unsure of what she means. "I already talked to him."

She half-nods, but it's not convincing.

We sit in silence, each of us mirroring the other's hunched mug clasp. It reminds me of when my father died and she'd sit me down at this same table those nights when I would wake up crying. She never showed her reaction to his death, just kept going tick tock tick, dependable. I was thirteen and so bereft of him. Seldom a week went by that first year that I didn't have the same nightmare about my mother getting washed away at a picnic. We'd be at Cape Split—Mom, Dad and I—and we'd finished eating but the tide came thundering in too fast. Dad and I scrambled up to the cliff, but my mother floated out to sea on the red-chequered picnic blanket. As bad as losing my father had been, I must have known I'd be lost without my mother.

The only thing that changed about the dream was the food at the picnic. Sometimes it was peanut butter and banana sandwiches, sometimes roast beef, sometimes heaps of corn nuts. Mom called the part about her floating away "stuff and nonsense" but she encouraged me to detail the food. She'd hear me sobbing and set the kettle on to boil. That was my cue to come padding into the kitchen. She'd rummage around in the cupboard for the box of digestive biscuits and dole one out, saying "I think you're just hungry."

My mother's still fussing with her breakfast but the colour in her face is improving. I try to casually mention another trip to the doctor but she snaps as soon as the words are out.

"You're not going to truck me all across Kings County looking for a physician."

"Will you at least book a physical? All I care about is blood work. It could just be that you're borderline anaemic, that's why you're tired."

My mother purses her lips. "I can tell you what the problem is—I'm getting old. That's all there is to it. My mother was the same way." She wipes a crumb off her lip. "If you insist on meddling, you can drive me down to Shoppers and I'll shove my arm in that cuff device."

The boys want to test their blood pressure as well. I leave them with my mother on the strict promise that they won't use the machine more than twice, then go wait in the pharmacy parking lot. The car windows fog up quickly, turning the vehicle into a dank cocoon.

Richard would have flown home last night and I try to picture what the house is like now that he's back. Ten to one, the luggage is still in the front hall and he's eating a late lunch in front of the TV, still in his briefs. I wonder if he's missing us yet, our family rituals, or if he's revelling in the space. It's been three days since we've spoken. He's chatted with the boys but each time I've begged off with some excuse.

There's a series of clunks as he answers, then silence. "Hang on," his voice calls, distant, like he's dropped the phone. When he gets back on the line the mechanical thudding's still audible.

"Laundry." The noise retreats as he walks upstairs. I didn't think he'd get to the washing for at least another day.

"How's the house?"

"Fine. Plants are watered. Mail is sorted. I stripped the sheets on the boys' beds."

"You've been busy."

"It's quiet." Richard's voice softens when he says it. There's a vulnerability he isn't trying to mask. "I thought I'd get another email from you."

"I've been distracted with my mother." I run him through the list of symptoms. Leaning into the phone, hearing his breathing on the other end, it doesn't feel like we're so far apart. The distance of the fight, of the trip, bridged by these data transfers and sound waves.

He tells me he misses me.

I miss him too. I ask about the conference.

"The folks at McGill are applying for funding to bring me on as a consultant. We're going to try to run a section of the lab as a satellite research station, bring some grad students on. The best part is there's whole outcroppings of the stuff. Even if it's not the oldest, it's a significant find. There's already a lot of directions for spin-off investigation. How do you feel about a sabbatical in Montreal?"

It's hard to fight down the welling jealousy, keep my reply jovial. "Sounds cold."

"The boys can learn French. We'll get fat on croissant."

I rub my arm against the window to clear the condensation. No sign of the boys yet. "Have you started on the article?"

"Tomorrow." He's nervous about it. Probably the only thing he doesn't excel at, career-wise, is writing in laymen's terms. *BBC Science* wants the hard research, but it's general readership. At home, Richard's got shelves devoted to all the popular science new releases in hopes that one day he'll write a similar volume on geochronology and the origins of life. He's been courting periodicals like *BBC Science* for a long time. "Can I email you the draft as I go?"

"Sure."

"My goal for the end of next week is an outline."

"It's only twenty-five hundred words, right?" It's a dig I shouldn't have made.

His speech stiffens. "Have you started looking into winter postings yet?"

He knows I haven't.

"How did the conversation with Prescott go after all?"

Richard doesn't answer right away and there are noises in the background again.

"Don't get angry."

He's back in the laundry room. The starchy transfer of wet clothes into the dryer fills his silence.

"It sounds stupid now. I thought once you got out there— it'd be a new perspective."

He hasn't told Prescott.

"It was stupid, wasn't it?"

I'm not going into the whole argument again.

"You applied for me. You can quit for me."

His voice itself is an apology but I don't give a shit how contrite he sounds. The boys are walking across the parking lot, waving their blood pressure printouts in the air like lottery tickets.

"Drop the courses." I pause. "Final word."

The next stop is the library for the boys to check their email and my mother to pick up a mystery paperback. As they scatter to their separate purposes, I'm glad to be alone with my rage. I log onto the express terminal, my body thrumming, and cancel the flights we still have for later this summer. There's a fifty dollar fee on each ticket, but I'm happy to swallow it. Next, I look up the address of Dr. Marc Morris, an old acquaintance from an agro conference at Guelph. It's hard to keep my hand steady enough to navigate the mouse. Marc's now acting chair of Acadia's Earth Science department and I drop him a quick note to ask if he has time to meet. Acadia's about as wide a net as I can cast.

At the soccer field in New Minas, Stephen bounds over to the coach. I scan the bleachers for Bernie, still unsure how to pay the registration fee. He's over on the far side of the pitch with Linda. She doesn't wave back.

"Forgot there's a game today," Bernie says when he reaches us. He looks down at Luke. "You ready to kick the ball around too?"

Luke shies beside me, eyes popping.

Bernie absently brushes a bit of fluff out of his hair—he must have come straight from work. He's wearing tight jeans with holes in the knees, stains spattered on them and his T-shirt tucked-in. He holds his hand out to shake my mother's. "You're looking well, Lynne."

"Not according to my daughter." She points across the field. "You sitting over there then?"

"Yeah, that's Linda—third row up."

My mother takes Luke's hand and the two of them cross the field.

"Cute kids," Bernie says.

"Thanks."

"Ellie and her pickaninnies."

The term catches me so off guard that I stop walking and have to stumble to catch up to Bernie. My eyes dart to Stephen and Luke, worried they've heard. I'd forgotten the way people out here can be. Bernie glances at me to see why I've slowed our pace. "We never use that word."

Bernie shrugs an apology. "Lindie says mulatto."

"I don't like that word either." We usually say "multiracial" even though it sounds like my sons are human versions of Expo's "Cultures of the World" pavilion.

"Cute kids anyway."

This high-school reunion may have been a mistake. A wall of anxiety builds as we reach Stephen.

The team has already started their warm-up. The boys are doing jumping jacks in a double line, the coach in front, barking out the count. Stephen's already wearing the team jersey but the coach has him waiting at the side.

Bernie makes the introductions. "This here's Donnie. Donnie, Ellie."

Donnie's a short man, bald and marble-eyed but with hulking calves and biceps. He stands with his feet wide apart, hands on his hips, wearing an outdated neon windbreaker.

"Thanks for letting my son join the league."

Bernie shifts from foot to foot and Donnie looks up at him. "Well, Bernie mentioned it, but I told him to talk to the Parks and Rec. I'm not supposed to put a kid in without the paperwork."

"Donnie," Bernie says, "you know what the Parks and Rec people are like."

"Tighter than the bishop's ass come Sunday morning," he chortles, checking for my reaction. "But I don't want to get in trouble with them."

Again, I glance over to make sure my son hasn't overheard.

"My brother already gave him a shirt." Bernie lowers his voice. "I figured we could make an arrangement like we did with Max."

Donnie frowns and checks his watch. "Your boy work hard?"

"Soccer's pretty much all he's got on his mind."

Donnie snorts, then scratches his thigh, near the crotch. He nods towards Bernie. "You can explain about the payment. If anyone asks, I'll say I lost the form."

Bernie claps him on the shoulder and Donnie looks up at him, subtly flexing his muscles. On the way back, Bernie tells me that he'd already agreed to as much, but he likes to jerk people's chains. I just have to pay him the registration fee under the table.

Stephen catches my eye as we walk past and I give two thumbs up. Donnie walks over to him and kicks the ball back and forth a few times, testing his reflexes. There's not much time for an evaluation, so Donnie just whistles and starts running the team through drills.

As we make for the bleachers it strikes me once again that my sons are the only black kids on the field. It wasn't as noticeable when we were just running errands, but now that there's an assembly of people, the homogeny is overwhelming.

Nova Scotia's always had a strong black community but it's also been heavily segregated into predominantly black towns outside of Halifax. My mother used to tell me about a high-school friend who briefly dated a black Dalhousie student. When her parents found out, they kicked her out of the house for a week. That was in the late sixties, around the time the government bulldozed through the town of Africville to make way for the MacKay bridge.

Up ahead, my mother's parked on the lowest bench with Luke.

"Come on sit up with me and Linda," Bernie says. "Lisa's at her Nan's."

"Your mom's?"

"Her father's actually."

I stifle my surprise.

"I didn't tell you the other day—Linda and I've only been together for the past four years."

"You all seem to get along really well."

"Tryin'," he says. "Just trying." He calls to Linda and she gestures with her hands, what? She exhales her cigarette smoke, clearly annoyed and marches down the bleachers.

"Hi, Linda."

"Yep." She's wearing tight tapered jeans and a cropped tank that shows off her belly ring—a pink rhinestone heart. I feel ancient around her.

"Well," Bernie says, "the boy's on the team." He puts his arm around Linda's waist and pulls her in to kiss the top of her head. She leads him up to her group of friends.

Luke wants to sit up higher too. Linda and her friends begrudgingly move their feet down from the bench to make room.

Linda points her cigarette at the other women. "Gail, Diane, Sandra."

"Hi," I say.

No response.

The ref is young—seventeen tops—with the run of an adolescent whose limbs have outgrown his coordination.

Linda hollers at him. "Get going, will ya."

One of her friends adds, "Don't go soft on Kentville."

The ref doesn't hear them and continues chatting with the coaches at centre field. The kids are in position, all ready to go and I notice that Stephen's off to the side, near the back. I can't remember the names of the positions but it's defence. Max's front and centre.

"Quit your moaning, boys," Gail calls. "I want to eat dinner before it walks off."

The poor ref is getting an earful from the Kentville coach and Donnie looks ready to punch. The coin toss hasn't even happened yet. Finally the kid pulls himself together, pushing the two men apart and blows firmly into his whistle. The bleating temporarily stuns them.

"Course Donnie's only pissed because his wife's left him again," Gail drawls.

Linda swivels around and I watch her discreetly. "I heard they were back together. I heard they tried that couples' therapy."

"Nah," Gail says. "I seen her just last week at the Cineplex with that guy from the service station sucking face at *The Da Vinci Code*."

"That new guy at the Irving?" Sandra cackles, then mouths, "Hung like a fucking horse." She spreads her hands a good two feet apart.

Luke leans in and asks, "What's sucking face?"

Linda answers, "That's eating popcorn."

He looks up at me sceptically. I just nod and point at the field, where the play has finally begun.

The kids on the Kentville team are about a foot taller than most of Stephen's teammates. Their brawn alone is going to make it difficult for our team to win—apparently they creamed the Canning boys last year. One of the Kentville boys bludgeons his way through a wall of our players and instantly scores a goal. Max tries to kick it out from underneath the player, but gets knocked down by the kid's shoulder.

Linda screams out encouragement. "You get up and show them." The other women whoop in solidarity.

"You been out here before?" Bernie asks Luke.

Luke doesn't answer, just scoots onto my lap.

"Shy. So where were you working this afternoon?"

"Over at the fields near Evangeline Beach."

"How many acres you working these days?"

"About 250—there's the fields around the poultry op, the ones out by the beach and we inherited sixty acres from my uncle a few years ago. Linda's got some cousins we've got an arrangement with—so that's another eighty."

"What are you growing?"

"Corn mostly and rotating hay through."

"Grain or fodder?"

"Feed corn." The sun is in Bernie's face, his hand a visor over his eyes. "You want to know what seed we use too?"

The ref whistles—Kentville's offside. The coach nods to Stephen for the free kick. There are a couple of Kentville kids in front of him and Stephen pauses, rolling the ball back and forth under his foot, unsure where to aim. He fakes to the side and gets the ball up and out.

"Nice one," Bernie calls out, clapping. Linda's friends make eyes at each other. One of them points her finger down her mouth, pretending to gag.

Bernie ignores them. "Now you're a teacher, then."

"Yeah, now I'm a teacher."

A few feet over from our bleachers, the Kentville parents are as menacing as the kids. There's one father who keeps screeching out directions to his son Brad, a freckled kid with a headband, waving him over to instruct him on plays. It's irritating the coach. Brad isn't a particularly talented player but you can tell he's doing his best.

Kentville scores another goal. Stephen's team manages a few shots, but only one of them connects. Our cheering section sags into silence for the remainder of the game. I expect Stephen to be disappointed by the loss, but when he jogs over with Max, he's in a good mood. Max's just as fanatic about the sport and the two of them are instantly at ease with each other.

Bernie suggests we all go to the Pizza Delight in New Minas. Linda's face sours and my instinct is to decline. Max, however, mentions that they have a sundae bar and the boys look up expectantly. It will be good for them to spend time with other kids.

Bernie offers to give Stephen and Luke a ride in the back of the truck and they jump at the chance. Linda shifts her weight to her left hip and snarls up at Bernie. "Going to be a packed ride."

Bernie suggests that she ride in the car with me. It reeks of a set-up.

"Sure," I say, playing nice. "Plenty of room."

Linda gets in the back seat, behind my mother, and scratches her nail along the upholstery. "How long you had this for?"

"Four years."

"Thought it looked older. Looks like my dad's old one."

My mother grabs the headrest and cranes around to face her. "Max is pretty sharp on the field, goes right for the ball."

"He's scrappy."

"You ever play sports?"

"Sure, volleyball up until grade eleven when I dropped out."

"I tried to get Ellie into sports, but it never took. Which high school did you end up at?"

"Horton."

"Been redone, hasn't it?"

"Looks like a mall now."

"Same with Cornwallis, that's where Ellie went."

"Yeah, Bernie mentioned that."

"It's funny," I say. "How much Max looks like Bernie, even though he's not his."

Linda rolls down the window and spits her gum out. "Oh, they're his kids all right, even if it's not by blood."

"Hard raising them on your own," my mother says.

"What do you know about it?" Linda snaps.

"My husband died when Ellie was thirteen."

Linda nods. "This guy split after Lisa was born." She pulls her cigarettes out of her purse. "Mind if I smoke?"

My mother answers for me. "Just keep the window down." We're close enough to the restaurant that I don't feel like protesting. "Of course," she continues. "You bring them up and then they fly the coop. That's hard too."

Linda takes a deep suck on her cigarette and exhales out of the corner of her mouth, so most of the smoke funnels out the window. She looks at me in the rear-view, catches me eyeing her. "Yeah," she says. "It's a sin."

My mother's family was from Dartmouth. Dad's was from Digby. They settled in Canning because it was a few hours away from both of them. Dad didn't want the daily interference of living in the same town as his in-laws, but wanted to be close enough to drive. They'd thought there'd be regular visits when they had kids, but both families expected Mom and Dad to do the travelling. One Christmas, we wiped out driving from Digby to Halifax in a blizzard. After that we only visited for funerals.

When my move to Toronto became permanent, Mom didn't want the same estrangement. Shortly after Stephen was born, she arranged to take a month off from the grocery co-op to come live with us. She'd packed her suitcase full of baby essentials—onesies, cloth diapers, jumbo safety pins and a large tub of Zincofax cream—as if she'd been worried they didn't stock them in Ontario.

Richard and Terrence had both taken time off work too and I could tell that their presence put her on edge. My own father had gone back to work the day after my mother came home from the hospital because they needed the income.

Terrence had also missed out on raising a newborn so he was eager to help change diapers and do bottle feedings. My mother didn't mind sharing at first, because Terrence was so charming to her and deferential—he let her demonstrate how to fasten the pins, how to cradle the baby's head. My mother didn't want me to have to keep up with the housework so she did all the dishes, kept a pail of bleach-water by the backdoor for soaking diapers and did all the laundry, separating everyone's out in crisply folded piles and leaving them on our respective beds.

It made Richard uncomfortable. He said it was like having a nanny, which he vehemently disagreed with. Years later we'd have a cleaning lady and he wouldn't complain, but being a father was new and precious and he wanted to do everything himself.

My mother indulged my breast-feeding for a week, but then started preparing infant formula and using it whenever she fed Stephen. I wanted to continue on the breast exclusively but when she'd had me, the nurses told her that formula was more nutritious. She took offence when Richard showed her articles about the importance of breast milk.

Then the Trinidadian cousins and aunties started coming over to meet the baby. We only saw the extended family at big holidays or at Caribana, but it was important to Terrence and I didn't mind. They always brought sweets and curries and the conversation was full of banter, especially when the older folks came over. It didn't take much to get someone keening into an old story, or singing to the baby. It reminded me of when I'd have dinner at Bernie's—the same boisterous exuber-ance I'd wished I'd belonged to all the time.

My mother never said much when the relatives were there. She was shy; they all knew each other. She'd never said anything negative about my marrying Richard, but I don't think she'd realized he came with a family. She kept pulling me aside to ask, "How are there so many of them?" Back home, everyone she knew was white. Most of her friends had never travelled out-side the province or lived in a city and they held to the same fixed ideas as their parents, grandparents. Coming to visit was the first time my mother had ever taken an airplane.

By the end of the second week, tensions were frayed. My mother asked if we might have a few days to relax, just the two of us and the baby. Richard was angry at being excluded, but he knew that accommodating my mother was important to me. Once everyone left, however, we didn't have much to say to each other.

Dad was the talkative one in my parents' marriage and I often wonder what our family would have been like if he'd sur-vived. I took after my mother, quiet. People like us need some-one else to prod us along, open up the doors to social contact. Without it, we clam up. I'd never doubted the current of attach-ment between my mother and me, but our communication had calcified over the years.

For the three days, all I did was give Stephen every other feeding because my mother wanted to take care of everything. Enough was enough. I told Richard we should all go to a base-ball game and Terrence got us cheap seats in the nosebleed sec-tion of the Skydome. The men drank beer and ate unshelled peanuts and my mother fretted the entire time that a stray ball was going to kill her grandson. She took the train home four days earlier than planned. Richard didn't hide his relief on the way back from Union Station and I couldn't blame him. Part of me was equally relieved to be back to our family unit, but the other part was angry with myself. I should have been more patient. I should have found a way to make her feel like she had a place with us. On the surface, her goodbye was as it should be, but something had changed between us.

We offered to fly her in for Christmas. She said she couldn't afford the time off.

5

I T'S ONLY QUARTER TO TEN when I hit Wolfville, far too early for my meeting with Marc Morris. The waiting cranks my anxiety and I kill time driving around campus. The conference was over three years ago and we only spoke briefly. He'd mentioned in his presentation that he'd grown up in Sheubenacadie and we'd chatted about the connection. At the time he was doing research on grass hybrids for wetland soils but I don't know what he's working on now.

Acadia's changed so much that I barely recognize my old residence at the top of the hill. The exterior's been reskinned, but it's still the same five brick towers connected by concrete hallways. The campus makeover's followed the Georgian style of the older buildings, which is lucky. It could have gone the other way and skewed towards the boxy '60s monstrosities like the Vaughan Library.

Marc's office is on the third floor of the Huggins building, at the end of a hallway lined with student posters. A lot of the names on the doorplates haven't changed since my undergrad. Through an open door, I think I see Marc hunched behind a laptop but I'm not sure. At the conference, I could have sworn his hair was blond. Now it's dark and clipped tight to hide a thinning patch on top. He catches me hesitating in the doorway and rises, sliding his black wireframes up the bridge of his nose.

We are wearing his and her versions of the same outfit—khaki pants, white shirt and a Mountain Equipment Co-op fleece. It breaks the tension immediately.

On the walk to the new botanical gardens, Marc tells me he's only been with the university about four years. "There's talk of amalgamating with geology to become a giant Earth Sciences department." He looks over his shoulder as he says it, but the only other people around are school kids in bright T-shirts—day campers. "A lot of the old guard are changing."

"I noticed that Schaffer is still around."

"Don't get me wrong, but we're trying to take the department in a new direction. Start bringing in grad students, generating more research. What's it like at Guelph these days?"

"Competitive." I skate past my recent layoff. "You know how it is, some of the branches get hot and the others scramble to preserve their budgets."

"We've had that problem here—constant pressure to water down first year courses to inflate enrolment." He rolls his eyes. "Rocks for jocks."

He opens the door to the Irving Centre and I'm shocked by the span of the place. We veer right in the foyer to a little café. Marc hands over a travel mug and introduces me to the attendant, one of his undergrad honours students. "This is Dr. Ellie Bascom. She's a visiting scholar."

The girl flusters, keen as I was at that age, doesn't charge for my coffee.

I fumble for change to tip her.

We stroll out to the public greenhouses just off the main entrance. They are so bright, white and clean it gives the impression of a plant hospital.

"I was really excited to get your email because we're going to try a pilot agroecology course next year—upper-year seminar and labs," Marc says. "I'm still developing the soil unit. I'd love to pick your brain about it."

"How long a unit are you planning?"

"Only about a month and a half."

I offer to walk him through some soil profiling and sampling labs.

"I've got a couple of grad students around for the summer and I've still got some discretionary funds. If you're interested, I could bring you in for a few hours as a consultant."

Marc fiddles with the key chain carabiner on his waistband. "We're doing some tests on soil contamination in the experimental garden, but I really want to branch into agroecology. There's the college in Truro, but—we're the biggest school this side of Halifax, we've got the Kentville Agriculture Centre down the road, we're surrounded by farmland—why shouldn't we be leading the research?"

Exactly.

"What are you working on at Guelph right now? I looked up the website, but couldn't find your page."

When I tell him, Marc seems genuinely concerned. "Where are you in the fall?"

"Still determining that." I study the terracotta planter across from me and wait too long before answering again, the silence choking the earlier familiarity. When I do speak, I gesticulate with my hands like a bombing vaudevillian trying to rouse the audience. "I'd been investigating applications for poultry manure fertilizer and soil conservation best practices."

"So we've caught you as a free agent." Marc smiles, unfazed. He surveys the near-empty room. "It's never this quiet. I should have been coming here all spring."

"I think that every time I get down to the beaches in Toronto."

"I never made it past YYZ. You like the city?"

"We're in a nice neighbourhood. But it's good to be back."

"My wife, Margie, and I always thought we'd settle in Halifax, but I like the pace here."

He leads us out to the formal gardens, which are spectacular. Looking towards the treeline, there's no sign of the town behind, as if this really were the lawn of some grand English estate. If I worked on campus, I'd teach every class out here. This is what I can never articulate to Richard, who thrives on the constant abutment of city-life—buildings on top of buildings, growing out of one another like nurse logs. He doesn't understand how it can be exciting to be silent, to be small, to be surrounded by green.

*   *   *

Bernie's found a good deal on a small forklift out by Peggy's Cove and calls to see if the boys want to come along for the ride. My mother already has plans to take them into Wolfville for Mud Creek Days, but Stephen's iffy about it, worried he's going to be the oldest kid there. When I ask him if he'd rather hang out with Bernie, Stephen pulls a face. "He's such a hick."

"I don't want to hear that word again."

Luke diverts the argument by asking his brother what he should get the face-painter to draw—koala or giraffe?

Stephen decides he'd rather not stick around doing kid things after all and my mother offers to take Lisa to the fair along with Luke.

Bernie's other errand is delivering a puppy from the neighbour's litter to one of Linda's cousins. It's a squirming sandy-brown thing—part lab, part shepherd. Stephen and Max sit in the back of the truck cab, trying to get it to sit still in its cardboard box.

Stephen wants to know if Max gets to keep one of the puppies himself.

"Ask Bernie." It's the first time I've heard Max call Bernie by his first name. I wonder if Linda's asked him to call him Dad.

"It's your mother you're going to have to convince."

"She'll say yes if you do."

"No way is Linda going to let a mutt mark up her floors." Bernie swivels around to Stephen. "We got a couple more—you could take one home."

Stephen picks up the puppy and arranges its front paws over the seat back. He ducks down and moves the dog's legs like a marionette, his voice part Scooby Doo, part urchin. "Say yes! Say yes!"

"Your father's allergic."

"Can't you get shots?" Max asks.

"Get shots! Get shots!"

I lie. "Richard has a thing about needles."

We drop the dog off at the cousin's then get the forklift. The seller's got a crane at the back of the house and he uses it to hoist the machine into the pickup. The house is run down—a squat wooden rectangle with a sagging shingle roof. There's a bigger garage where the construction equipment's stored, but it's also ramshackle. There's a Hustler calendar next to the light switch that's still displaying Miss April 1983's plentiful bush. Stephen glances at it and quickly looks away, jamming his hands in his pockets.

Max is used to all the machinery and gets right in there, helping tie down the straps and opening the truck gate. The seller even calls Max over and lets him operate the crane levers. Stephen and I stand back, watching. I can tell he's nervous. He'd thought Bernie was rough around the edges, but it's nothing compared to the forklift owner's seedy beard, his white T-shirt yellowed with sweat.

"I saw a crane get stuck in the mud when I was growing up," I tell my son. He's scanning the scene in front of us, half-apprehensive, half-entranced. "One spring at Bernie's place. It was so muddy that the treads just made a big rut in the ground. They used to get tractors stuck in fields all the time if the thaw came too quick."

"How'd they get it out?"

"Usually had to wait until the ground drained and hardened. Sometimes you could wedge a plank or something underneath."

Stephen hasn't spent a lot of time outside the city, except for a weekend or two at a friend's Muskoka cottage. "I can't believe you hung out on a farm."

"I practically lived at Bernie's."

"How come I've never heard of him before?"

It's a fair question and I want to answer it honestly. "We grew apart for a while."

Stephen squints over at me. "Was he your boyfriend?" The boys know that their father was married before, but I've never talked much about my past.

I shake my head. "No, Bernie was more like a brother."

On the way to the cove, Max asks Stephen if he knows about the Swiss Air plane crash.

Bernie glances at me, appraising whether or not he should let Max continue.

"Did people die?" Stephen asks.

"All of them," Bernie says. "The whole area was shut down for months." He pulls into a parking lot a few kilometres away from Peggy's Cove and I realize it's the memorial site. We file out of the truck and Bernie maps the plane's trajectory with his hand. "They crashed over there."

Max sidles up to Stephen and points across the bay. "That's where the forensic tents were set up."

I'm curious as to how Max knows so much about something he's too young to remember but I don't want to push the conversation any further in case Stephen develops a fear of flying. We reach the twin stone memorials and mull around for another few moments, unsure of what to say. Back at the truck, Bernie pulls some small metal spheres out of the ashtray compartment. I roll them around the palm of my hand. Bernie's looking mischievous now, waiting for me to identify what they are.

"Ballpoint pen?"

He shakes his head. I hand them to Stephen. He guesses they're for jewellery.

Bernie returns them to the tray. "Ball bearings," he says. "From a woman's torso."

"That's not even funny."

"It's true," Max says.

"I got them from a buddy on the forensics team—he showed me all the photos from the investigation. People started trolling that area looking for scraps pretty soon after."

"Since when are you hanging out with forensic scientists?" I ask sharply, appalled by his souvenir.

"One of Chuck's cousins. Went through the program at Dal." I flush at the mention.

We were on sabbatical that year and travelling in Trinidad, so we missed a lot of the coverage. There, the story was just a blip—a report on the night of the crash and a follow-up a few days later. They played some BBC feed with a journalist commending the Canadians for the hospitality they showed to the bereaved. That's the thing about Nova Scotia, people'll give you a blanket right off their own bed and go out scanning the beach for mementoes the same night.

When we reach Peggy's Cove proper, Bernie lugs out a cooler and hands us each an apple juice. He opens his own bottle in an efficient twist, the palm of his hand flat on the cap. It reminds me of the way he used to be at bonfire parties, always able to crack off beer caps with his belt buckle or wedged against the side of a log.

Max leads us down the granite boulders, past where you're supposed to stop and I don't want to say anything that will make Bernie think I'm being picky again. We get as close to the water as possible, where you can see the barnacles and mussels on the rocks, like a mottled black frosting. Suddenly Bernie twists around and picks me up, so my head is lower than my feet. "Stephen, do you think I should toss your mom in?"

He laughs. Max hollers, "Give 'er."

Bernie pretends to heave, one, two, three, like he's going to really swing me into the ocean. Then he whirls me around and plants me back down. "Better not."

The boys sprint back up the rocks. If Richard was here, I'd say something—don't run, don't slip. Instead, I scramble up the slope alongside them. They're too fast for us. At the crest, Bernie and I sit at angles so we can keep an eye on them. I take my shoes off to feel the heat of the granite against my soles.

"What are you going to do with the forklift?"

"Move things."

I punch his shoulder.

"Use it for packing away the hay, maybe start storing other things on skids." He leans back on his palms and squints up into the sun. "It was a good price. Max'll be able to drive it."

"He's working on the farm already?"

"A bit," Bernie says. "May as well hire him myself than have him get some shitty job in back of Tim Hortons. I don't let him work too much during school." He pauses. "Lindie wants him to go to college, like you did."

"He wants to be a scientist?"

"No. He likes the farm." Bernie turns to face me straight on, "There's way more papers now, more certification, inspection. He can learn things at college—restructure the whole op."

"If you want, I can call some colleagues from Guelph— they might know a consultant out here."

Bernie waves me away. "I've got ideas. It's Dad doesn't want change." He scratches absently at the back of his neck. "Later on, if things work out, we're going to get a hatchery going."

"Linda doesn't seem like a farm girl."

"She's as good as you are with the chickens." Bernie grins. "But she's got a head for keeping the books. Lindie likes the Superstore though—she's not giving up the benefits when the kids are still young."

It's strange picturing the two of them together, Bernie and Linda. She's nothing like the kind of girl I thought he'd end up with, too hard, too brash. I wasn't lying to Stephen earlier—I'd never imagined Bernie and me together. For eight years or so of my life I felt closer to him than almost anybody. But I desperately wanted out of the Valley. Even in high school I knew Bernie'd die on the same ground on which he was born.

The boys have circled back now and Bernie calls a race to the pickup. Stephen almost makes it first but Bernie grabs him and spins him to the side so he can win. Stephen pretends to slug Bernie's arm and Bernie cuffs Stephen's hat off. Both boys turn on him and start play-fighting.

Bernie's so much taller, all he has to do is keep one arm out to deflect their punches. After a few minutes he groans and hangs limp so the boys fall back. Max looks worried that he's actually hurt him, but Bernie springs up and jumps into the truck, locking the door. We stand in the parking stall as Bernie backs out. He lets us catch up to him, then accelerates forward a few feet at a time, until there are cars behind us, honking.

Bernie doesn't linger when he drops us off. He gets Lisa settled in the truck, her face still made up to look like a tiger and then shuffles out into the lilac bushes at the far end of the property. He pauses there, facing the trees for a good minute.

"You need anything?" I call out.

He waits another moment, bends his knees then straightens up. When he turns around he winks.

"We have a bathroom inside."

"Nah, just track dirt in." He jumps into the truck, reaching out through the window to tap on the hood.

Luke and Stephen grin back and forth at each other, disgusted and delighted.

That summer before university, we had a big Labour Day party over on Evangeline beach. We'd brought tents and set them up in the campsite, along with three two-fours of beer and some homemade panty-remover from one of the guy's uncles. Chuck and I were more or less an item by that point. There was a tacit agreement that we'd hook up at some point during parties, but we didn't go on dates in between. Chuck still flirted with other girls, but everyone knew to keep a distance. Mostly I'd hang out with Bernie and Jason until Chuck got drunk enough to come over and start giving me attention, feeling me up in front of the other guys and pretending it was a joke.

That night we got drunk fast, before the sun had even gone down. Some people were doing shrooms, but I wasn't on anything and I don't think Bernie was either. After a few hours, we ran out of firewood and we volunteered to search the wooded area up from the beach.

There was a road through the forest leading to a string of cottages, a dark Hansel and Gretel trail. Bernie kept silent until we were well out of the campground. The end of summer was on both our minds; I was moving into residence in a few days. He'd be continuing on at his dad's farm, same as ever.

"Must be expensive."

"Cheaper than buying a second car. There's the scholarship too."

Bernie reached over and tousled my hair. "Too smart for your own good."

I grabbed his hand and pulled him off the trail and into the woods. It was hard to make things out in the trees. The moon was up, but it was a thin crescent and the clouds were blowing in from Blomidon. I grabbed some underbrush and started piling it into the crook of my arm. Bernie's boots made a clomping sound as he walked over the mossy patches. We couldn't have been more than ten feet apart, but he kept reaching out to me every so often, making sure I was there.

"Are we going to see you any more once you're at school?"

"What do you think?" I reached for his hand again. It always felt good to be next to Bernie. It felt like nothing bad could happen.

"You scared?"

I shook my head and pulled away. He held on. "It's okay if you're scared." We found a tree that had snapped and Bernie hoisted it up onto his shoulder, the height dragging behind. I just carried branches—nothing that would burn for long.

It was strange to come back to the group. The forest had been so quiet and we hadn't said much to each other on the way back. When we crested the bank, the fire was blazing and everyone seemed to be having a good time. Someone was playing guitar and a couple of the girls were dancing. Chuck was sitting next to some blonde, someone's cousin from Bridgetown. "You'd better take care of that," Bernie said.

I shrugged.

"What are you two doing anyway?"

"Chuck's Chuck." I raced down to the beach, not wanting to get into it. It turned out Jason had chatted with the manager and had bought logs from him, so what Bernie and I had gathered wasn't needed. Chuck waved when he saw me. The blonde shied away.

Around midnight someone suggested a swim. Evangeline beach isn't really a swimming hole—the shore is pebbly and the ocean cold, but everyone stripped down anyway. Some of the girls took everything off, but the bonfire was too bright and I was embarrassed. Chuck tore off into the water. I unzipped my jeans and noticed Bernie staring at me. I pretended not to see and took off my T-shirt so he had a full view of my bra. Jason ran over, picked me up and tossed me into the water. The naked girls stayed in longest. When they ran out it was into the shadows farther down the beach, their clothes clutched to their chests. I was lucky that my underwear was navy, and may as well have been a bikini. I was aware of Bernie watching me again as I dried off by the fire.

He looked down at the sand when I caught his eye. Chuck saw and grabbed my waist. "You'd better dry off." He spun me around and slapped my back, his hand making a loud smack against the wet cotton. He grabbed my clothes and I sped off after him into the parking lot. I thought we were headed for the pup tent we'd set up, but he led me to Bernie's truck instead. We climbed into the back of the cab and lay on top of an old blanket, fumbling drunk. Chuck started taking off my bra with one hand and rubbing between my legs with the other. Chuck was good with his hands and he'd got me to the brink when we heard the door open. I stopped dead, afraid to breathe.

It was so dark that Bernie didn't see us. He sat in the cab for a minute and there was a metal clang, like he'd undone his belt buckle. Chuck started to grin.

He shoved me upright.

Bernie veered around. He thudded against the door, grabbing for the handle.

Chuck seized Bernie's shoulder. He kept him pinned there, against the seat back and Bernie froze like a dumb dog in the middle of the road, his cock out of his pants, erect.

"Go on, Ellie," Chuck said. "You did this to him." He pushed me so I was half over the front seat, bent over.

"Bernie, you want me to leave?" I looked him in the eye, but he just sat there, mute.

Chuck repeated, "Help him out, Ellie. I don't mind." Then he moved my hand over to Bernie and jerked it up and down. Bernie stared at me, pleading.

I kissed him. He shifted so it was easier and I kept pumping him. He grabbed my breasts, massaging them between his thumb and palm. Bernie kissed differently than Chuck, more clumsy, but more earnest. Then I felt Chuck enter me from behind, but Bernie and I didn't stop. Chuck started pounding, driving hard in a way that was becoming painful. He reached around and played with my clit. In spite of everything, I came. Chuck groaned against me, staying inside and watching over my shoulder as I finished Bernie off. It got all over the steering wheel and dashboard.

If it had just been us, I would have let him hold me against his chest, laughed as we dabbed up the mess. Instead, any connection that we'd had was broken and Bernie slumped, his head in his hands, refusing to look up. That sight is a shame I've carried with me my whole life.

Chuck knelt on the seat, tucking himself back into his pants. He took his time pulling on his shirt, his face plastered in a self-satisfied grin. Chuck let me out of the truck first then leaned in and patted Bernie's shoulder. "Cheer up," he said. "Maybe next time she'll suck you off."

Richard's always treated my life before we met like something cramped and adolescent that I'd shed, snakelike, out of necessity. He's right. I don't know why I get so defensive about it. With this summer's excursions, I have to ask myself what proud heritage I'm trying to pass onto my sons. The Citadel, the church at Grand Pré, even today's drive to Peggy's Cove—they're all stunning examples of the Nova Scotian landscape, the province's cultural heritage. But they're not where I grew up.

*   *   *

Stephen's using the cornfield's wooden fence as a gymnast's bar. It jiggles as he somersaults forward, hooking his legs behind him and dismounting into the rear field. He springs back up and sits straddling the post, watching me secure a pile of Ziploc bags under a stone. I've performed this dig dozens of times but I still mumble through a rehearsal and triple check my inventory, lining the shovels up so the handles are level.

Bernie has staked off a 4 by 4 section of the field for us right on the border of the cultivated area. The terrain is moderately sloped and a valley creek separates this field from the far hill like the spine of an open book. The corn is already waist high.

If we'd been doing this project in Guelph, it would have taken months to set up, but Marc located several LaMotte testing kits in storage and Bernie offered his field, so I've only had a week to prepare. Smaller school, smaller bureaucracy. Stephen leaps down from the fence and stands at my side as Marc's red hatchback cruises down the access road. With our serious expressions and the stockpile of shovels we look like mother and son undertakers.

Both of Marc's grad students are so unabashedly enthusiastic it makes me feel like a minor celebrity. Melanie is tall and blonde and has a Swedish naturalist look, her hair pulled back into buns on either side of her crown. Tom is olive-skinned and slightly elfin, small hands and ears. Unlike my usual undergrads, they've come equipped with clipboards and graph paper. No one's surprised that I've brought my son. While we're unloading the vehicle, I overhear Marc chatting with him, comparing the Nintendo DS to the Sony PSP.

We have the site prepared by eleven, the profile edges nice and clean so we can see the layer-cake striations. This soil is almost a textbook example of a humo-ferric podzol with a nice ashy band under the topsoil where the minerals have leached out. Underneath the ruddy, iron-rich b-horizon, it gets darker as it approaches the parent material—glacial till over sandstone. There's a little bit of mottling, patches of a rusty brown, which can mean the soil isn't draining well.

The first step is to touch the various layers of soil, get a rudimentary feel for the composition. The more silicate or clay in a soil, the more it will clump together as you knead it between your thumb and forefinger. With some marsh clays, you can form a long ribbon.

The horizons on the sample we've dug are on more of an angle than I'd expect. The a-horizon, which has the bulk of the organic matter, is thin. As the rest of the group works through a soil classification flow chart, I take a shovel and dig over in the first furrow, where the crop's failed to thrive. The soil there is worse, the b-horizon close to the surface, indicating significant erosion. There's also the start of a hard pan. I feel a bit like a dental hygienist, poking away, checking for receding gums.

Clarence startles me as I'm examining the patch of earth. "You just go digging in people's fields now, Ellie?"

I rise to greet him but he just stands there peering down into the hole, nodding. "Bernie didn't tell you we'd be here?"

"Maybe he did and maybe he didn't but I'm right curious to know what you're doing."

Marc jumps to his feet and holds out his hand to Clarence. "Thanks so much for letting us use your field."

Clarence looks Marc up and down, not sure what to make of a man who wears new clothes to dig up dirt. Clarence himself is wearing an old pair of jeans, a plain white T-shirt and a flannel vest, even though it's a warm day. "Mind telling me what you're up to, Eileen?"

"Jump down there and I'll show you." I slip into the first pit. Clarence and I always got along pretty well when I was growing up, but I can tell he's gotten protective of Linda.

"I can see from here."

"Alright, suit yourself." I go through the same information that I gave the students, pointing out the bands of minerals. Clarence doesn't look particularly interested, so I focus on the top soil. "How've your yields been?"

"Can't say as they've been one way or another. Some years good, some bad, same as always."

"You've got a nice layer of humus up here." I point to the side where it's thickest then walk to the smaller hole. "But it's pretty thin here. You ever sat down with someone to talk about alternative management practices?"

"When you start speaking English, I'll start listening." Clarence pulls out a cigarette. Healthy, holistic Melanie tries to keep smiling but I notice her shifting out of the line of exhale. I go back to the original site and show Clarence a hard pan that's been forming where the soil's been compacted, probably from plowing.

He's still unmoved. "Looks to me like you're doing an autopsy on my acreage."

"I am, Clarence, I am."

"Thing is, it ain't dead yet." The ash on his cigarette has grown to the size of a knuckle.

I lead him over to some vials of solution and he eyes the equipment suspiciously. "When you're through all these tests, where are you sending the results?"

I toss him a set of safety glasses. "I'm not the Board of Health."

The experiment is a crude test of the soil's organic content. I assign Stephen the task of shaking the sample, which he executes with the vigour of an electric paint mixer. When the colour's settled I get Clarence to match the shade to the test swatch.

He adjusts the brim of his hat to accommodate the goggles. "Two?"

The vials are passed around and the rest of the group concurs.

"It's good. That's medium."

Melanie notes the findings. Clarence just stands there, his brow pinched, bewitched by the scientific equipment.

"This stuff works?" he asks, as if I'm peddling snake oil. "I'm an old dog, Ellie. I'm done learning new tricks." Still, he lingers as I finish up with the experiment, helps us fill the hole back in.

At the end of the day, Marc shakes Stephen's hand, extending it into a high-five and fist bump. If it was me, Stephen would groan, but he plays along with Marc. "So do you think your Dad would let us steal your Mom for a semester? We could start with a six-credit soil intro and build up a whole agroecology program."

Stephen's flinches as though what Marc's proposing is a real possibility. I tousle my son's hair, keeping the mood light. "I don't know about Richard, but I could be persuaded."

We swing by the library on the way home, so Stephen can check his email. I'm so buoyed by the day that I browse some job sites and fire off a resume to a posting at the Kentville Agricultural Centre. It's too far, but it'd be good interview practice. At the very least, it's another chance to get my name out.

"So you finally got our son interested in science," Richard says. Stephen's given him the play-by-play. It's the first time we've said more than a perfunctory hello since the car argument and his voice sounds lubricated with a stiff scotch.

"He was great out there." I slide off the fact that I hadn't mentioned getting in touch with Marc, let alone setting up the lab.

"It sounds like you're making some good contacts."

"Yep."

"Good for you." He continues, chipper, as though nothing's shifted between us. "Dad and I have started clearing out the basement. He's got an idea to excavate some of the backyard so it's partially above ground so we can put in two rooms with standard windows."

Finishing the basement so the boys can have separate bedrooms is a project that resurfaces every few years but has always been postponed.

"I wanted to ask how you'd feel about having your own office down there. That way you can have your own space if you're going to be looking for teaching or doing freelance contracts. Dad's measuring up a shelf for your soil samples."

In contrast to his manic pitch, there's a heaviness in his pause. "It's all settled with U of T. They're bringing in one of our recent grads."

The defeat in his tone makes my question redundant but I ask anyway. "How did it go?"

After severe erosion, there's a process called isostasy that causes the underlying bedrock to rise up to fill the void. It works like a raft on water—as weight is removed from the Earth's crust, it floats further up from the mantle it rests on, providing parent material for future soil. However, it's not a simple equation of loss and replace; it can take tens of thousands of years before the soil achieves its former depth and fertility. All I can think as Richard details the plans for the office is that this is his botched attempt at isostasy, maintaining the equilibrium with an inadequate offering.

*   *   *

My mother nods at a couple on the other side of the bleachers. "Those are the Hartley's kids." Stephen is already across the field, warming up with the rest of the soccer team and Luke's jogging on the spot next to them, imitating the exercises.

"Who?"

"You remember a few concessions over when you were growing up?"

"They look younger than me." By a lot, I think.

"Louise got breast cancer you know."

"I don't remember her."

"Full mastecto-whatever."

"Chemo?"

My mother makes a face and waves me away. "I don't know. Sold their house and moved to Mexico—some kind of witch doctory centre. Mumbo-jumbo along the lines of what you want to sign me up for."

This morning I suggested she book an appointment with a naturopath since she's still adamantly against a physical.

The coach kicks a spare ball over to Luke and he tries bouncing it on his knee like the older boys. Stephen's shifted to the far side of the line-up, getting the maximum distance between himself and his brother, mortified by the attention he's attracting. I rise to call Luke back, but my mother stops me. "Just leave him. He's got to sit through the whole game, doesn't he?"

There's still no sign of Max or Bernie. At five to seven Max sprints out from the parking lot and apologizes to the coach. A few minutes later, Bernie arrives and chats with a few other people before joining us.

My mother asks where Linda is.

"Took Lisa to her Mum's."

"Luke will be sad," I say.

"He getting sweet on her?"

The whistle blows and the ref waves Luke over to call the toss.

I scoot to make room for Bernie but he motions for me to stay in place. "I've got to head out. Linda wants me to pick up some roast chicken for dinner."

When he's left, my mother whispers out of the corner of her mouth like a ventriloquist, her eyes still facing the field. "It's because of you, you know."

"What?"

"Bernie not staying."

"Why?"

"Linda's had two guys run off on her before. She's laying down the law this time." My mother frowns. "I'm not saying anything, Ellie. But Linda's mom is going to have words with Bernie—Mary Hutchins told me."

"Fat Mary?"

My mother lowers her voice to a hiss. "Be nice, Eileen."

"You've called her that for years." She must have heard this at the co-op yesterday. I should have known—she was gone two hours getting fruit.

Our team scores and a father on the other team, the same one from the last Kentville game, calls out, "Come on Brad, wake up." His son wipes his hands on his shirt then runs a bit faster.

Stephen looks at me as he jogs back to the starting line and motions like he's clicking a camera. I'd forgotten that I'm supposed to be taking pictures to send Richard. I focus on the viewfinder, happy for the excuse to ignore my mother.

Stephen passes quickly to Max, who gets the ball out and over the centreline. The dad on the other team calls out, "Brad, keep your eyes on the black one."

Christ. The freckled kid tries to close the distance between himself and Stephen, but my son is too fast. The play nears the bleachers and I'm able to snap a few action shots of Stephen sneaking the ball past his opponent.

For a long stretch, neither team can manage a play. As the ref blows the whistle for half-time, Max gets the ball and cocks his leg back to shoot. The play's dead, but he kicks the ball anyway, frustrated.

My mother's busy eating carrot sticks from a yoghurt container.

"So what did you tell Mary?"

She waves a carrot to show me her mouth's full.

"What do you think?"

She shrugs the question off as if she can't remember her end of the conversation. It's this kind of gossip that makes small towns so claustrophobic.

Across from us, Brad is busy receiving a lecture from his father. Brad doesn't seem too interested in soccer at this point, just kicks at the sod while his father blusters. "You can't let them take the ball from you like that. Blackie's a ringer, you've got to take him out."

That's it. I leave my mother and walk right up to the man. He's taller than I'd thought. I only come up to his chest. The father nods to me. "Yeah?"

"You can't call my son 'blackie.'"

His upper lip curls into a snarl as if to say, he's yours? Brad's mortified. "He's black, isn't he?"

"He's Trinidadian-Canadian."

The man's head is slightly oblong, the skin acne-scarred, a ball of pastry dropped on the floor and carelessly brushed off. "You get knocked up from one of the seasonal workers?"

My arms go rigid from the adrenaline. The man watches, amused, as I struggle to keep my voice low and level. "My husband is a professor at the University of Toronto."

"So what's your problem?"

"I'm not going to have some asshole screaming at my son from the sidelines."

"What's wrong with the word 'blackie'? He hulks over me. "I didn't call him a nig – "

My fist connects with his collarbone. He catches my wrist and I hang in his grip like a dangled fish. "Why don't you just piss off? Your son shouldn't even be on the team."

"Because he's black?"

"No." He draws out the vowel. "Didn't register in time. You blow Jason McInnes for a jersey?"

The ref jogs over, same beanpole kid from the first game. He gets in between us, forcing the man to release me. The ref looks him straight in the eyes like he's staring down an aberrant dog. "I'm giving your son a red card if you don't settle down."

The rest of the field snaps into view. Everyone is staring. There are people ten feet across from us in every direction eyeing the spectacle. No one has stepped in to restrain him.

"I'm just trying to give my son a few pointers and this bitch is telling me what I can and can't say."

"You can't talk like that, sir." This kid can't be more than nineteen, can't weigh more than a hundred and twenty pounds.

The man spits on the ground and grabs his son's jersey. Brad's eyes are welling. "We'll be complaining to Parks and Rec." He pokes at the ref's chest. "I want you fired. And I want this cunt and her son out of the league."

The ref blows the whistle so loud we have to shield our ears. He presses a red swatch against Brad's chest. The father grabs his elbow and raises his fist, *up yours*. He drags his son off the pitch. It's obvious Brad's going to be in shit tonight. That part I feel badly about.

I march over to my son, the whole team tracking my approach. I angle my body so they can't see his reaction when I ask if he's all right. He doesn't answer.

"We should call it a night."

Stephen glances at Max then at me. "Can I finish the game?"

I wait another moment to make sure it's what he wants.

On the way to my seat I notice that my wrist is starting to bruise. There's a red welt on my hand from where my fist balled up around my wedding ring. Luke is sitting on his hands, next to my mother, tears running down his face. My mother isn't making any effort to comfort him. He wraps his legs around my waist and leans his head into my neck. "It's okay," I repeat, rocking him against me. "It's okay."

Play resumes. Luke stays on my lap. I worry about whether I should have called the police, whether I'm guilty of assault because I threw the first punch, whether a cop out here would understand that kind of provocation.

My mother catches my eye and shakes her head as if she's asking me if that was necessary.

"What?"

"Was that the big city stuff you were telling me about?"

Ten to eight and no sign of Bernie. We mill around the parking lot so that Max won't have to wait alone. He and Stephen pass the ball back and forth to each other like it's a Hacky Sak, never letting it touch the ground. I think they're talking about the soccer dad but they're a ways off and I can't make out what they're saying. I scan Stephen's movements—the force he drives into his kick, the timbre of his laugh—trying to ferret out any injuries beneath the surface.

I didn't realize how hard it would be for the boys out here. How much they would stand out. Back within the confines of our house walls, we've always felt like a family, same as any other. It's a primal bond, not something I appreciate other people throwing social theory at. But what I'm realizing more and more is that once we open the front door, the world comes rushing in, filing us into separate categories.

Most of the other families are gone now. We pack the soccer ball and the backpack in the trunk and my mother sits in the front seat, the door open and her purse on her lap, irritated by the wait. Luke leans on the car hood watching the older boys.

Max raises his arm, takes a sniff and then recoils. "Onions."

Stephen laughs and pokes his nose into his own armpit. He groans.

The truck pulls in a few minutes later but Bernie doesn't get out of the vehicle. My mother's probably right—Linda's laid down the law. Instead, Lisa runs over to Max and he wipes his sweat on her arm. "Special delivery."

She stomps on his foot, disgusted. He swings her over his shoulder so her face is in line with his armpit. "Sniff it," he says, with a voice like character in a zombie movie. He staggers with the weight of her all the way to the truck. "Sniiiffff iiit."

We pull into the ice-cream stand just as it's closing. My mother stays in the car to eat hers, but I lead the boys back to the menagerie just off the parking lot. We stroll over to the goat cage. It's just a pen now, with pigs in a stall next to them, but there used to be a whole jungle gym set up for them with planks and steps for them to climb. Luke wants to feed them, but I refuse to deposit a loonie in the dispenser. Undaunted, he leans up against the pigpen, trying to call the sows over.

Stephen licks his cone staring out towards the duck pond.

"I got a good picture of you playing that you can email your Dad."

"Thanks."

I put my arm around Stephen. "I'm sorry you had to see that."

Stephen nods. "Max said that he was the coach last year but he got fired because the parents complained that he was always yelling at the kids. So he took Brad off our team. Max says Brad's pretty okay, it's just his Dad who's. . . ."

"A fucking asshole." I put my finger in front of my lips and roll my eyes towards Luke. He's still squatting happily by the pigs, trying to lure the piglets over with a high-pitched oink.

Stephen smiles conspiratorially. "I was just going to say jerk."

"He's jealous," I say, crunching up the waffle cone. "It's because he knows you're talented." I wait until he's looking me in the eye. "If you don't want to play soccer anymore, you don't have to."

Stephen shakes his head. "It's just him. The other kids are okay. The coach thinks we have a shot at the playoffs this year."

"Because of you?"

He balls up his napkin and stuffs it in his pocket, nodding shyly. "But they wouldn't be until late August."

"If you want to stay, we can stay."

"Dad too?"

"We'll call him as soon as we get in."

We wander over to the peacocks. They've gotten worn down since the last time I saw them, although maybe it's not the same birds. Their tail-feathers are molting and dirty, penned in by their too-small enclosure.

Lying in bed, waiting for Richard to call back, the physical reality of the fight hits me. The ring and pinkie fingers of my right hand have doubled in girth, the bruises like strawberry stains. There's a dull throbbing, but I can articulate all the digits, so I probably haven't broken anything. My biceps are sore from straining and my stomach muscles are starting to tighten, but the full reckoning probably won't hit until tomorrow morning.

Richard talked to Stephen for a solid hour when we got home, until he had to drive Terrence to the train station. I thought I'd done a good job of defusing the situation but there's such a marked contrast when Stephen gets off the phone that I realize he'd still been on edge. It's a reminder that as Stephen gets older, there are places I won't be able to follow him.

Between that thought and the pain, I'm feeling pretty melancholy by the time the phone rings.

As I run Richard through the incident I get a clear picture of him ticking through the minutia of bedtime. The familiar sounds—his weight on the mattress as he changes, the bathroom taps, leather slippers on the tile floor—narrow the distance between us.

"Do you think you should go to the clinic?" he asks when I tell him about the bruising.

"What are they going to do?" I flex my hand instinctively as if to reassure myself. "Even if they're broken, they'll just tape them. Anyway, they're not broken."

Richard mumbles his relief. We lapse into silence.

"Boys get to bed okay?"

"Yes."

"Good." Again, pause.

It's obvious that Richard isn't giving himself permission to speak what's on his mind. "Just say it."

"What?"

"Whatever it is."

Richard still hesitates. He pronounces the words carefully, as if they're fragile items he's unpacking from a crate. "Ellie, I haven't told you all the names I've been called over the years. In anger, in jealousy, a cruel throwaway. More times than I can remember. I've never raised a hand to anyone." His voice is soft and empty of rebuke, but I'm mortified.

"If it was our son?"

"I understand why you hit him."

"You think I shouldn't have."

"What if you'd been hurt? I mean seriously, physically hurt. The last thing I want is for my wife to, God I don't even want to think about it." Richard falters. "It's just not worth it. I don't want the kids getting into fights. I don't want them putting themselves in danger."

"Do you think I should have called the cops?"

"It would have been better."

"Do you think I should call the cops?"

"Not at this point. There's not much you can charge him with—if he'd grabbed before you struck, maybe. Probably better to let him cool off. Besides, who knows if you're going to see him again."

"What's that supposed to mean?"

"Don't you think it's time the three of you came home?"

"Because of what he said?"

"Partly."

"Not everyone out here is like that."

"That's not what I'm saying."

"Stephen told me he wants to stay."

"Stephen is thirteen. This is between the two of us." Richard pulls the reins on the tension. "Ellie, it's been a hard day. I'm not going to push it. But I'd like to talk about it."

When he hangs up, I'm left with the aftertaste of being chided. I wish I could have spoken to Terrence instead, wish I could have heard him tell me that I'd done the right thing. I go to sleep thinking of my own father, wishing for the first time in years that he were still alive to say the same.

We drive to Martinique beach a few days later. Linda rings me at eight and asks what food I'm bringing for the picnic.

"We made some ham and cheese."

"With mayonnaise?"

"Yeah."

"Lisa doesn't eat mayonnaise."

"We also have some peanut butter and strawberry jam."

"Did you bring any fruit?"

The kids are squabbling in the background. Linda covers the mouthpiece and yells for Max to cut it out.

"Bernie wants me to make fruit salad," she huffs, irritated by the demand.

"We'll make do without it. We can stop on the way if we have to."

"Yeah, that's what I told him but he said you were making sandwiches, so I'd better bring something too." Lisa's started wailing.

"Don't worry about it."

"I've got some macaroni salad."

I can hear her open the fridge and what sounds like the lid coming off a casserole.

"Christ, Bernie, did you get into the macaroni?"

When Linda hangs up, she doesn't replace the headset on the cradle, and the line stays briefly engaged so I can hear Bernie's muffled apology. I head down to my mother's cold cellar to see if there's anything else I can salvage. The cellar's only lit by one bulb, hanging from old, loose wiring. It always feels as if the socket is going to give before the light flicks on.

There's a flat of pop left over from our last visit. I pack the cans into a crate, feeling badly that Linda's worried about the potluck. If I weren't on vacation, I wouldn't have made anything either, I'd have just picked up chips and salsa. Besides, it's her one day off this week. I doubt she wanted to spend it at the beach with me in the first place.

It's already quarter past eight so I call up to the boys, who were sent to change into their swim trunks. No response. When I reach the landing, they're standing outside my mother's bedroom. At first I think they've broken something, their bodies rigid like they're expecting punishment. When Stephen turns to me, however, his face is afraid, not guilty. My mother's naked, standing in front of the bed, staring at her bathing suit. Oblivious to the three of us.

"Mom?"

She tilts her head to the sound, but doesn't respond.

I close the door to shield the boys. "Mom?" I touch her back tentatively, like she's a strange animal I don't want to startle.

She turns around, unperturbed and unaware that she's naked. I'm arrested by the sight of her body, even in the midst of my concern, by the way my frame is a replica of hers. The rounded "W" of her chest, her narrow gymnast's hips, the frown of belly over her hysterectomy scar—it's like skipping ten frames forward on a film of my body's trajectory.

She's still staring at the suit.

"Do you need help putting it on?"

"No. Don't be silly." She grabs the teal suit, holds it against herself, and examines her reflection in the full-length. Her lips are moving, as though she's having a vigorous conversation, but no words come out.

I should call an ambulance. I lay my hand on her forehead to test for fever.

The contact snaps her out of it. I reach for her wrist to check her pulse but she bats my hand away. She presses the suit against herself, covering up and sharply asks for a bit of privacy.

Downstairs, I question Stephen about how long my mother was standing there.

"Five minutes."

Stephen asks if she's going crazy.

"No," I say. "She's just getting confused." I send the boys out to pack up the car then call the doctor's office. The receptionist is curt. I outline the morning's symptoms and ask to speak to the doctor. I'm told she doesn't do phone consultations.

"It was like she didn't know I was there." I need to know if I should bring her in right away.

Her response is dry as an automated recording. "If this is an emergency, go to the hospital."

I book the first available physical.

My mother is in the upstairs hall, dressed in her suit and sarong. She's been listening to my conversation. The colour in her face is better, but it wouldn't be a bad idea to run her by emerg.

"I just need some breakfast."

She sits down at the table, her arms folded over the straw placemat. In the cupboard, there are a couple of digestive biscuits and I put a few on a plate for her. I grab a mug and an Orange Pekoe tea bag, hoping the caffeine will revive her. One cream, two sugars. It could still be anything benign—mild hypoglycaemia or adult-onset diabetes.

The phone rings. It's Linda. They're ready to leave.

The day's alternatives spread out like diverging squares on a board game. If there's a problem, Martinique beach is very remote. I'm not even sure that they have a professional ambulance service. On the other hand, getting my mother to the hospital will be a fight.

Linda is waiting for the go-ahead.

"Give us ten minutes, then we'll be on the road." We'll be driving near Halifax, so I reason that's an hour in a confined space for observation. If there's any question about her health, we can take a detour.

I step outside to round up the boys. At the sound of the door closing, their heads pop out of the far shrubbery. I call across the lawn, "You two need to use the bathroom."

Luke looks at his brother sheepishly. This is what they've been doing in the hedge.

We're twenty minutes from the beach when we pass a surfboard rental shop and Stephen asks me if we can take a look. There's no way that I'm going to let Stephen try surfing, but we settle on a boogie board. Luke, of course, wants to have what his brother is getting. I get him a flutter board instead. He's got a hand-me-down life jacket, so it should be okay.

"Do you think Max and Lisa will want one too?"

Linda's annoyed when we pull into the parking lot. She's smoking beside the truck cab, wearing an orange bikini with a white mesh top and jean cut-offs. "We were about to go back to see if you got lost."

Stephen's already brought Max's board over to him.

The kids run up the stairs to the boardwalk but Linda hollers for Max to come back. She nudges his ribs and gestures towards me with her cigarette.

"Thanks, Mrs. Bascom."

"No problem."

Linda nods at me. The kids sprint ahead and we follow behind with all the stuff. Linda hauls a lot of the gear, despite her espadrilles, which twist out from under her once we hit the sand.

My mother takes out her book and sets up a towel over by Linda, who's rubbing on tanning oil. I throw some sunscreen on my legs, my top covered by one of Dad's old button-downs.

Martinique beach is white sand with marsh grass growing at the top of dunes. It's an endangered sandpiper habitat and before going in the water, I call Luke over to point out the signs describing their migration patterns. They're not the same variety as at Evangeline beach, but they're virtually indistinguishable. These birds are fattening up for the three thousand kilometre flight to South America. Breeding season's passed, so I promise Luke we'll look for old nests when he's finished swimming.

Back on the beach, my mother and Linda are deep in conversation. When I get within earshot, my mother falls quiet, like a kid caught by a teacher. For a moment neither of them say anything. Then my mother starts chortling, her hand over her mouth, body rocking back and forth. Linda's howling as well.

"Useless as teats on a steer."

At first I think they're talking about me. I lie on my towel, pretending not to notice.

My mother finally slows to little hiccups of giggles. She looks at me and says, "Did you know that Linda works with Barry Sheffield now?"

I can't place the name.

"You know, Barry from the co-op. The one with the moles?"

I vaguely recall a manager or something when my mother was still there.

"You know," Linda says. "The one with the damp spot—" It's too late for her to get the words out because she's laughing again. "I swear one of the girls caught him in the office." She cups her hand, pretending to jerk off.

My mother hunches over laughing again and then straightens up and reaches out to touch my knee. "I might not have told you about that."

Linda pulls out her cigarettes and offers one to my mother. She shakes her head and then shrugs. "Why not?"

In thirty-nine years, I've never seen my mother smoke.

Linda looks over at me. She already knows I'll refuse. I expect my mother to start coughing, but she doesn't, just drags on the cigarette and lowers the corner of her mouth to exhale. For a second she's thirty years younger, the way she looked when Dad was still alive.

"When did you quit?" Linda asks.

My mother looks sheepish. "Oh, I haven't smoked much since Ellie was two or three. I started up again a bit when Mackenzie died—still keep a pack around the house."

Linda nods as if she's seen this all before. "Smoked since I was fourteen," she says. "The only thing that bothers me is my nail." She holds her index finger out to show the half-moon stain of nicotine.

"You just got to bleach it out," my mother says. "Just a dab or two when you soak your nails. Might take a while, but sure."

Linda nibbles a bit of cuticle off and smiles.

"Do you smoke, Ellie?" My mother leans back on one arm and stretches her legs out. "Wouldn't it be funny if we'd been keeping it from each other all these years?"

Linda raises an eyebrow, waiting for my response. It's like being the only one at a sleepover who doesn't want to make crank calls. This is my chance to join the rapport between my mother and Linda, but I blow it. I don't smoke. I don't want to smoke. I find it embarrassing watching my mother lighting up. Mostly I want to ask if she's been keeping it from her doctor too.

"Bernie told me Ellie was more of a drinker." Linda smirks at my silence, ashing her cigarette in emphasis. "She'd be two sheets to the wind and he'd have to drive her home."

They slip right back into their one-on-one.

Even though there's nine years between me and Richard, the distance between Linda and Bernie seems unfathomable. On Friday, he'll be forty. She's in spitting distance of thirty.

"Bernie's a natural with those two," my mother says.

"Bernie takes to kids pretty quick. He felt pretty bad about what happened to your Stephen the other night. Drove over to Dougie's house as soon as Max told him."

I watch Linda in my peripheral vision.

"Blocked the car in the drive and started laying on the horn."

"He come out?"

"I guess. Bernie wouldn't tell me. Just said they came to an understanding." She shakes her head. "Fucking stupid if you ask me. Not his fight. That's the way Bernie is though."

"He's a natural," my mother repeats, still oblivious to the implications of the altercation. "You two going to have any of your own?"

Linda holds up her ring finger. "I want to be hitched first next time."

At the end of the day, it's Linda and me left packing up while Bernie herds the kids to the toilets. She separates out our food and hands it over with a forced politeness. Everything smells plastic after the day in the cooler. We won't make it through all of the coleslaw that's left so I suggest she keep it for the party she's throwing for Bernie's birthday. She holds the container up to the light, checking for an expiry date.

"We just got it yesterday."

She tosses it in their fridge bag. "You know the time, right?"

I didn't know we had an invitation.

"Seven-thirty, at the house." She works an elastic around a deflated bag of cheese curls. "Bring your man too, if he's in town."

The comment catches me off guard. "Richard's still in Toronto."

"Max told me he's flying out."

"Not anytime soon. Not that I know."

She shrugs. "Stephen told him he was flying in on Friday."

Her tone makes me suspicious—not about a surprise visit, but that she's on a fishing expedition. "Wishful thinking, I guess."

"The boys must miss their dad."

We rise to fold the picnic blanket, a corner in each hand. When we meet in the middle, she towers over me in her heels. "You missing him too?"

Definitely fishing. "Of course."

My first visit here after Richard and I were living together, I thought about him so constantly that he might as well have been travelling with me. Everything I saw, even the most familiar things, I saw with double vision—my own perception and his imagined reaction. We spoke on the phone every night, each goodbye counting down the days until my return.

This time, I'm feeling his absence, but it's not the same. Instead, it's an anxious feeling, like watching a tree being felled and not knowing where it's going to land.

On the drive home, my phone starts vibrating—a text from Richard asking me to check my email and give him a call. It's brief, but the message feels like a good sign, an answer to my rumination. I drop my mother and the boys at home and drive back to Wolfville on the pretext of picking up take-out. Waiting for the email to load, a pop-up ad covers the screen and I almost swear out loud trying to find the close button. When the screen finally clears, I find that the message is a forwarded travel itinerary from Westjet. Linda was right—Richard's booked on an afternoon flight two days from now. At the bottom of his message he's written one line: Thought I'd keep it a surprise but then realized I'd need a ride.

If it's a surprise, then why do our sons know?

After dinner, I pull Stephen aside. It doesn't take much cross-examination.

"Dad booked his ticket Saturday morning."

The day after the fight on the soccer field. This trip is a rescue mission to bring us back to Toronto. What's so unfair is that it's not the first time the boys have been witness to this kind of ugliness. In school, there's a no-tolerance policy and the teachers have been good at cracking down on students using racial slurs. But it's happened after classes and not just with kids. Once, Luke overheard a friend's parents discussing the supposed medical dangers faced by kids of mixed parents. Even within the family, one of Richard's cousins has always had a problem with him marrying a white woman and wasn't afraid to discuss this in front of the boys until Terrence shut it down. I'm furious that Richard doesn't trust my judgement. For Linda to know first is humiliating.

When everyone has gone to sleep, I open my bedroom window and slide out onto the porch roof, hoping that the outside chill will offset the rage that's building. My jeans scrape against the shingles, one of which comes loose and jangles down to the lawn. A few bats make passes down from their nests under the eaves.

It's the underhandedness, the fact that he involved our sons. We're right back to where we were at the beginning of the summer—he's making decisions unilaterally that should involve me. I text him back one line: 6:15, arrivals.

The phone rings half an hour later, but I don't pick up. Richard doesn't leave a message. I sit on the roof for a good while, feeling like a petulant teen, wishing for the first time in twenty years that I had a fat joint to spark and some White Shark to chug. I'd like to see what Richard makes of that.

6

WHEN SHE OPENS THE DOOR, Linda's arms are looped with streamers. She's asked me to bring the kids over to keep Max and Lisa occupied while she preps for the party. We've come bearing videos—one picked by Stephen and one by Luke because after thirty minutes, I gave up on consensus. They have their whole lives to learn about compromise.

Linda's got a friend at M&M Meats who's helping with the catering. She's been saving the frozen appetizers nearing their expiration dates and is selling them to Linda half-price. She was supposed to drive them over later tonight but got called in for the late shift. Linda looks at me like she doesn't want to ask. "You mind driving to the mall? Here, I'll give you some money." She digs around in her wallet, crushing the draped crepe paper, and hands over a hundred dollar bill.

"Bernie out?"

"He's supposed to be at Gail's watching the baseball game but he's got to work late at the autoshop. He doesn't really like baseball anyway."

"Neither does Richard."

"He coming in tomorrow then?"

It's a wide-open target but Linda doesn't take the shot. "Boys must be excited." She thanks me again for running the errand.

The mall parking lot is almost empty when I pull in except for a collection of abandoned carts crashed along the perimeter. The meat store's got the same sterile row of freezers that all the franchises have, same orange trim, same air conditioning set to Tundra. There's a blonde girl with a long face leaning over the counter reading a gossip magazine and chewing gum. She looks up but doesn't straighten to greet me. The magazine is open to a fashion spread where readers are invited to choose which celebrity wears the same look better. I don't recognize any of the people.

"You Eileen?"

"Ellie, yes."

Her name tag reads "Tracee." She's decorated it with a metallic heart. "So you know Bernie pretty well?"

"We went to high school together."

She points to a picture in the magazine. "Think this one's handsome?"

"Sure."

"Wouldn't touch him with a ten foot pole." She flips the page. "He's a dog. Left his wife six months pregnant."

I wait for any indication that she's planning to provide further customer service. She's absorbed in a good/bad plastic surgery photo-spread, unfazed by the silence.

"Did Linda leave you an order?" I ask, worried because she didn't give me a list. "Or am I supposed to choose?"

· Tracee rolls her eyes, colder than the air-conditioning. "Linda's had this planned for months. She isn't going to leave it to an ex-girlfriend."

"Bernie and I weren't together."

"That's the word going around." She slouches back to the stockroom and comes out with a mountain of frozen items. Tracee's been hoarding all the sale items. The money ends up covering 100 burgers, 3 dozen sausages, cocktail rolls, a few boxes of assorted appetizers and a few trays of squares. There's no chance that they'll all fit into the cooler.

"My mom wanted to buy something for Bernie too."

She retrieves another five dessert boxes and offers me the employee discount. "You need a hand carrying this?"

"No, I'll make a couple trips."

"Yeah, I can't leave the cash."

I leave the bagged items and haul the cooler out to the car. When I come back in, Tracee's on the phone. She puts the receiver to her chest. "Linda wants to know if you can stick around and pick up the cake. The bakery at Superstore won't have it until quarter to ten."

It's seven twenty.

"Will the meat be okay in the car?" I don't feel like driving back again.

"I'll give you the work cooler."

"Sure. Tell Linda I'll pick the boys up at the same time."

Tracee covers the phone again to ask if I'm going to stick around the mall.

"I might head into Wolfville and read at a café."

Tracee relays the information. "Just make sure you talk to Len, 9:45 at the back of the store." She shuffles around the corner and hauls out an oversized neon cooler. She sets it down in front of me and returns the phone to her ear.

I wait for further directions, but Tracee just stares back. "Nice to meet you." It's my cue to leave. When I drop the cooler by the car trunk, I look back and catch her leaning against the window to spy on me.

As I'm driving out, some asshole revs up behind, then pulls alongside to pass, laying on the horn. I roll the car window down to give the driver an earful.

It's Bernie.

"Giving me a heart attack, McInnes." My accent creeps in, thickening my vowels. "I thought you were working."

He waves towards the Canadian Tire. "I needed a part."

"I don't think you're supposed to see me here."

"Nah, I already know about the special deal."

We're holding up traffic. Bernie waves me into a U-turn and we park on the far side of the mall. We speak through our open windows, like bus drivers crossing enroute. "You heading back?"

"No, I've got to stick around for another errand."

"My cake?"

"Is there anything about your party that you don't know about?"

Bernie laughs. "What time are you going to the Superstore?"

"Quarter to ten."

"Want to hang out at the shop?"

"I brought a book."

"They don't have the part anyway. Let's go for a drive." Bernie lays his hand on his chest, scouts' honour. "I'll have you back by 9:30."

We head towards Wolfville and I guess we're going to the dykes.

"Linda's putting on a big party. You excited?"

"Just means another year older."

"It's the big 4-0."

"You still look like when we were in high school, Ellie."

"You're full of shit."

We take a turn up past Horton High and get onto Ridge Road. Maybe he's heading to White Rock. "I took the boys out here for a swim a few weeks ago and it looked like the power plant had closed the place down."

"It always was no trespassing," Bernie says, glancing over at me and shaking his head. "They just got newer signs."

"I guess I thought it was a regular swimming hole."

"Pretty much everywhere we went as kids was off limits." Bernie turns the other way along the road. We're headed to Three Pools. Bernie winks. "It's no trespassing here too."

We park the pickup and climb around the gated entrance to the gravel lane.

"You come down here a lot?"

"Almost never."

The heat of the day has passed and it's settled into a comfortable warmth. It doesn't take long to reach the water towers, now covered with graffiti at the base. We walk along, Bernie on the road and me on the water pipe. After a ways, the path curves off and it's a steep descent to the water. I skid on the gravel and Bernie catches the back of my shirt, hoisting me up by the excess material.

We reach the first pool and rest on the outlying rocks. Bernie takes his shoes off and dips his feet, the water dark as tea from the sulphates.

"You ever miss this?" he asks.

"The valley?" I kick my foot and watch the splash. "Didn't realize how much until this summer."

"How come?"

"Didn't spend enough time here I guess."

We scramble up the rocks to the next pool. Bernie stands in the stream, where the water falls down over the edge and pretends to slip.

"Don't even joke about that," I say, grinning.

He repeats the performance, adding exaggerated "ooohs."

Across from us, there's the old rope swing and a makeshift firepit circled by upended tree stump stools. In the centre, there's an old six-pack, the cardboard sunken and the bottles littered around it. We reach the final pool and climb to an overhanging boulder. The sun will be up for another hour at least but it's darker in the forest.

Everywhere is covered in vegetation—mosses carpeting the rocks and trees, ferns growing out of last year's dead leaves, tree saplings wedged between cracks in the boulders. On the forest slope there's a cascade of dried pine needles.

I run my fingers over some lichen. "Did you know this is actually two plants? A fungus and an algae. They can produce acids strong enough to dissolve rock."

"I wouldn't know about that," Bernie says. "Science and I never really understood each other." He moves up closer to me.

"Last time I came here a kid dove in and cracked his head open. Must have been five, six years ago, before I met Linda. Kid came out of the water with this bug-eyed expression and then the blood started pouring down his face. I wrapped a towel around his head and we drove him to the hospital."

"Was he okay?"

"I think so. I mean he could speak. Dove in right over there. The nurse at emerg gave him a hard time—I think she was his mother's second cousin or something. Reminded me of all the stupid things we used to get up to."

Bernie walks over the rock where Chuck and I first had sex. I head the other way, up the steeper boulders, conscious of blushing. Bernie follows, sitting farther down and leaning back so his head's between my feet. I play with his hair and he strokes my legs. Bernie's hands are calloused and I feel their roughness against my calves. I shaved a day or two ago and the stubble catches against his skin. I wonder if it makes a sound at some high frequency, inaudible to the human ear.

My skin gets raw after a few moments and I reach down to take his hand, not wanting to stop the contact, but knowing that I should. He rubs his thumbs against my palm.

"You want to go for a swim?"

"I don't have a bathing suit."

"That never stopped you before."

Linda wouldn't appreciate that, I think, especially since she's spending the evening prepping his birthday party. Richard wouldn't appreciate it either.

"Come on," Bernie teases, noticing my reticence. "They going to kick you out of the university if they catch you?"

"I'm not really at the university anymore."

"I thought you were a professor."

"I got laid off."

Bernie crosses over to a far rock and takes his shirt off, his back to me. He unbuckles his pants and drops them to the ground. I turn my back and take my shirt and shorts off too, leaving my bra and underwear on. My body almost disappears beneath the darkness of the water.

Bernie's on the far side of the pool near the waterfall. "I don't know how you live in the city. No way to cool off." He hoists himself so he's directly under the stream. He's so sure of himself, of his balance on the rocks, so unselfconscious of his body.

I dip my hair under the water and swim to one of the rocks where I can hold on by spreading my arms out and kicking to stay up. My chest stays just below the waterline. "Do you ever wonder if things had turned out differently? I mean what if I'd gone to Dal or something instead of Toronto."

Bernie mirrors my pose on the opposite side of the pool. "Different how?"

I raise myself out of the water a bit.

Bernie swims over, close enough that as he treads water, his legs brush mine. We pause, unsure of how to proceed. There's a water strider crossing between us and I point it out, giving the Latin genus Gerris remigisi.

"I always liked how smart you were." Bernie grasps the rock on either side of me, his thighs between mine. His eyes are the colour of the wet stone.

"Apparently, I'm a failure as an academic."

Bernie slides my bra strap off, then raises me up. He takes my nipple in his mouth. "You're not a failure," he says, his teeth and tongue on my areola. His nails scratch my thigh as he tugs my underwear off.

We're crossing a line, but right now the consequences are too abstract. Instead, I'm hungry for the act, the rush that comes from smashing things. I pull him into me without thinking it through. I grapple his head against my chest, moving him the way I want it. He's the one who slows down halfway through, holding me still and kissing me like a lover, like something sincere. I don't let it last long before rocking back and forth to a conclusion. I close my eyes and I am eighteen again, wishing it had been Bernie all along.

Shortly after, Bernie's cell rings, the sound magnified in the quiet of the pool. He shimmies out of the water and manages to answer in time. He talks quickly on the phone, trying to end the call as soon as possible. I get out of the water too and head to the other side, wringing the excess water out of my underwear as best I can. Bernie waves his hands for me to stop, but I slip on my shirt and shorts, the cotton sticking to me uncomfortably. By the time he flips the phone shut, I'm already halfway down to the next pool.

"Linda?"

"Canadian Tire."

"I've got to pick up your cake."

"Ellie, I don't want to go yet."

The wet has soaked through my clothes and my hair is dripping. Bernie's covered in damp patches as well. He runs his hands through his hair, shaking it out like a dog. We head back up to the water pipes, not saying anything and keeping to the opposite edge. When we reach the truck, he opens his door first, then leans over to pull up the lock on mine. It's only nine. Bernie slides over and reaches his hands up under my shorts, playing with the band of my underwear.

This time it's fast and rough as Bernie presses down on me, careful that we can't be seen. He manages to reach around to pet me as we screw, bringing me to climax quickly. It makes me wonder who taught him how to do that. When he's done, he grins, pleased with himself and we clean up as best we can with some Kleenex in the glove compartment. He doesn't ask me what I'm going to tell Richard and I don't ask him where this is going. Instead he flicks on the radio and we listen to Top 40 country tunes all the way to New Minas. We get to the mall parking lot and Bernie parks close to the Canadian Tire. "Just in case Tracee's watching," he says. "You coming tomorrow?"

"Should I?"

He squeezes my hand because we can't kiss and then I slide out of the truck. As I walk across the parking lot, I'm aware of how bedraggled I look, how the damp from swimming has seeped into my clothes. There's one of Stephen's hoodies in the car and I pull that on, ashamed to be wearing anything of my son's. As I wait out the remaining quarter-hour, I think about how this doesn't feel much different than losing my virginity to Chuck. So, you've just cheated on your husband, I repeat to myself, but I still can't feel anything.

The rule of thumb in soil science is that it takes nature five hundred years to form an inch of soil but only decades for humans to lose several. We're that efficient.

I make my way over to the Superstore back entrance. A paunchy, middle-aged man opens the door, wearing a white lab coat with the name "Len" embroidered on it. "You here for the cake?"

He looks at me and then back towards where I've come. "Not raining is it?"

"No." I don't offer further explanation.

"Just to the right." He leads me through the stockroom, past flats of cereal boxes and a cold room for the produce. "Tell Linda it's on the house. We had a birthday cake called in and we wrote the wrong name on it, so we made them a new one and patched up this one for Bernie."

There's a skinny high-school kid sweeping up behind the ovens and he stares at me as Len opens the fridge. I'm conscious of the damp circles still visible on my clothes. Len hauls out the rejected cake—a massive rectangular slab with chocolate icing, decorated for a kid with bright balloons and bicycles. "Better than rosettes," Len says. There's a giant chocolate chip cookie with Bernie's name on it covering up the original recipient's. "Linda need anything else?"

I shrug.

He leans his hip on the fridge. "Haven't seen you around before. You one of Linda's girls?"

"I'm an old friend of Bernie's. Just back in town visiting my Mom."

"You want me to call Linda to see?"

"Sure."

He slides over to the employee phone. "Linda? Yeah, it's Len. She's here. Nah, it's free. She'll explain. I've got some cupcakes with vanilla frosting. You want me to throw them in special too? Some people don't like chocolate." He hangs up and asks me, "You got any change from the M&M?"

"I've got a twenty."

"Just take them. I'll give you a hand."

Len calls over to the young kid and makes him carry the cake with half of the cupcakes stacked on top. Len carries the other tray so I don't have to carry anything. He lays the cake across the car's middle seat and straps it in with an elaborate cradle of seatbelts. "I've seen enough cakes ruined from sudden stops," he warns. "You going straight to Linda's?"

"Yeah."

"Go easy on the brake."

He doesn't make any motion to leave, even though the kid's already back at the door, waiting for Len to unlock it. "So you going to be at the party I guess."

"Yeah."

"Not going to pop out of the cake?" Len laughs, wheezy.

"My youngest might fit in there."

"How many you got?"

"Two boys."

"Married?"

I nod.

"That's nice. I got twin girls, but I'm going through the divorce."

"Sorry to hear that."

"Sure thing."

I sink down into the seat and wave goodbye. Len steps away from the car but stays to watch as I pull out.

When I get to Linda's, the kitchen is covered in balloons and banners and the kids are in the living room finishing up a movie. Linda, Gail and Linda's mother are in the backyard, smoking on the edge of the deck. "Everything go okay?"

"Where should I unload?"

Linda gets up to help. When we reach the car she says, "Christ, how much did you get?"

"Your friends give a lot of discounts. Some of the squares are from my mom."

We carry the load over to the mudroom, where the chest freezer's set up on a plywood base. I can't look her in the eye. "I'll thaw them out in the morning," she says and we pack the food inside.

Linda's at the corner closest to the door and when we finish she pauses and pulls it closed. She stands there, hand still on the knob, steeling herself to say something. Bernie must have called. I'm terrified she'll make a scene in front of the boys.

"What did you do for the wait?"

"I brought my book," I say, feeling it out as I go. "Then I ran into Bernie. We drove around while he waited for a part."

"Thank Christ." She exhales. She uses her nail to flick a tear out of the corner of her eye and smiles at me. "My friend at the M&M saw you guys drive off together and I thought you were going to lie to me." She looks a bit searching, apologizing for being suspicious.

"I know it's silly," she says, "because Bernie's always said you were like his kid sister."

*   *   *

Even if we'd started going together, there's no way Bernie and I would have lasted throughout my undergrad. There was a tangible divide between Wolfville town and gown. What would he have done, come to residence parties and tried to blend in, smoking up with the philosophy majors in Members Only jackets?

Bernie showed up at my dorm in late September and asked if I'd like to go for a drive. It was already nine-thirty.

"Where?"

"Don't know. Just thought we could go for a ride." He opened my door first, then walked around to his side, whistling.

"How'd it go at the hatchery?" I'd heard through my mother that they were starting on turkeys.

"Got about a hundred chicks. Ten extra for insurance."

"How's it going working with your dad?"

"Sure," he said, not elaborating further. We rode in silence for a while, neither of us wanting to bring up the last time we were in this vehicle. "You happy at school?"

"I guess."

"You'd better be, all the money you're paying."

"I'm on scholarship."

"It's not just the money you're spending, it's also the money you're not making." He turned up Ridge Road and we drove past the old Rotary park. "Even if you're not losing money, you're still losing pay."

"I just want to get a degree, Bernie." I was surprised at his lecture. He'd never really pushed me about anything before. "I need it to get the kind of job I want."

"Like what?"

"You can't just get a job as a scientist."

"What about in Halifax?"

"Not out of high school."

"Good thing I'm a farmer then."

Good thing. I rolled down the window to get a breeze in the cab. It was too cold, but the hum of the wind distracted from the conversation.

Bernie and I'd never had trouble finding things to talk about
in high school, but now it felt like we were on a terrible first date.

"You been to any parties lately?" he asked.

"Not really."

"You don't have parties at school?"

I shrugged.

"Heard you broke up with Chuck."

We were way up in Gaspereau now, the roads twisting along
the river. Bernie pulled a hard right into a driveway and parked
a little way up. I could see an abandoned wooden house outlined in the headlights.

"What do you think?"

"I don't know what I'm looking at." There were toys scattered throughout the yard, including an old swing set and see-
saw with moulded lamb heads for the handles. The house paint
was weather beaten and from what I could see of the roof, it had
a swayback worse than glue horses. It wasn't anywhere I could
imagine living.

"It's my uncle's old place. He's got a new house out closer
to the farm, so he sold it to me cheap. Going to fix it up myself.
All goes well, I'll have it renovated by the time you get done
school." He slid over and put his arm around me. "It's only
twenty-five minutes from your mom's."

I must have guessed his meaning, but didn't know what to
say. "I don't have a car."

Bernie brushed his stubble against my cheek and tried to
turn my chin up to kiss him. I let him at first, but then he
started feeling me up, trying to unbutton my jacket.

I wasn't about to lapse into quick fucks in the back of a truck.

He backed off right away, retreating to his corner of the
cab. He sat there in the dark, his hands on his thighs, unsure
where he'd gone wrong. Then he sprung out of cab and came
round to my side, opened the door and lifted me out, like a
groom at the threshold.

I squirmed until he dropped my legs, my feet hitting the weeds on the overgrown drive. He grabbed my hand and led me around the back of the house. "I'm going to dig a ditch around this side so the water drains better. That way we can extend the cold cellar, maybe put the laundry machines and a workshop down in the basement. Over there's a good patch for a garden." He pointed out a mound of dirt that had been banked up near the swings. "Barbecue can go right here, and I'll cut another door out of the kitchen, put in a deck."

Bernie'd figured it all out—the walls he'd tear down to expand the master bedroom, the best way to lay the plumbing, the cabinet he'd build for the stereo. I got a picture of us twenty years down the road guessing along with Pat Sajak at the vowels in a Before & After puzzle. This life he was planning had nothing to do with me.

He led me back into the truck and waited for my reaction.

I sat, worrying a small hole in the upholstery. "I don't know when I'm going to be done school."

"It's just four years. You could come up on weekends."

"If I do grad school," I trailed off. "I don't know where I'm going to be."

"Like Halifax?" He reached over to squeeze my hand. "I can't leave the Valley."

"Toronto. Vancouver, maybe."

Bernie looked at me hard and kicked his leg against the inside of the door. "Maybe you and Chuck aren't done with each other after all." He reversed out of the driveway and started speeding towards Wolfville, dropping me at the base of the hill, nowhere close to my residence.

After six years of celebrating at the McInneses', I spent Thanksgiving with my roommate's family in Halifax.

*　　*　　*

The highway to the airport is completely clear. It's easy to play and replay the scene at Three Pools, fixating like a school kid on her first kiss. It's a movie spooling in slow motion and I'm watching from an editing booth, trying to pinpoint the exact frame where everything shifts. The loop is so incongruous from the rest of the film. It feels like footage from a separate reel, something easily excised, something with no bearing on the present story.

Richard's flight has been delayed forty minutes. I try calling my mother on the cell, but there's no answer and she doesn't have a machine. It doesn't matter; we'll make up the time on the way back.

I wait by the baggage carousels, looking through the glass wall to arrivals. Richard's one of the first people down the escalator, his khakis and salmon button-down wrinkled from the flight. He's grown his goatee again. It's always suited him, shown off the geometry of his jawline.

Neither of us knows how to act when he reaches me. He awkwardly wraps his arms around me and kisses the top of my head. He's wearing the aftershave the boys gave him last Christmas.

We move out of the way of the other passengers. The kids in the family next to us are holding cardboard signs with "Welcome Home" spelled out in glitter letters. The father's got a camera in one hand and a camcorder in the other. The mother's carrying a bouquet of flowers. We wander to the other side of the baggage conveyor and watch them swarm an elderly couple in matching CN Tower T-shirts.

"Stephen and Luke wanted to come to pick you up."

Richard puts one foot up on the rim of the carousel and we wait for the blinking light to turn on. There are only a handful of other visible minorities in the room, a fact that only bolsters Richard's argument. It's a quick out, leaving. For a moment I consider caving straight away, never mentioning last night's lapse.

A warning buzzer sounds and bags start to funnel through the flaps at the far end of the belt. We wait in silence as people crowd around us, lunging at their suitcases, until Richard's red hard-case finally arrives.

Normally Richard likes to drive, but I get in the car before he's finished closing the trunk. I take a different turn at the 103, heading west towards Truro, because I'd rather take the 14. It's a winding patch of asphalt, running through forest and pasture and it's twenty minutes longer than the freeway.

He asks if we usually come this way.

"Scenic route."

Richard nods vaguely and stares out the window. Neither of us wants to be the first to start the fight.

There's construction on the road just past the turnoff and a line-up of stopped cars curl all the way over the next hill. It's harder to ignore each other without passing scenery. Richard drums his thumb against the inside of his knee. Other than the tic, he acts calm.

My façade is less successful. When I check the rear-view, I realize I'm squinting, my eyebrows pulling my forehead into deep lines, my jaw clenched. Waiting for the traffic to progress, my stomach goes into spasm and I'm distracted from deciding whether or not to tell Richard about Bernie by the fear that I'm going to need a bathroom. I conduct a desperate scan of resources, Kleenex in the glovebox, no tree cover in sight, an old barn a half-mile off.

"There was a great seat sale," Richard says. "Monday's the Civic Holiday anyway."

"Is that how long you're staying?"

"I haven't booked a return-ticket yet."

The traffic is starting to move and we coast forward a half-kilometre, within sight of the flag turner. If I'm going to stop at the barn, I'm going to have to park the car now.

"Stephen told me that you asked him to keep the visit a secret."

Richard braces himself against the handbrake and leans against the door frame. "Stephen also said that you've been impressing the faculty at Acadia. That'll be a hell of an expensive commute."

"I guess that depends on the point of origin." Richard twists his head to see if I'm being serious. "I haven't been offered a job."

"Thank, Christ." He slouches into the seat.

"Did you think?"

So that's what this is about. Stephen must have misinterpreted Marc's comment about bringing me on staff. Acadia's a small school—I'd be stunned if they had the budget to hire another sessional, let alone a tenure-track professor. "You should have confirmed with me before booking a ticket."

"You weren't willing to talk about coming home."

"That still doesn't excuse—"

The flag girl smiles and nods as we pull through. I smile back, as if even though our lives have only collided for a few seconds, I'm obliged to keep up appearances.

The clot of traffic fans off after a few minutes. The abdominal cramping's subsided but I still keep my eye out for exits.

"So what's the plan?" I ask. "Are you just here to scoop us up?"

"I want us to go home together." Richard lays his hand on my thigh. It's a tender gesture but it irritates me. I'm not ready to be soothed.

"There's my mother, there's Stephen's soccer."

"I'm not going to lie. What happened on the field really shook me."

"What if you stayed out here with us?"

He shakes his head. "The BBC article."

Now's the time to tell him, to explode the whole damn thing and clear the air. The spasms start again, this time more insistent. Shifting position doesn't help.

Richard stays silent for a long time. "If this is about earlier—you don't break up a family over a job."

Of course he's right, but the comment strikes me as absurd. "It's not the job," I start to say.

I find a spot twenty metres ahead—a field access road that's concealed by trees. I winch the car into the lane and the tears roll through me. Richard reclines his chair and takes off his shoes, waiting it out. He looks tired, the fight already drained out. I reach over and hold his hand. He strokes the skin over my knuckles.

We don't say anything for a long time and several cars pass us on the road.

"Fifteen years," he says.

I don't know where we go from here.

"I'm sorry."

When I lean over, it's like kissing a stranger, filled with the same charged unknowing. He pulls me onto his lap.

With one hand he grabs the back of my head, working my ponytail undone, twisting my neck so he can kiss where it meets my shoulder. At the argument's impasse, it's as if only our bodies are capable of communication. We bite and scratch each other out of our clothes. Before, he's always screwed me like something delicate, something he has to take care not to crush or break.

Once it's over, the conversation stalls again.

I get us back on the highway. Richard stretches his legs and whistles a few bars from a jazz ballad I can't quite place. This time it's still light when I drive through Windsor but the tide's in, so I can't see the mud flats clearly.

"Do you want to stop for food?"

He shakes his head. "Whatever you've got at the house is fine."

"My mother's cooking chips and fish sticks." I expect him to groan but he doesn't. I ask again.

"Your mother's cooking won't kill me."

It's almost eight-thirty by the time we drive through Port Williams and Richard straightens out his clothes in preparation for seeing the boys. We only have a few more minutes to ourselves but neither of us wants to launch into another discussion. There's a tacit agreement to get home and deal with this later.

Fifteen years. One night out of fifteen years. We're better off striking it from the record.

My mother's house is obscured from the road by a tree break, a line of poplars at the end of a field two properties over. It gives me a rush of anxiety and relief when I spot it, knowing we're so close. At the last stop sign on the concession I squeeze Richard's knee and ask if he's ready. He nods and rolls up his window like we're on a plane and he's making the final preparations for landing. Outside, it smells like one of the neighbours is having a bonfire. We slow as we reach the trees and I flick on my indicator, the metronome click amplified by our silence.

The house snaps into view as soon we pass the trees. Bernie's truck is in the drive. There's a police cruiser in behind. George, the RCMP officer from down the lane, is taking notes on the cruiser's trunk. There's no ambulance, but no sign of the boys either. I misjudge the distance and have to brake too hard to turn into the drive, jolting us forward. Richard grabs my forearm and points at the house. Thick bands of soot streak the walls. The living-room windows have blown out. There's no sign of the boys. There's no sign of my mother.

Burnt plastic, burnt synthetics, burnt wood. There's an undertone of something off and sulphurous, like the stench of burning human hair. Some Smokey the Bear voice plays in my ear, *Stop, drop and roll.* I stumble across the massive tire treads plowed by the fire engines. Richard stops my fall. We look at each other. Neither of our voices is working. Let Stephen and Luke be okay, I plead, racing over to the officer. Let them be okay, whatever's happened to my mother. The house is still standing. They must have gotten out. The PSA starts again, *In a fire, the smoke is as dangerous as the flames.* Let them have gotten out in time.

George drops his pen and papers.

Already my heart is thudding in my ears.

Richard restrains me so that I can't run into the house, grappling both arms, holding me tight against him. My hands lock onto his wrists, needing every point of contact while we get the news.

George raises his arms to stop us. "The boys are fine. They're in the truck."

I jolt forward, desperate to see them. Richard holds me steady.

"Lynne was using a pan to deep fry," George explains. "She had her scanner on and a car crash got called in—a couple died on the 101. She tried your cell but couldn't get through and panicked. Your boy said when the grease caught fire she tried to pick up the pan and burned her hands on the metal. The fire spread from there."

George pauses, letting it sink in. "She's got second and third degree burns on her hands and the hospital's keeping her in overnight because of the shock. The paramedics said she was lucky the oil didn't spill on her."

There's nothing he's saying that I can grab onto. It all slides away, slippery and surreal.

"Your son called 9-1-1 right away. They were able to put the fire out. Bernie was going to bring them back to his place."

"Do they know we're okay?"

"They haven't released the ID of the victims but we found out an hour ago that they were both Caucasian." George nods at Richard as though he's apologizing for bringing it up.

Richard leads me to the truck cab. Luke's sobbing against his brother, who's got his arms wrapped around him. As soon as Stephen sees us, he starts to cry himself. He bolts from the truck and throws his arms around his father. I reach in and pull Luke out and hold him while he cries. Richard strokes the back of our son's head. "We're fine, we're fine."

Bernie opens the front door, carrying the boys' backpacks. "Ellie, Jesus Christ." He jogs across the lawn and draws me into a hug, Luke between us.

"Bernie." I wipe my eyes. "This is my husband, Richard."

Bernie's got soot on his hands and streaks of it all the way up his cheek. He nods at Richard. "You'd better have a look." The fire department escorted him through before they left so that he could grab a few things but they don't want much traffic inside until the building inspector can investigate.

Richard loosens Stephen's grip. He asks if I want to go inside with them.

I can't. Not tonight.

"Is there anything you want us to get out?"

None of the stuff that we've brought is worth saving. It's the tin of photos of my Dad that my mother keeps in the basement that I want. We've never had much money, so there aren't any heirlooms. All we've got to remember Dad by are those pictures and the house itself, the details he put so much work into. I tell them where to find the boxes. As they're heading in, I call out, "And my mother's crocheted blanket from the bed."

The two of them leave me with the boys. Luke has his face pressed into my neck, sucking on my shirt collar, like he used to when he was little. Stephen slumps against my side, holding onto my waist. I kiss his forehead over and over.

"You called the fire department?"

Stephen nods, his chin rubbing my shoulder.

I nuzzle the top of his head, trying to reassure myself he's safe.

George paces back over to us. "I called the hospital. They've told your mother that you're fine."

"Can we see her?"

He checks his watch. "Visiting hours close in ten minutes." He dials the hospital again and hands the phone over.

The nurse explains that they've given my mother a sedative so she won't be able to talk, that the shock was severe, but they think she'll be just fine. "We're going to run some tests first thing in the morning, but you can come see her after eleven-thirty."

"There's no way I can see her tonight?"

"I'm sure we could bend the visiting hours. She's going to be asleep though."

Luke has finally calmed down enough to raise his head from my shoulder. If we can't talk to her, it doesn't seem worth upsetting the boys again. "She's really fine?"

"We're taking good care of her. You're going to want to bring her some clothes tomorrow. We saved the ones she was wearing, but you'll probably need to throw them out."

When I hand the phone back to George, he tells me that he's already sent word out to keep an eye on the place tonight. There's no way we can stay here until it's cleaned out. I'm going to have to contact my mother's insurance company first thing.

"You're lucky it didn't spread to the wires," George says. "Whole structure would have come down."

When he emerges from the house, Richard's shaken. He takes Luke so that Bernie can show me what's been saved while he starts calling hotels.

I haven't ever seen Bernie this grave. "The fire stayed in the kitchen, but the heat melted the upholstery on the couch in the living room. There's smoke everywhere. The frame's probably sound, but a lot of the interior's lost." He opens the truck's passenger door and deposits the photo box in the foot well. It survived because it was in the basement, on the opposite side of the house. The blanket's melted to the sheets.

He's found her car keys and saved a few items that escaped the soot upstairs—the boys' backpacks with their video games, my mother's jewellery box, her Royal Doulton Fair Lady figurine and, from her bedroom wall, my diploma.

It's the Natal Day long weekend and there are two conferences in town. George and Richard are both on the phone to motels with no success.

Bernie offers to let us stay with him.

We need to be alone as a family. I slide it off, saying we don't want to impose.

George holds the cell to his chest. "They're saying the closest place is Windsor."

"We've got a spare room," Bernie insists. "I'll call over to Linda and she'll make up the pullout couch."

I look over to Richard to see what he wants to do.

"It's a half-hour to Windsor?"

George says they can't hold the room past ten, giving us twenty minutes. "Better to be with people."

Richard's warming to the idea. He waves for George to let the room go.

"Did they say how many rooms were left?" I ask.

He shakes his head.

Richard thanks Bernie for the invitation.

Considering last night, I'd rather drive to Windsor and get our own room, but I wonder if seeing their friends will be a good distraction for the boys. Besides, it will be closer to the hospital tomorrow. I angle Stephen aside and ask if he'd feel more comfortable at a hotel or if he'd like to see Max.

Stephen would rather go to Bernie's.

There are cars lined up all along the road when we reach the house. I'd forgotten that it's Bernie's 40th.

We wait in the car, unsure of what to do. It's quarter past ten and neither of us wants to drive for another half-hour without a guaranteed room. My cellphone is dead, which is why my mother couldn't get through.

"We may as well stay." Richard asks the boys if they're okay with it.

Linda opens the door wearing a tight summer dress— ruched white cotton with thin strings that rise up from her cleavage to tie around her neck. She's gotten her hair done, half pulled up and half left down in side ringlets. Her nails are

French manicured with a palm tree decal airbrushed on her pinkie. She tells me she's sorry to hear about the fire, sorry about my mom. I notice that her mascara has started to flake at the corner of her left eye. She's been waiting. Because of us, Bernie's already missed half his party.

Bernie kisses her cheek. "I told them they could stay."

"Sure."

"I'll show them to the spare room."

"No," Linda snaps, then catches herself. "Just park your bags at the front, we'll sort out the sleeping arrangements later." She grabs Bernie's hand and leads him through the house, towards the backyard. "People have been here for three hours." She whispers but we catch it anyway. "Gail was about to cut your cake herself."

There's a small deck, no more than three feet wide off the kitchen's sliding doors and when Bernie steps onto it, everyone cheers. I suddenly wonder if he was meant to have changed. Everyone else is done up for the occasion and he's still in his jeans and T-shirt, still dirty from the fire. He raises his hands up to accept the welcome. Someone calls out, "Late to your own funeral!" There are a few more whoops and hollers. Richard and I stand back, not wanting to be up there with Bernie, awkwardly receiving the applause. Richard takes my hand. It's such a relief to hold it.

"One beer, one hour, then we'll crash."

All around us, the party is throbbing but I'm so zoned out, I barely taste the beer as I swallow.

Bernie's folks are a few feet over, each nursing a can of *Labatt 50* and I steer Richard over to them. Irene looks the same, except that she's gone all grey now. She's wearing a pretty flowered dress with leather orthotic sandals. Clarence's red button down is tucked into his jeans, his old cowboy hat perched on his head.

Irene shakes Richard's hand politely then gives me a big embrace. She rubs my arms as if I've just come in from the cold and need warming up. "This one was like a daughter to me. I've always wondered what happened to you, girl. My boys told me you were in town, but I couldn't believe it until I set eyes on you myself."

When Irene smiles, you can still see the beauty she must have been at eighteen—a rural Farah Fawcett, her hair still feathered out around her sun-baked face. She's a slight woman with a body like a piston, all primed for industry. "I remember the first time you came to dinner and you sat there so sweet and well-behaved. You were just a little pint-sized thing the wind could've blown away."

"Heard about the trouble over at your mother's place," Clarence says. "How's she look?"

"We can't see her until tomorrow."

Clarence's slouched to one side, his thumbs in his belt loops. "The house?"

Richard exhales slowly. "We won't know until the insurance people come through." He tells them how grateful he is that Bernie and George were there.

Irene's visibly upset. "Your poor mother."

"I'm just happy the boys got out." I start to stutter an addendum, worried that it sounds unfeeling, but Irene shushes me.

She puts her arm around my waist and makes me point my sons out, even though it's pretty obvious which they are.

"Some cute that they're playing with Linda and Bernie's kids." She takes a sip of her drink and gazes at the assembled guests. "Took our boys a while but it's worked out. Linda's been good for Bernie."

Clarence downs the last of his beer and crushes the can. "Hell of a fancy party she's organized."

We all look around, surveying Linda's efforts. The whole backyard's been transformed. There are white Christmas lights strung from the trees and streamers everywhere, as well as a few Chinese lanterns. It's a big lot but there's no empty space. There's food everywhere—picnic tables with potluck items, an industrial-sized barbecue, a cake stand. Everyone is drinking.

Jason McInnes comes up from behind, boisterous as he was as a teenager. He gives Richard a perfunctory introduction then turns to me. "You've already got a drink?"

I raise my beer can.

"Good, you'll need it."

I glance at my husband. He's watching our interaction, bemused. He tilts his head towards Clarence, signalling for me to go on without him. Irene releases her grip on my waist. "You can borrow her. As long as you bring her back."

Jason leads me to a clutch of people hovering near the chips and salsa. "I told you she'd be here," he says to the group. "Long lost Ellie Lucan."

We're ringed by Cornwallis alumni. There's Debbie, who sat with me in Grade 12 English, Trevor who I mostly remember from parties and Mikey K., a jock who hasn't aged well.

Trevor holds his hand up for a high-five. "Where the fuck have you been hiding yourself?"

Jason answers for me. "She's moved to Toronto. Teaches science, PhD and everything."

"That true?" Mikey K. asks.

"Well, I'm currently unemployed." I say it like it's a joke.

"That's the fucking truth," Trevor says. "I got turfed from Frito Lay, even though they had me take all these bullshit upgrading courses."

Debbie's a dental hygienist in Windsor. She married one of the guys in our class but left him a couple of years ago. "I should have known when he spent thirty bucks on seventy-five cent bar shots at the rehearsal dinner."

Mikey K. asks if she's going to give him a chance now.

"I don't date men who don't get six-month cleanings."

"How about you, Lucan?" he asks. "You divorced like us yet?"

He's teasing, but the question still catches me. "That's my husband over there." Richard's still chatting with Bernie's folks.

"Handsome," Debbie says.

The guys look back and forth at each other, smirking. Mikey K. hums a few bars from *Ebony & Ivory*.

"You're still a pack of horse's asses the three of you," Debbie says, saving me. "Go get us another drink before you choke on your own feet."

Debbie doesn't look much like how I remember her. In 1984, she had a massive brown perm and the tightest jeans in the county. She's blonde now, with hair in soft layers to her chin like a news anchor, her nails the same petal pink as her tank top. "So you're living in Windsor?"

"I got a place there, but my boyfriend's in New Minas. I'm always driving back and forth."

"Did we go to school with him, too?"

"No, he's an accountant. I cleaned his teeth for two years before he noticed me." Debbie reaches into her purse and pulls out his card. "We're both divorced, so we're not rushing in."

"You got any kids?"

"Three. They're with their father this weekend. You?"

"Two. They're running around here somewhere."

"They tanned?" she asks.

"Yeah."

"You never can tell. At work I get all kinds of people—you'd swear they were Mexican but their mom's Chinese and their dad's Italian."

Trevor and Mike return, carrying a stack of beer cans. Jason follows with a nail. He distributes two cans to each of us. "Shot gun the first in under ten seconds," he says, "and we'll let you nurse the next as long as you want."

I protest—the first drink's already going to my head and I haven't eaten in hours. They heckle me to play along. I don't want to have to explain about the fire.

Debbie winks. "Your husband can take care of the kids tonight."

We keep our fingers pressed over the holes in the cans until everyone is ready. Trevor counts us down, crowing like an auctioneer. The beer spews foam over my chin and down my shirt. I'm too busy wiping my face off with the back of my hand to notice someone bully up to our group. His voice startles me with its proximity. "Ellie Lucan, twenty years later and you still can't swallow."

Chuck.

As I walk away, I can hear his refrain. "What'd I say? What'd I say?"

I meet Richard by the beer bathtubs. He looks down at my damp shirt.

"Never mind," I say. "Have you seen the boys?"

"Food table."

Stephen and Max are loading up paper plates so high that I'm not sure they'll hold together. Richard and I follow their lead.

"Bernie's folks are nice," Richard says. It's still jarring seeing him here among all these faces from my past. "Irene thinks a lot of you. She wants you to go back and have another look at the field. I didn't realize that's where you did the dig."

We eat perched on a railway tie that's being used as garden edging. We just sit there shovelling the food in, exhausted. The party is barrelling along but we're in a strange limbo, buoyed by the collective exuberance and weighed down by the day. Everything blurs—the crowd of bottles reflecting the lights, the neon food on my plate, the vibration from the speakers. Everything leaves us numb.

After a while, Debbie comes over and introduces herself to Richard. I leave them talking and go back over to the claw foot to see if there are any water bottles left. As I'm bending over the tub, fishing through the water, Bernie holds a cold can of beer against my neck.

"Christ, Bernie." I splash him and he backs away laughing. He's already wasted. He reaches out to grab my hand. I pull away, looking around to see if anyone's watching.

He catches my concern. "If I can't hold hands with an old friend on my fortieth birthday, then what's the point?" Still, he backs off.

"Thanks for taking care of the boys today."

He shrugs off my gratitude and waves for me to follow him, handing me another drink. We end up in the kitchen. His brother's there, along with Trevor and a couple of other people. They're trying to toss bottle caps into a pail on the other side of the room. Luke and Lisa are picking up the ones that miss. It's almost eleven. Luke should be in bed by now.

Linda's made up a pullout couch in the living room for the boys to sleep on. The room's got doors on each side, so the noise shouldn't be so bad. I stay with Luke for almost half an hour, rubbing his back to settle him down. By the time he's asleep, I'm ready to crawl off to bed too.

"Lucan, you can't avoid me all night." Chuck intercepts me on the way over to Richard. He holds his arms out. "Come on, Ellie, give me a hug for old-time's sake."

Reluctantly, I let him crush me into his Coors sweatshirt— probably won in a bar draw. Bound in Chuck's thick embrace, the veneer of the person that I've spent the last two decades trying to become peels away.

"What are you doing with yourself?"

"Working at Michelin." He swats a mosquito away from his ear. His hair's thinned—his shag reduced to tufts that feather down to a full beard. "Still playing hockey—Kentville pickup league MVP two years running." He makes a "boo-yah" cheer and holds his fist up in devil horns. If I could change the past, give a frantic message to my eighteen-year-old self, this is the snapshot I'd send.

Linda and Gail stumble over to us. "High-school reunion?" Linda drawls.

"Heard you two used to be sweethearts."

Chuck grins and puts his arm around me. Twenty years on, he's still acting like my personal Christopher Columbus. "We should get a picture of this."

"I think we could make that happen." Linda hollers for Bernie. He's not far off and he turns around, surprised to find Chuck and me standing together.

Bernie stalks over and Linda snuggles up to him. "You got your camera?"

"Don't bother." Gail pulls out her cellphone. "One, two, smile."

At the last minute, Chuck leans over to kiss me. I push him off and wipe at my cheek, the way Stephen would when he was little. Gail and Linda erupt into hysterics. Bernie's well gone from the booze and seething. He stumbles over to Chuck. Chuck just grabs him and spins him to the side. "Gail, get another one with Ellie in the middle." Bernie shoves him hard and Chuck struggles to keep his balance. Bernie lunges in to take another shot but Linda grabs him and leads him away, asking what the hell that was about.

It's way past Stephen's bedtime and I haven't checked in with him in a while. I walk through the crowd, now dancing to Van Morrison's *Brown Eyed Girl*, and make my way through the house. Someone's making out up against the fridge, but I don't stick around to investigate. I look in on Luke and am relieved he's fast asleep. No sign of Max or Stephen. I open the front door and hear giggling down under the porch. Stephen, Max and a couple of other boys are sitting up against the siding.

"Hi, Mrs. Bascom," Max says.

I don't want to embarrass Stephen in front of his friends by sending him to bed, so I say his father wants to see him. When he gets up, the light catches on something between Max and the wall. A trio of beer bottles. The boys look at each other apprehensively. Max hands them over.

"Are there any others?"

"No."

"Stand up." I collect four more and lead my son over to his father. Richard's gone back to eating. He waves for Stephen to come sit next to him.

"I missed you, buddy."

I hand the bottles over, explaining where I got them.

"How many did you have?"

"Two." Stephen looks like he can't decide whether to cry or laugh.

"Did you do anything else?"

"No."

I'm too drunk and too tired to handle the situation.

Richard takes him inside.

I make my way over to Bernie and find him sitting with Linda on his lap. Max has already come around and is lingering near his mother. He looks at me, afraid of what I'm going to say. Linda put a lot of work into the party and there's still a big crowd, so I'm not going to ruin that. I sidle over to the two of them and tell them I'm heading to bed.

"Come on," Bernie says, bouncing Linda up and down on his knee. "It's early."

"Long day."

Linda could care less.

"Thanks for having us over."

"Sure," she says, leaning back to suck on Bernie's earlobe.

The Last of Barrett's Privateers comes on and the crowd reacts like it's the Maritime anthem, everyone rising to belt out the chorus. When it ends, the air feels charged, the cold of the night setting in and everyone stumbling. Beer cans and bottles litter the yard along with discarded paper plates. I check my watch and it's past one. I wonder if the cops will come because of the noise then remember that Bernie's friends with most of them.

In the bed upstairs, I pass out waiting for Richard. I wake up when he comes in, feeling the same weird exhaustion that I used to feel at high-school field parties when I stayed up to watch the sunrise. Richard undresses at the far side of the bed, drops down to his boxers and socks. He tosses his T-shirt across for me to sleep in. My bra unhooks mechanically and I drop it on the floor, balled up in my shirt.

"Considering what happened today, I think we can give Stephen a free pass."

Agreed.

This is the first moment that we've had to ourselves since the car ride. It feels like weeks have passed since then. Richard holds me, cradling me into him. Nothing that came before seems important now. Everything is steady, my back against his belly, feeling the rise and fall of his breath as his body slows to sleep. He is still, still, still.

"What if they hadn't gotten out?" I gasp, smothering the noise with my pillow.

"Don't," he says, gripping me tight. "Don't."

7

*S*EVEN-THIRTY in the morning and I'm on an Easter egg hunt of the damned, stumbling around the backyard, picking up stray cans and bottles. Every time I stoop then stand, my brains shift to the other side of my skull. Richard's still horizontal, only a thread less hungover.

The beer cases have gone soggy overnight and disintegrate when I grab their handles. The grass is wet and my canvas joggers and pant legs are soaked before I've covered half the yard. A lot of the cans are filled with cigarette butts, which I empty into a separate bag, trying not to get a whiff of the beer-soaked tobacco.

After about fifteen minutes, Linda comes out cradling a cup of coffee. Bernie's already taken the kids into town. "Your husband's up. I don't have anything in the fridge for breakfast."

"Is that place still open next to the Irving?"

"Yeah."

"I'll take them there."

Linda's relieved but still somewhat hostile. On a whim I ask if she wants to come too, my treat.

"Really?"

I wonder if it's a mistake, but Linda's already taken off back inside.

We're out of the house by quarter to nine, which leaves plenty of time to swing by the mall to get my mother some clothes. The restaurant is packed, but they know Linda, so they make up a table for us. As we take our seats, Linda waves to two other couples.

Richard asks if she's ever considered running for mayor.

"I've been working cash so long at the grocery store, you get to know people pretty quick."

"That was my first job too."

I've never heard this before. Stephen looks up at his dad, waiting for the story. Luke's busy colouring on the kids' placemat.

"After school at No Frills. First I was just the checkout boy. Then I got put on cash. Most people in the area knew my dad, so they were pretty friendly to me. It's where I met my first girlfriend."

"That's how Bernie and I met," Linda says.

The waitress comes back with juice cups for the boys, coffee for the rest of us. I catch a glimpse of myself reflected in the napkin dispenser. We should have had showers at Bernie's since there won't be water at the house.

It doesn't take long before the waitress brings our food over, laying an immense stack of pancakes in front of my husband.

"You ever think of moving out here?" Linda asks.

"I like the city too much," Richard says. "Being able to walk to work or to the boys' school."

"I'd like to live in Halifax one day but Bernie—" Linda sighs. "How much longer are you staying?" Stephen and Luke look at us, wanting to know the answer too.

"Not sure," Richard says.

"It's going to depend on a lot of things."

"We're not leaving before the soccer tournament, are we?" Stephen asks.

"I'm not sure," Richard repeats. "I've got a few things coming up at work."

"It's only three weeks." Stephen's smile drops.

"Christ, that reminds me," Linda says. "I've got to get the schedule from the coach for that weekend. I want to ask for some time off work."

"It'll depend on my mother too. How long it takes to fix the place up."

"Your mom's a nice lady." Something in the way Linda says it makes it sound like a comparison in which I come out lacking. When we leave the restaurant, she makes us wait while she runs across the road to the gas station convenience store. She returns with a box of Ferrero Rocher. "I was hoping they'd have a plant, but I know your mom likes these."

Any lingering hangover is iced by the walk through the hospital's double doors. Richard and the boys wait in the car. I follow the receptionist's directions down the hall to the ward room my mother's sharing. Around every corner, there's the waft of hand sanitizer.

In 309, there's an elderly lady asleep in the far corner with several IV bags draining into her arm. The bed next to her is empty. On the other side of the room, the curtains are drawn and I peek through the gape. Both areas are filled with families visiting their relatives. I speed to the nursing station, worried my mother's already been discharged and is waiting out by the entrance.

There are two RNs at the desk, one of them absorbed in filing medical charts and the other typing absently at the computer.

"I'm Ellie Bascom," I explain. The chart-filer looks up. "My mother, Lynne Lucan, was brought in last night. Has she already been discharged?"

The nurse at the computer stiffens. She starts to speak but the other nurse silences her with a hand on her shoulder. "Lorraine, page Dr. Bellingham." She leads me into a small consulting room to the left of the nursing station. I try not to panic as she opens my mother's chart.

"I'm afraid your mother's had a stroke." The nurse keeps her voice very low and even, and I wonder if it's a technique she learned in nursing school. "We've been trying to get in touch with you, but the only emergency contact on your mother's file is a Toronto number."

"Is she...?"

"She's in stable condition. We don't know about the extent of the damage. Dr. Bellingham will be able to give you a clearer picture."

"When did it happen?"

"During the night. She was sedated for shock, so the effects took more time to be noticed." She reaches out and touches my knee. "I'm sorry. If there's anyone you need to phone, you can use the one in here."

"Can I see her?"

"You'll want to chat with Dr. Bellingham first." She stands and hovers a moment, negotiating between her apparent sympathy and the need to get back to the station. "Can I get you a coffee?"

I shake my head.

"I'll bring you a juice." The door clicks closed.

I feel an overwhelming need to see my mother right away, to have physical confirmation that whatever's happened, she's still here. I'm still clutching the plastic bags with the two sizes of jeans and three T-shirts. I slowly hoist them onto the couch, beside a couple of kids' books—their pasteboard covers curled up at the edges. I wonder if patients' children did that, worrying the pages while their parents received grim diagnoses, or if they were donated that way, used and comfortless.

There's no Kleenex left in the box on the side table. I wipe my nose like a kid against the inside of my shirt, realizing too late that we won't have laundry for a while. Dr. Bellingham catches me like that, my shirt exposing my belly. "Oh," she says and pops out again. She's back a moment later with another box of tissues. "That's better." It's cheap institutional stuff that's coarse against my skin. I blow too hard and it breaks through onto my hand.

Dr. Bellingham waits for me to compose myself. She's an older woman, not much younger than my mother with salt and pepper hair combed back in a ponytail. "Have you noticed anything different about your mother's behaviour lately?"

"We took her to the doctor but all that came back was high blood pressure."

The doctor nods. "We've done some scans and it looks like your mother was having some blood flow blockage to the brain. We call it transient ischemic attack, TIA." She pulls out a brochure from one of her folders and hands it over. "Unfortunately, TIAs are often a warning that a full-on stroke is coming. The acute stress of the fire likely triggered it."

"Is she okay?" It's such a childish question.

"It wasn't a severe stroke, but it was significant," Dr. Bellingham says. "We're putting her on medication that should prevent more stroking. She's lost some motor control on her left side, but still has feeling in the limbs. Once she starts rehab, we'll be able to see how she progresses." She hands me another pamphlet. The front has an illustration of an elderly couple exercising. It still smells like printing ink.

"How long will she be in hospital?"

"It could be a few weeks or longer, depending on how quickly she responds." She pauses. "It's sudden, but you're going to want to think about long-term options."

"We're going over to the house today to clean. Once we get in touch with the insurance broker, we'll hire the reconstruction company."

The doctor lays her hand on the chart. "It's not just that. Some stroke patients aren't ever able to live unassisted. Do you live in the area?"

"We're visiting for the summer."

"We'll book you an appointment with a social worker right away." She makes a note of this and then turns back to me. "If you want my advice, I'd call the Health Board line today. Unless your mother has extensive health coverage, you'll want the Single Entry Access program."

My mother has lived uneventfully on her own for twenty-five years. What the doctor is suggesting sounds impossible.

"Hopefully, she'll have a fast and complete recovery." She prints the phone number on the back of the brochure. "But if she needs to move to a home, then you'll want to be on the list right away."

The first nurse comes back to let me know they're moving my mother into a semi-private down the hall. I wait for her there, flipping through the pamphlet, my anger towards Dr. Archibald flaring.

When the nurses wheel my mother in, her skin is waxy and washed out by the pale blue of the hospital gown. As the nurse adjusts the bed, my mother doesn't meet my eye, just stares at her limp hands. I bring a chair over so I can sit holding her arm, careful to avoid her bandaged hands.

"I'm here now," I say and stroke her face.

She's dazed and unresponsive to my touch. After a few minutes, I realize I'm holding her left arm, the wrong arm. I switch to her right, hoping she'll be able to register my presence better this way.

My mother winces and shakes my hand away. My eyes dart to the door to see if the nurse is around, unsure if she needs immediate aid. She's covering her brow, the cotton gauze a mitt around her hand. She's crying. Her voice is hoarse and speaking sends her into a coughing fit.

"It's fine," I say, pressing my nails into my palm to keep from tearing up. "The boys are fine. Everyone's fine." It's the only word that comes.

She shakes her head. She says something but it's hard to make out what it is. Her hair is askew from the pillow and I root around in the nightstand for a brush. There isn't one. I do my best combing through her hair with my fingers, smoothing her fringe to the side. I'm not sure what else to say or how to act. She drifts in and out of sleep.

I decide she might like some water. I wander back to the nursing station to find out where I can get a Styrofoam cup and an ice cube but am told they still don't know if she's capable of swallowing. The best I can do is dampen her lips with wet paper towel. In the bathroom, I notice there are bars along all the walls—by the toilet, by the sink—the whole room is a mobility aid. My mother's always been so adamant about not needing assistance. I can't see her living in the kind of nursing home with grips over the fixtures.

My mother nods in thanks as I pat her mouth with the towel. It's one-thirty. I've been here almost two hours and should check in with Richard. I tell her I'll be right back. She lets the wet paper fall on her gown and a water ring blooms around it.

The day passes quickly attending to the hospital administrative business—setting up the room phone, ordering TV service, letting them know the name of my mother's health carrier, a rainbow of Xeroxed forms. My mother isn't awake for most of the day, but I stay by her side as much as I can. The nurses make the rounds every few hours, diligently checking her vitals and assessing her response. They assure me that she just needs to rest.

Richard picks me up at eight. The first thing he does is hand me a new pay-as-you-go cellphone because my charger melted, along with the cordless landline. My mother's broker is closed for the long weekend but Bernie was able to recommend a restoration crew and they're already at the house.

"It's quite the production," Richard says. "They've got the commercial dehumidifiers going—apparently mould's the biggest concern right now." The power's still shut off. They're also running a HEPA filter to start the odour removal.

He and the boys have eaten but we swing by the drive-through to get some takeout for me. We're all exhausted and I ask if they managed to find a place to stay. I'm shovelling the fast food in, biting into the chicken fingers before they've properly cooled. All I can taste is the bland tang of plum sauce.

"Bad news and good news," Richard says.

The boys are giggling in the back and I take this as a good sign—the situation needs all the levity it can get.

"Bad first."

"Even Windsor's booked up now."

"And the good?"

"There was a sale on camping equipment."

The tent's already pitched at the far end of the property, near the hedge. It's a six-person dome tent—bright purple with a grey fly and there are four sleeping bags laid out inside, visible through the mosquito-net door. "All this for only one-fifty." The neighbours have offered the use of their toilet.

"Can I grab some clothes from inside?"

Richard shakes his head. "We're not supposed to go in until they've done more work. Right now the whole place is toxic." He's bought a change of clothes for me from the mall, as well as sleepwear for all of us. We are all sporting different sizes and patterns of old man pajamas. Lined up outside the tent, we look like a demented barbershop quartet.

George stops by at ten-past-nine, when we're already rigged out in this new uniform. He scratches his stubble to hide his smile.

"It's okay," I say. "You can laugh."

"I'm just coming off shift and thought I'd stop by to see how you're making out." He's seen the copy of the fire report and walks us through how the fire spread. We pace the opposite edge of the lot as he explains what happened, so that the boys don't have to hear the details.

They say that in a plane crash, there needs to be a convergence of bad luck. Pilots are trained for error—electrical system failure, tire blowouts on landing, loss of cabin pressure. Catastrophe only strikes when there's a string of smaller crises. Swiss Air was lost in Peggy's Cove when the arcing of wires on the in-flight entertainment system didn't trip the circuit breakers. A fire spread in the insulation with no instrument warning so by the time it was discovered, it was already too late— the displays had failed and the smoke quickly overcame the pilots.

George keeps telling us how unlucky we were—my mother's misdiagnosis, the accident coming over the scanner, the fire that could have been put out so easily with a pot lid, the stroke. With each profession of sympathy, however, I start adding up a separate tally. The oil didn't spill on her. She didn't throw water on the flames, which would have sprayed the fuel across the room. The fire stayed smouldering for a long time—the progress slowed by Dad's tile backsplash, an old asbestos panel and the stove's location in the room. George says the men down at the station are still talking about Stephen's presence of mind. Not many kids, he says, would call EMS right away, let alone get everyone out, close the doors and start pouring water on his grandmother's burns. If any of those things had gone the other way, we'd have lost the whole structure. Or worse.

George is sombre when I tell him about the hospital visit. "She taking visitors?" he asks.

"Not for a few days."

He nods. "I'll spread the word." I'm not sure who there is to tell, considering how small my mother's circle has become.

After George leaves, Richard and I sit on the tree stump that marks the end of the driveway. It's gotten cooler out and the pajamas are a thin cotton. He wraps his arms around me and the heat of his body is a comfort.

"Did you go in today?" I ask.

"They fitted me up with a mask and walked me through. I think they have to for insurance."

"What's it like inside?"

"Because it smouldered for so long, there's more residue. Less structural damage, but more soot."

"Can any of it be saved?"

"The kitchen's gone," he says, softly. "The living-room furniture's pretty badly stained from smoke. The dining room will be fine."

I start to make mental lists of things that will need to be dealt with in the morning. I wonder who I need to call—what family my mother's still keeping in touch with.

"Everything in the kitchen's really gone?"

"Anything plastic melted. The cabinets that didn't burn outright are scorched."

My mother kept her address book stacked with the phone directories in the cabinet next to the stove. I think about her meticulous list of Christmas card replies—all of her careful notations gone.

"Did they give you an estimate?"

"They deal directly with the insurance company. They've worked with your mom's broker a few times."

"You've been busy."

"It's the most productive day I've ever had with a hangover."

Richard squeezes me. I feel his usual shift to tickle my waist, waiting for his fingers to start wiggling into my ribs. His hands drop to my hips. Part of me wants to pick them up and make him keep going.

"Thank you for doing this," I say, leaning my head back onto his collarbone. "Thank you for all of this."

He nudges me up so that we can talk face-to-face. "I also called the BBC people. I let them know there's no way I can get the article to them."

"Can't it be delayed?"

He frowns and shakes his head. "They understood the circumstances."

I start to protest that we can work something out but he silences me. He's made his decision.

"I'm sorry." I reach around to run my fingers across the nape of his neck. His hairline's straight as a ruler. I tell him that I'm so happy he's here.

That's all that matters right now, that the four of us are together.

"Part of me's worried it wouldn't have happened if I hadn't insisted—"

It's my turn to shush him. If I hadn't had to pick him up at the airport, if I hadn't gone alone, if my mother hadn't made fish and chips . . . if I hadn't lost my job. It's pointless.

It's a tighter fit in the tent once we're all inside, lying in our neon sleeping bags like parallel glow-worms. Luke and I squish into the middle, where there's no room to shift to a different position. Despite the disastrous past two days, with all of us huddled under the cheap nylon dome, it feels like we're at a family carnival.

I lie on my back staring up at the intersection between the tent poles. "I just want to say that I've never been more proud of the two of you boys. Especially Stephen."

"Here, here."

Stephen unzips the opening of his sleeping bag and starts flapping the top.

"Too hot?" Richard asks.

Our youngest starts shrieking before Stephen can answer.

The reek hits. It's like he's digested a rotten egg.

Stephen howls, "You smelt it, you dealt it."

The fast food strikes us all over the next half-hour. There's only a brief moment of calm, the four of us finally closing our eyes, before the next person erupts. Luke props his little bum against me through the sleeping bag and forces out a stinker so bad I can feel the heat against my leg.

"Check your pants," Richard says, leaning his face against the mosquito netting like a fish bobbing for air.

It feels like I don't sleep at all, but I must, because at half-past four I'm woken up by a crying Luke. He's had a nightmare about my mother's burns and I take him out of the tent and into the car so the others can sleep. He wants to go home. I make him sip some bottled water and try to explain that we can't leave until my mother's better. He's equated going home with every-thing returning to normal and it's difficult to convince him otherwise. By the time he falls asleep again, the dark's already thinning.

*   *   *

My mother is with the physio when I get to the hospital. In scrubs and sneakers the physio looks impossibly young, her corkscrew curls bobby-pinned off her face—more candystriper than ther-apist. Her name badge reads Joanne.

The colour in my mother's face is much better and she's vastly more alert. When she speaks, it's only the very bottom corner of her mouth that still dips towards the chin. "This is my daughter Ellie."

"Spitting image," Joanne says.

Apart from our similar build, I've never really thought of my mother and me looking much alike. I'd always thought my face was closer to Dad's but there's something comforting in Joanne's assessment, even if it's just an aside.

"Now, Lynne, I'm going to get you to close your eyes." Joanne tests to see if my mother can identify where her body's being touched. She does well as the physio taps her arm but my mother doesn't have much leg sensation. Joanne moves my mother's big toe up and down like a light switch but she can't tell if it's on or off.

"You're doing really well," Joanne says, still cheery. She gives my mother a ball to see if she can hold it with one hand. She can open her fingers, but can't quite make them grasp the circumference. Her foot she can't lift at all, but she can wiggle her toes a little bit. Finally, Joanne gets my mother sitting up on the side of the bed, showing her how to safely support herself. The whole process tires her out. She needs assistance to lie back down.

After the session, I follow Joanne into the hallway. "Did she do all right?" It comes out wrong, like I'm grilling a coach about my kid's tryout.

"Baby steps."

My mother can barely sit up. I think about what Dr. Bellingham said yesterday—get her on the list. I take the phone outside and make the call, feeling guilty as hell. It's decades off from the time when I should be stepping in to make decisions for her. But even if she makes a speedy recovery, the house won't be ready. They're not going to send a stroke patient home to a tent.

By late afternoon, the nurses have done a swallowing test and my mother's placed on a liquid diet. She sucks away at a strawberry flavoured energy drink, the alarming pink travelling up the bendy straw. Her bandages have been changed so only the more severe burns on her palms are covered.

Now that she's looking more herself, I broach the subject of notifying family. I take a pen and paper out of my bag and pause like an old-time stenographer. "Is there anyone you want me to call?"

She shrugs, noncommittal.

"When you're ready, Richard wants to visit."

She slumps into the pillows. "I don't want to see the boys."

"They're fine now. They're doing okay."

"I'm so embarrassed." She looks at me to see if I understand.

I don't know what to say to her. I remember the chocolates from Linda that I left in the nightstand yesterday. She takes the package and tilts it so the sunlight reflects off the plastic top and onto the cloth room divider.

"My favourite."

"They're from Linda."

She drops the box on her lap and uses her good arm to shift her right elbow across her body. Her shoulder's been bothering her all day. She opens her bad hand slightly, then tries and fails to make a fist. She wants to know about the house.

It's too soon to describe the extent of the damage. "We've got some people in to fix it up."

"Get the plates out," she says. "The ones with the ships. And the pictures on the fridge."

The decorative plates were a wedding present from my grandparents. They would have fallen from their display above the stove early on. The photos curled up and flaked off like dead leaves.

"I made such a mess," she says, shaking her head and trying desperately to make her fingers work again. "And after you did all that scrubbing. Sin."

There's no room to park in the driveway. It's half-past seven and the crew is still at it, laying out the debris on massive blue tarps like it's Hell's garage sale. The crew leader, a tall man with an Australian accent, tells me we need to decide what to keep. They'll truck it off to storage and cleaning and send the rest to the dump.

The big appliances are all out. The dials have melted off the stove and the plastic on the display panel's poured across the element. The fridge is also charred, the plastic handles completely gone. They've taken what's left of the cupboards out. Only a few pieces of wood from the far side are really recognizable, even the ceramic tile surface is cracked. There's a separate pile of obvious garbage: plates, coffee pot, glasses, and a clump of plastic and metal that I only recognize as the blender because of the pitcher.

I walk through the rows like a magpie looking for anything shiny to grab onto. They are bringing the couch out from the living room, the synthetic green upholstery melted down. I stop one the workers before he goes back in.

"Is the coffee table okay?"

"Mostly just soot damage. You can refinish it."

"What about the hutch and dining-room table?"

"Same."

They're all pieces that my father made or stripped and finished himself. They're the only things worth saving. The rest can be carted away.

Richard arrives with the boys as they're loading up the truck for the dump.

"Shouldn't you wait and ask your mother?"

At this point I don't want to worry her. Once she's out of the hospital, we'll take her shopping. With the insurance money, she can come home to something new.

The holiday Monday, the restoration crew only works a half-day. The bulk of the dangerous work is finished—the downstairs completely gutted and the few things we're saving already in storage. The team leader gives me a company brochure and an itemized list of work completed, along with an estimate for the remainder. I'll need it for tomorrow's meeting with the broker. After only two and a half days, they've worked through eleven thousand eight hundred dollars worth of restoration.

It's only a third of the total repairs and doesn't cover cosmetic work like repainting, let alone contents replacement. There's still no electricity or running water but it's now safe for us to go inside.

There's a soccer game in the evening and I'm hoping it'll be a bit of normalcy for the boys. Since they're playing Windsor, there's no danger of Brad's father making an appearance. Stephen spends the drive catching his father up on the games so far, like they're episodes of a serial that Richard's missed.

On the pitch, Max's nervous when I greet him. He doesn't make eye contact or ask questions like he usually does and it takes a moment to register why—I'd almost forgotten about catching him drinking. I wasn't going to say anything, but there's no way to let him know he's off the hook. The past few days I haven't thought much about what happened with Bernie, but Max's embarrassment sparks my own dread of Richard finding out.

Bernie has brought baseball gloves and a softball to play catch with the younger kids while the soccer teams warm up and Richard quickly joins in. The two of them have hit it off, I suppose. I know Richard's grateful for all the help Bernie's given us. There's something so incongruous about watching the two of them together. I catch glimpses of past and present versions of myself and it's hard to imagine either interacting with the other. Six months ago, if Bernie had run into me downtown, what would we have had to say to each other?

Linda slouches next to me on the bleachers and lights a cigarette, asks how my mother's doing.

"Coming along." The boys are out of earshot, so I add, "The doctor's told us to look into long-term care."

Linda scrunches up her face. "Like a nursing home?"

"Or a seniors' residence. Maybe just until the house is fixed."

"I'd rather be shot than thrown in one of them. Before I started on at the Superstore, I worked food service at a home over on Main. Most depressing thing I ever seen—all these old people parked at the tables. The management's got it arranged so the droolers are all at the same table, the shakers at another." She jerks her hand in a spastic twitch, getting ash on her jeans. "Soft food, real food, self-feeders, assisted-feeders, all separate.

They had to do it so the ones still with it wouldn't get depressed. All the food was shit."

Richard tosses Bernie a pop fly and he has to lunge to the right to catch it. The exertion almost knocks his cap off and he grabs his hat with his free hand to steady it. The whole thing has a vaudevillian effect. Linda yells out encouragement then turns back to me. "You wouldn't really put her in a place like that would you?"

"It's not my first choice."

"You got room in your house in Toronto?"

"She wouldn't want to live in the city."

Linda seems to agree with me. "Probably best to leave her where she is. Maybe rent out a room to a nurse or something. Sometimes people do that with cops."

Ever since Richard's arrival, Linda has relaxed around me, has almost treated me like she would Gail. It surprises me how quickly I sink into an ease with her, how I feel almost sisterly towards her. Of course, after Three Pools, I don't have the right to think of her that way.

Early in the second half, Stephen steals the ball on a forward rush and quickly pivots to his own net. He passes straight across to Max and the two of them zigzag up the field.

"Hustle! Swerve it!" Richard calls out, already impressed with how well they work together.

We all cheer as the boys advance up the field. Twenty yards from the goal, the other team pens Max in, but he pops the ball up and over the crowd. Stephen leaps past a kid who's lunged feet first at the ball. Stephen regains his balance and drives the ball hard towards the net. The keeper is off by a foot. We all whoop like it's the playoffs, waving our arms above our heads and shrieking. Stephen scans the stands for his dad.

When we settle back down, Bernie leans against the rear bench, resting on his elbows, and I do the same. Richard and Linda are upright, still clapping. Bernie smiles at me, the first real interaction since the party. We're surrounded by people, but I quickly look away. For the rest of the evening I try to avoid meeting his eyes.

After the game, as we return to our respective vehicles, Richard keeps turning back to wave goodbye. There's a lightness to the interaction, as though the eight of us have been friends for years. When we hit Port Williams, however, the weight of the day sets in. We pull up to the gutted house and go about our new rituals of getting ready for bed—brushing our teeth by the bushes, taking turns pissing in the shrubbery, passing around wet-naps.

Tuesday morning our luck gets worse. My mother has no insurance.

I'm informed by her very concerned ex-broker that she did have an insurance policy for almost thirty years, but it has been lapsed for the past ten months. The brokerage tried to get in touch with her after she failed to return the renewal payment, calling and sending letters. My mother doesn't have an answering machine and never replied to the correspondence. In the end, he decided she'd gone with the competition.

"A lot of people get those deals at the grocery store or through their bank now," the broker explains. "Sometimes they see a number on TV."

He ushers me into an empty office so I can call the hospital. My mother's in a state. Her shoulder's bothering her a lot, she's fed up with the soft food and she hates needing assistance to the bathroom. She says she's not sure if she wants to go on if this is what going on is like.

It's an annoyance when I ask where she has her house insurance.

"Allen's in Kentville. Almost thirty years."

"Do you know when you last paid the premium?"

"No," she says, getting defensive. "Just ask for Barb. They all know me in there."

I walk back into the broker's office, hoping against hope. Barb retired a year ago.

I drive back to the house and tell the restoration crew to stop. Richard and the boys aren't there—he must have taken them for a swim over at Lumsden's. The crew head is alarmed when I relay the situation. He wants to know who'll pay the bill.

"Just send it to me." I'm going to have to get power of attorney over my mother's finances. She's got a pension through the co-op and some RRSPs but I doubt she'll have that kind of cash accessible.

As quickly as the crew got here, they're gone. They take their tarps off the driveway and leave the charred contents on the gravel. After they drive away, I realize that they still have my father's furniture.

Bernie drops by with some leftover cookies from the party while I'm still waiting to hear from Richard. "I'd have brought squares too, but you don't have a fridge." He looks around at the debris on the drive. "Boys on break?"

I shake my head. "Murphy's law."

He gapes when I tell him how much it's already cost.

"We can't afford to keep going."

He puts the cookies down on the roof of the car. He looks up at the house with his hands deep in his pockets and his body tilted to the left, like he's battling a strong wind. After a moment, he starts to whistle softly and walk towards the door.

I've avoided entering the house before but I follow him into the hall, now emptied of the usual line of shoes. The living room's bare except for a box of my mother's records still in the corner. At the back, there are a few that haven't melted but father's favourite album, Kris Kristofferson's *Me and Bobby*

McGee, is concave. As I flip through the LPs, Bernie raps on the walls. He raises his eyebrows at the different sounds, like he's conducting a private interview with the carpentry, able to interpret the wall's thudding replies.

We can see the bathroom through a hole in the kitchen ceiling. Bernie sighs. We visit the damage up there but he doesn't say anything. Whatever they used to remove the odours has worked well, but the soot's still everywhere. The mosquito coil rug from my old room has been tossed and my clothes have been bagged. They'll either need to be heavily laundered or destroyed. The boys' room and my mother's have been left untouched by the crew because the damage was so minimal.

"Okay," Bernie finally says. "You've got to start with the electrical. I've got a buddy, he'll do it quick and right. It'll cost, but I'll get him to knock it down to something reasonable. I can help with the plumbing. Then it's just getting some boards sistered onto the one wall in the kitchen."

He sounds like a coach giving the last-ditch play to a losing team.

"Once that's done, it's drywall and a bit of work in the bathroom. The rest is cosmetic. You're going to have to primer everything. Best bet for the bathroom and the kitchen, at least until you've got the money, is to get some second-hand fixtures. I've got a toilet and a bathtub from the dump. I'll keep my eyes open for appliances."

We walk back outside and sit on the lawn near the tent.

"First thing you're going to need is a building permit."

"Don't they take a long time?"

"Chuck's cousin's the permits guy," Bernie says. "There won't be a problem."

Everything about his confidence is reassuring.

He can't stay because Clarence is waiting for him on the farm. It's awkward saying goodbye. Bernie hugs me with his hands low on my hips, fingers stretching towards my ass. I look around, conscious that Richard and the boys could pull in, wishing that Bernie would let the whole thing drop. He asks if I'd like to go for a quick drive. "I'm not pushing," he says, but it still feels like a bargain's been struck.

The nurses have helped my mother into one of the sweatsuits I bought and she's brushed her hair into a ponytail. The difference between today and Saturday is astounding. The physio is there again, finishing up an exercise, watching my mother point her toes up and down.

"Go ahead and tell your daughter," Joanne says.

My mother rolls her eyes at the prompt.

Joanne waggles her finger. "Come on."

"I stood up."

"That's right." She gives me a handout of some exercises I can get my mother to practice—tapping her fingers, spreading her toes, sitting up with an assist.

My mother dismisses the progress as soon as Joanne's left. "What am I going to do? Have someone propping me up all my life?"

I don't want to bring up the insurance before talking to Richard, so I turn my attention to the line of greeting cards and potted plants on the windowsill. There's a mini-cactus garden with a card that reads, "Our Lynne – from your family at Co-op Foods." George or Bernie must have phoned the store to let them know about the stroke.

"This is lovely."

"A few of the cashiers came by."

The cards are covered in signatures and promises to visit. Almost everyone's written "Don't be a stranger." I'd never considered my mother to be particularly linked into the community but working at the co-op eight hours a day, five days a week, she'd have been at the centre of a social hub. Retiring must have been a huge shift for her.

Richard peeks his head in and waves hello before shepherding our sons around the curtain. It's their first time visiting anyone in the hospital and they're apprehensive. Richard leads the way, holding my mother's wrist below the bandage and leaning down to kiss her cheek. Stephen and Luke shuffle towards the bed with a bag from the hospital gift shop. Inside is a white bear with a red heart between its hands that says *Get Well Soon, Grandma.*

"Thank you, dears." She gives each of her grandsons a hug. As Stephen straightens up, she reaches out to touch the raised lettering on his T-shirt. "Is this new?"

He glances at his father for guidance.

"We bought them a few things over the weekend."

Luke does not pick up on his father's discretion. "We bought a tent too!"

"You did?"

"We're camping in it."

"You mean you're going camping in it?"

"No," Luke says. "We're staying in it."

"Just for a few days," I say. "While they're cleaning out the house." We'd told the boys not to tell her about the extent of the damage but forgot to include the current living situation.

Thankfully his interest diverts to the medical equipment. My mother patiently answers his questions about the IV drip, the blood-pressure monitor and the emergency call button. She perks up with the boys there and when Stephen brings out a deck of cards, I think it's safe to pull Richard aside.

The hospital cafeteria has the same concrete institutional architecture as the Guelph Student Union. I link my hand through Richard's, wishing we were there, wishing my news was more benign. Richard's still stiff from sleeping on the ground and both of us are showing the effects of exhaustion. We line up for the automatic coffee dispenser and watch it spit out a French Vanilla Latte.

When I tell him, Richard waits a long time before responding. I sit, staring at the thin, stale coffee, trying to restrain myself from giggling. I'm so tired.

"You sent the guys home?"

I nod. "I'll ask her about power of attorney tomorrow. Then I'll see what financing I can get."

Richard shakes his head. "We'll pay it."

We don't have that kind of cash.

"However it shakes down. In the end, if your mother needs it, we'll pay it." He rubs his thumb against my palm. "It's family."

"Bernie thinks we can do most of the repairs ourselves."

"You already told him about the insurance?" I hadn't anticipated Richard feeling slighted, but he does. He drums his fingers against the Styrofoam cup and forces a smile.

"He caught me right after I stopped the reno guys. I tried to call you a few times."

He taps his cell through his breast pocket. "Swimming." On the way back to the room he casually flips through the call history.

Tonight is the worst night in the tent. The boys forgot to zip the screen door in the morning and bugs have gotten in. We kill fourteen mosquitoes before we turn out the flashlight, but I lie awake, unsure if the buzzing is inside or outside.

8

Y MOTHER'S LUNCH is still on her tray table.
She's eaten half an egg salad sandwich but is
ignoring the rest to rummage through her purse.
Before I can sit down, she draws out her chequebook. "I want
you to tell me how much it's going to cost to fix everything."

"We'll take care of it," I insist, not wanting to rattle her.
Thanks to Bernie's electrician, we've got power back, but we're
running out of clothes and are going to have to go to the laun-
dromat if we can't get water soon.

"It's my house and I'm going to need it fixed up. Please, just
tell me how much."

"We don't know yet. Richard went to buy some lumber
today."

"Save the receipt for the insurance people. I want it all
sorted out as soon as possible." She's in a snit. I reach over to
pat her arm but she shakes my hand off.

We've spent the past two days washing the walls down with
a solution of detergent, bleach and phosphate, our hands sweating in rubber gloves. Richard and I do the first wash and the boys
wipe the walls with a damp cloth afterwards. They've gotten
bored quickly. We have too, but the sooner we clean the place,
the sooner we'll be out of the tent.

I suggest that we talk to the bank to get me temporarily added onto her accounts. My mother holds up her good hand and delivers an emphatic no. "The social worker brought that up too when she came by to plan my discharge. I told her that there's nothing to plan—I'm going straight home. I'll be able to handle my finances just fine from there."

"When did she come by?"

"This morning."

That's why she's so riled up.

"There's a meeting in a week."

"When?"

"If you want to be there, fine. But it's not going to be a big production. I'm going home and that's it. I want to be able to rest up in my own bed without being prodded up and shipped off to exercise twice a day."

"Did the physio come again?"

My mother shakes her head. "No, they wheel me down to the room now. Stand and turn, sit and stand. It's exhausting. They want to throw me in the pool next."

"Did the social worker mention anything about a rehab hospital?" We're going to have to let the discharge team know that the house won't be ready for weeks, if not longer. There's also no bathroom on the first floor and I don't know if she can handle stairs.

"Ellie, you can't kick a person out of their own home."

"Did they think you'd be able to manage?"

"Of course. I told them you'd be there to help me."

When I get back from the hospital, I go into Dad's shed at the far side of the yard and start gathering tools. Everything's arranged by size—jacksaws, hammers, wrenches. There's a shelf at the far end with mason jars full of nails and screws, their sizes labelled with masking tape. I run my fingers over the labels but they fall off, the adhesive long since dried up.

Richard comes in and sits on my old stool. The smallness of the seat gives him comic proportions and his legs bend off like a giant arachnid. "Everything go okay at the hospital?"

"It's going to be a battle."

"No idea yet about the prognosis?"

I shake my head.

"Well, if she can't climb stairs."

"Knowing her," I say, "she'll probably want to put in an elevator."

"She won't be able to afford that."

I hold up my hands. I know, I know. "I'm going to check the basement later, see if I can find any financial records." Anything to let us know how grim the situation is.

"I talked to some of the guys over at Home Depot. By the time we replace everything. . . ."

"How bad?"

Richard leans against the wood framing and shifts his feet so our sneakers are touching, trying to get me to meet his eyes. "Even if we do it all ourselves."

"We can't sell my mother's house."

"I'm not trying to sell it from underneath her," he says. "But if she can't move back—the buyer's going to want to renovate anyway." He rubs the toe of his shoe against the dirt floor, like he's making a snow angel. He stops and knocks his foot against the door frame to clear the dust. "We might be better selling now."

It's a valid point but if my mother thinks she's got nowhere to go she's not going to get better. The past few days I've been running through all sorts of scenarios—in-home care, retirement residences, extended rehab—but none of the permutations involve selling the house.

"I could stay on for a bit to help her out."

Richard throws up his hands, exasperated. "Look, if you want to repair the place, fine."

"It's not meant as a threat."

He starts peeling a splinter from the grey door panel. "How long?"

"Even if she moves into a home, I'm going to want to get her settled. If you're worried about money, I can pick up adjunct work out here or in Halifax."

"I thought you weren't looking at jobs."

Richard doesn't understand that repairing the house has as much to with my father as my mother.

"It's not the money." He stands and brushes the dirt off his jeans. "If you stay, for what—a month, two months—what happens after? We're not moving out here. It can't go back to the way it was before."

"We don't know that," I say, my voice rising. He's right. I know he's right. But if this were Terrence instead of my mother he wouldn't be able to be so damn rational. "She's in physio several times a day. She's already standing and sitting with minimal assistance. Today she said they're sending her to Aqua-fit."

"Aqua-fit?"

"It's something."

"Do you know what happens at Aqua-fit? They strap floatation devices onto old people and get them to kick pool noodles across the water. Aqua-fit is not working any fucking miracles."

"My father built this house."

"Fine." He walks back into the yard before I can respond. That's the trouble with this summer—we haven't fought past the point where there's nothing to do but laugh and apologise. With our current living situation, the blowout's on permanent hiatus.

Bernie drives over around four-thirty, when the Home Depot delivery truck is finishing up unloading. Right away he wants to know why we didn't wait to order the lumber. "I could have got you some salvage pretty cheap. Or at Rafuse, discount."

"Richard didn't want to impose, I guess."

Bernie gives me a funny look, pissed off about something.

The Home Depot truck backs out of the drive and my husband comes over to shake Bernie's hand. "Ellie says you're a handy man."

"It's not my day job."

"Me neither." Richard laughs, not realising Bernie wasn't joking.

The two of them walk around the place together, not saying much. The boys and I follow behind. "Why'd you rip out the bathroom door?" he finally asks.

"We tried washing it, but the soot stuck to the varnish," Richard says. "Looked like shit." He doesn't usually swear in front of other people and it comes out strange, like he's trying on an act.

Bernie raises his eyebrows. "Coat of paint's easier than hanging a new one." He leans over the hole in the floor to tap on the shower backsplash, working his fingers under the grout to pry a few more tiles loose. "Your mom should have called me a while ago."

"I don't think she noticed."

Luke asks if he can start tearing the tiles off.

"Don't want to get that mould on you."

"I don't mind," Luke protests.

Bernie hoists him up into a piggyback. "I'll get you to help me lay the new ones in, how about that?"

Back outside, we have to wait for Bernie to unload the truck. Richard tries to help loosen one of the straps but Bernie waves him off—he has his own system. The two of them hoist the table saw off and lug it to the side of the house where there's an outdoor plug. It's a strain for Richard, but he puts on a brave face.

They get going measuring up the lengths of wood but our progress is stalled when Bernie discovers we don't have a framing gun. He rummages around in my father's shed for a few minutes and comes out with an ancient nail gun. He tries driving some nails into the discarded planks but it jams. "May as well go grab mine. It'll save time." He suggests that I go with him because his dad'll be there and he's got a question for me about the field. "Think you can spare Ellie?"

Richard thanks Bernie again for offering to help.

"Should only take an hour or so." It feels like a kid promising his date's father that he'll have her home by ten. As we get into the truck, I wonder if Clarence will be any happier to see me or if he'll be more suspicious, seeing the two of us alone together.

On the way to Gaspereau, Bernie pops a tape in the deck and Tom Petty's *American Girl* is barely discernible above the engine hum. Bernie sings along and puts his hand on my knee, squeezing my quadriceps in time to the music. The contact makes me nervous but I don't stop it. He changes the second chorus to "Canadian Girl" and looks over to check if I've noticed. He almost misses the turn and has to jerk his hand away and winch the wheel to make the corner.

We stop by the house first and Bernie leads me into the garage. He finds the nail gun right away but doesn't make to leave. Instead, he motions for me to sit up on his work-shelf while he goes to get a Coke. I ask about Linda and the kids, hoping to diffuse the tension, but he tells me they won't be back for several hours. Any idiot could see where this is going.

When he comes back, pop in hand, he surprises me by sitting a few feet off and asking how the boys are coping.

"We're trying."

He nods. "It'll be easier when you're back in the house."

"It's going to take a long time."

"What are you saying about my skills?" he asks, teasing. It's the first time tonight that he's smiled. He reaches for my hand. "You get the water going, the bathroom floor down, put in a fixture or two—it'll be functional. Baby steps." He sounds like my mother's physio.

We sit like that for a minute or two, each of us staring straight ahead, our hands the only point of contact.

Then he's between my legs, his hands on either side of my head, pressing my lips against his. I ask him again about Linda. He pulls back, annoyed by my hesitation. He repeats that we've got time.

Bernie looks at me, half-expectant, half-hurt, like he did when he was showing me his uncle's place. It's easier to just kiss him. He rushes this time, getting my shirt off and unsnapping my bra before we've even warmed up. I lie and say I've got my period to get out of screwing. Everything about this feels wrong. Bernie presses my hand to his jeans with a teenager's expectation. I let him fondle me while I jerk him off. As I pump him towards climax, I notice the haphazard tower of cardboard boxes, milk crates with extension cords spilling out around us, so different from my father's neat labelling. Bernie grunts as I rub him and when he's about to come, he grabs me off the bench and leads me down so he can finish in my mouth.

I clean up in the downstairs bathroom. There's a pair of Lisa's underwear crumpled next to the toilet. The print is tiny blueberries, the elastic a matching purple. Seeing them gets me so upset I have to run my wrists under cold water to stop myself from crying.

Over at the farm, we find Clarence in with the chickens. Bernie leaves us to talk while he looks for an extra crowbar. Clarence tips his hat to greet me, and I do my best walking through the poultry towards him in my cheap Zellers flip-flops.

As soon as I stop, the chickens get curious about my feet and start pecking at my toes. It doesn't really hurt, but it's not comfortable either.

"So you're going to fix the place up again?"

"Yeah."

"Too bad you don't have more relatives in town. Hard for Lynne being there on her own."

"We're trying to sort something out."

Clarence taps on the feeders and then reaches in to clear a blockage where the grains have clumped together. It takes him a while to gather the nerve to speak. "I've got a line of credit application coming up. Irene thinks it'd help if you gave us a consultation after all."

"Sure."

"Take your time. You've got your hands full with your mom."

When Bernie comes back, Clarence asks him if Linda will be bringing the kids over to the farm after the hospital.

"Is there something wrong?" I ask, worried one of them's had an accident.

Clarence looks at Bernie then back at me. "She's just in visiting your mother."

I'm too mortified to say anything. On the drive home, I stare at the red dots on my feet from where the birds were nipping. Already an hour and a half's passed since we left Richard and the boys.

Bernie asks if anything's wrong.

"You should have told me."

"About Lindie visiting your mom?"

"I never would have. . . ." I'm no longer convinced of what I would or wouldn't have done.

Bernie takes his frustration out on Richard. He's given all the grunt work while Bernie operates the power tools. At one point, Richard asks if what we're doing is safe—if the boards will hold or if we need new support beams.

"Let me guess," Bernie says, refusing to address Richard's concern. "Back home you hired someone for every leak and squeak?"

Later, Richard reminds him to keep track of his hours, to make sure we pay him for his time. Bernie asks if he's got a punch clock.

We're all relieved when he decides to pack it in at eleven.

We were hoping to have water back by Friday but the plumber's not as fastidious as the electrician and the afternoon comes and goes without progress. We've been invited to Marc and Margie's for dinner and, without laundry or our own shower, we arrive at their place dressed in shorts and Ts, smelling of our neighbour's Irish Spring.

Marc and his wife are sitting on the porch, nursing beers. Richard sighs as he unclasps his seatbelt and asks if anyone in this province drinks wine. Still, he's thrilled to be socializing with fellow academics. It feels as if we've arrived at a play date, all the same charged expectations and anxieties. Margie's wearing a black linen halter on a skirt like an over-turned camellia, plain black flip-flops and hair pulled back into a ponytail with a suggestion of bouffant. Their house is the same mix of elegance and IKEA.

They already have glasses and an ice bucket laid out on the kitchen island.

In solidarity with Richard, I ask for wine.

"We've got some Chardonnay chilling," Marc says with a sly expression. "But we've also got some microbrews in on special order from the liquor store." He reaches under the slate countertop and into a built-in bar fridge. "How about starting with a Weiss bier instead?"

"He's a bit of a brew-snob," Margie says, turning over two goblets. "We can open some Cab Sauv or the white."

"No, no," Richard says. "We'll try the beer."

Marc smiles and pulls up four bottles, smooth as a magician setting up a card trick. He pops the swing-tops and pours the beer in a slow, controlled drain.

Richard rubs his hand over the counter. "Where did you get the slate?"

"It's from Ontario." Marc hands over a coaster made from the same stone. "We got a deal from a company that used to make blackboards." He gestures to Margie like he's asking permission. "She made me promise not to do this but I think you might be interested. We've tried to incorporate materials from all across Canada into the architecture."

Marc leads us around the downstairs, pointing out marble, granite and limestone accents, along with different indigenous woods. The highlight is a large display of fossils on the living room mantel. The specimens are quite stunning—ammonite, nautiloid and knightia fish.

Even the backyard is immaculately landscaped—a container herb garden near the flagstone patio, six raised vegetable beds at the rear and a border of native grasses along the fence line. I ask who has the green thumb.

"Mark's the carpenter," Margie says. "But the outside is mine. It's taken the better part of five years to get the place in shape."

Home renovations are the last thing that we want to discuss tonight.

Margie keeps popping back into the house to check on dinner and her entrances and exits disrupt the already tenuous threads of conversation. It's the first time since Richard's been here that we haven't been dealing with crisis management and neither of us is able to relax. We make walk-me-through-your-CV small talk until Margie delivers the first course—gazpacho served in clamshell bowls with toasted baguette rounds and three kinds of tapenade.

I ask where she got the ceramics.

"One of the NSCAD fairs a few years ago. You should try to get into the galleries while you're here. Leave the kids with your mother. Make it a date."

"The last time we left them with Ellie's mother," Richard says dryly, "the fire department got involved."

The way he's set it up, they both think it's going to be some kind of amusing anecdote. As I tell the story, Margie's smile becomes more and more forced. "That's awful," she says quietly.

We all sit, spooning the cold soup, waiting before swallowing, not wanting to be the first to speak.

"Where are they now?" Margie asks.

"At soccer with an old friend from high school—Bernie. You met his father at the dig."

"And the house?" Marc asks. "Are you getting a contractor in?"

"No, Bernie and Richard are taking care of it."

"Do you have much left to do?"

Richard ticks through the laundry list of remaining jobs, a small fleck of coriander stuck in his left incisor. He could have brushed the question off, but instead he delivers an item-by-item estimate, which I suspect is directed at me because I was so inflexible about selling.

Marc grew up working construction with his brothers during the summers and he offers to come by to help.

I protest, but he says to think of it as compensation for future collaboration.

"The students just loved her at the dig. You two ever consider moving out here?"

Richard bristles, but Marc doesn't notice.

"Once we get the boomers out," he continues, not realizing Richard was born in 1958, "there'll be lots of spots coming open. You'll make a bundle just from the cut in housing prices."

Margie collects the plates, teasing her husband about sounding evangelical.

Marc points to Richard's empty glass and asks what he'd like as a refill.

"Perhaps I'll try that Chardonnay."

"By all means," he says, grinning impishly. "But I should warn you that we're having seafood and pasta and I've got a pilsner that will drive you crazy it goes so well with the garlic."

Richard pretends to consider it. "I might still switch to wine."

In the kitchen, Marc hands me a pilsner then pulls the bottle of Chardonnay from the back of the bar fridge and unscrews the cap. It's already been opened and he swishes the liquid inside before he pours. When I deliver it to Richard, his face sinks into a relieved smile, as if he was worried he'd get the pilsner after all.

Dinner is five perfectly seared scallops on a bed of basil and gnocchi. All Margie. I can't remember the last time we've had friends over for a dinner party, let alone invited Richard's colleagues over. Here I am slouching in three-day-old shorts and she's a blonde Jackie-O. I can't help wondering if Richard notices the difference between us.

The decadence of the food improves our rapport, mostly because it leads to easy-to-navigate avenues of conversation: recipe sourcing, local vs. organic, food self-sustainability, raising poultry in the city. Margie's a producer for a CBC science program, so between the four of us we can practically sleepwalk through the discussion.

After dinner, Marc brings out a set of dominoes with numbers up to double fifteen. In the dark of the backyard, it's difficult to make out the colours and digits, but it's a fun diversion. Half an hour into the game, however, I notice Richard making discreet eye signals. I'm ready to leave too but his impatience is irritating. As I start to make our excuses, Margie springs up, suddenly remembering there's still dessert. A few minutes later, she calls out to Marc from the sliding door, "Do you know where the blow torch is?"

With the two of them inside, Richard gets to work packing up the game, the dominoes' plastic collisions filling the silence. He whispers, "Eat quickly."

There is no fuel in the torch so Margie's doing the brulee in the oven. As we wait for the sugar to caramelize, Marc walks Richard through his agroecology course outline. It sounded so exciting when it was just the two of us, but in front of Richard, the whole project sounds facile. Over the course of his career, Richard's brought several million dollars worth of funding to the university, chaired the geology department and overseen the operation of one of the only geo-chronology labs in Canada. It gets progressively more embarrassing as Marc earnestly reiterates that he's lobbying for more Life Sciences courses and name-drops a few grants he's applying for.

We're saved by a loud crack in the kitchen and Margie rushing to the oven. A moment later we hear her muffled explanation. "The broiler cracked the cups."

"She warned me," Marc says, sheepish. He asks if she can save the dishes.

"What a shame," I say.

"We've got sherbet in the freezer. Mango or Limón?"

As soon as we're buckled into our car Richard asks, "Do you think she's going to let him have it?"

"Why?"

"The dishes. They were probably handmade by a vegan community in El Salvador. Do you have any Rolaids in your purse?"

I shuffle through the side pocket. "The scallops were delicious."

"You didn't have to drink vinegar with yours."

"Have the pilsner next time."

Richard turns left on Main Street and heads down to Front at the first side street. I think he's lost, but he makes a sharp right into the liquor-store parking lot. It's ten to ten and still open.

He comes out in five minutes with a case of something. He's got a boyish look on his face as he gets in the car.

"Was that necessary?"

He starts the car up and speeds back down Main towards Bernie's. "Even in the liquor store, half the wine was pink."

"Some people like blush wine."

"Is that what you drank in high school?" he asks, still horrified by the store's selection. "No wonder you moved to the city."

"In high school I drank White Shark."

"You really were a hick."

Richard doesn't seem to think that I should find this offensive.

"Is that what you thought of Marc and Margie?"

"Well, that's not how you play dominoes." He reaches over to squeeze my knee, trying to smooth things over. "They don't really think we'd move back here, do they?"

I don't answer.

"I mean, Regina has cheap housing prices, but you don't see me buying." He's warming up to his argument. "And that course—did he really think we'd want to move to teach that?"

"You wanted me to teach Geology 101."

"Same level, prettier veneer."

As pissed off as I am at his arrogance, I can't blame him for thinking what he does. U of T's got funding and administrative muscle that Acadia will never have. What Richard doesn't seem to realize is that for someone with my portfolio—strong on teaching, weak on research—Acadia's the kind of place where I could build a reputation.

He drives up Ridge road, taking the curves fast. "If there wasn't so much to take care of with your mother and the house, we'd be going out of our minds." He brakes at Bernie's and leaves the engine running, expecting me to go in to retrieve the boys. "Imagine living somewhere you couldn't get a decent roti? They probably think the Irish pub is ethnic eating."

"There's the Taj Mahal on Main Street."

"Oh, the Taj Mahal." Richard raises his hands in mock understanding. "And I bet over in New Minas we can get some food-court Moo Shoo Chicken."

"If I had said anything like this when we were in Trinidad."

"Not the same."

"No, it's not," I say, getting out of the car. "Because you didn't even grow up there."

The morning of my mother's discharge meeting I arrive early to help her get ready. She unties her gown, revealing her hysterectomy scar, her weight pooling away from it. I hold out her bra for her—it's so old the elastic doesn't spring back anymore. It flattens her breasts against her waist like two Phyllo triangles. Her right arm is too weak to reach around to the back to do up the hook and eye.

"I can stop into New Minas to pick you up some sports bras." I reach for the clasp.

"No, I can get it." It takes four attempts before she gives up. My mother knows that every step towards recovery is a step away from a facility.

She's better with her underwear. If she props herself into a seated position, she can slide the pair over her legs, then pivot back over the bed and shimmy them up. It's only the final pull that she needs assistance with, just to spot her while she stands. Joanne thinks she could be able to walk with a cane by the end of the month.

Once she's standing, I help her put on her jeans one leg at a time. This all feels like a dress rehearsal for a future role, one which my fifteen-year absence has left me distinctly unprepared for. The search through the basement yielded no financial records. If I'd lived closer, I'd have known where she kept them or been able to call up the bank myself to straighten everything out.

My mother's tired after getting dressed, but she doesn't want me to notice. Instead, she sits herself down and pretends to have caught something out the window.

In the conference room, the medical team is already waiting at the oak table, their pastel scrubs clashing with the coral wallpaper. Dr. Bellingham is the only one in civvies and she greets my mother casually, as if she were merely welcoming her to a ladies' book club.

It's the social worker who acts as both leader and secretary. She's got a clipboard and pages of forms that she flips through as she speaks. "In our previous meetings, we've identified the goal of returning to primary home residence."

My mother nods, encouraged.

"We like to start these meetings with a review of patient progress." She reads through the checklists supplied by the physical and occupational therapists, all my mother's basic motor functions broken down like a child's report card. Patient can sit unsupported. Patient can stand with a mobility aid. Patient requires assisted shower.

The list quickly runs dry.

"Dressing," my mother adds. "Independent dressing."

The social worker smiles. "You're close to the markers we use for assisted home living."

For a moment I'm terrified that they're going to release her home.

"However," she continues, "stairs are a problem because of the home layout."

"Can we get a stairlift?" my mother asks.

The social worker takes her reading glasses off and twiddles the lanyard between her fingers. "You'd have to evaluate those options financially."

Dr. Bellingham leans forward, propped up on crossed hands. "Most patients take several months to fully recover from a stroke. You're already showing lots of progress but the reality is that you're still going to need intensive physical therapy."

A bed has come up unexpectedly at a care centre outside Kentville. Because of the unique circumstances, my mother has been designated as a priority case. If she lived in Halifax, she could be transferred to a rehabilitation hospital. Here, a nursing home is our best option. The social worker explains that she'd be working with a dedicated rehab team and could take advantage of other seniors' health programs.

"Do I get any choice?"

"We want to find the solution that works for everyone."

The hospital needs the bed back.

"Can I talk to my daughter for a moment?"

The team hesitates before agreeing, because despite the breezy façade, they're all on a schedule.

"Your father always called those places glue factories," my mother says as soon as we're alone. "Can't Richard carry me upstairs?"

"The house is still under repair," I say gently.

"I don't mind a little clutter."She pleads. "Ellie, I haven't asked for a lot from you over the years."

We still don't have a working bathroom. There's nothing to do but to detail the rest of the damage, including the lapsed insurance policy. I should have told her all this sooner. Now, she can't take it all in. "Richard and I are going to cover the costs. Bernie's donated his labour."

"Did you talk to Barb?"

"We're going to take care of you."

She stares at the table. I try to get her to talk, to respond, but she won't. Too soon, the doctor knocks on the door and they all file back in, minus the OT, who had to see another patient.

My mother's face has set like plaster. The social worker interprets it as resignation. She slides a forest green residence brochure over for us to flip through. On the booklet cover, there's a photo of seniors at the entrance, posed as convalescent estate owners welcoming their guests. Inside, there are pictures of smiling nurses, residents playing board games and a recent trip to Neptune Theatre. The social worker opens to one of the pages with a floor plan of a basic 9' x 12' single room. "You can bring your own furniture. Anything that reminds you of home." She flips forward to a list of sample menus. "There's a choice of entrées."

Wednesday we'll have access to the room to move any items in and Thursday she'll be discharged. They'll lend us a wheel-chair so we can save the expense of an ambulance.

"Many people find it a relief after they first move in, not hav-ing to deal with the day-to-day chores," the social worker says, getting up to leave. "It's easier to focus on recovery."

We can reassess the situation in eight to twelve weeks.

I wheel my mother back to her room. This time she wants me to assist her in transferring back into bed, even though she's done it herself half a dozen times. She complains when I tilt the bed back upright. She wants me to prop her up with pillows instead.

"This isn't permanent," I say.

Her voice is full of rebuke. "People only leave those places in caskets. How do you think they got the spare room?"

There's a message from the Kentville Agricultural Centre when I get back—they want to bring me in for an interview the day after tomorrow. Richard delivers the information straight, no interrogation, just hands over the phone number on the back of a receipt.

"You've got to confirm a time."

I'd forgotten that I'd applied.

Richard doesn't ask, but I reassure him that I'm not consid-ering taking the position, that I only wanted to get my feet wet with interviewing again.

"Of course I'll cancel. I shouldn't have kept it a secret."

Richard shakes his head, calling my bluff. "If it's about prac-tice, by all means, go."

It's a first-round panel interview. They're looking for a research scientist to study methods of reducing agricultural runoff into local waters—not my primary area of expertise, but the meet-ing goes well enough. When I get back, the boys are on the front lawn staring up at the roof, flanked by Richard, Bernie and Marc. Bernie's fixed Stephen up with a tool belt and he's got it slung low on his hips, the hammer smacking his leg with each step. Richard's got a pen and paper in hand, looking like he's taking lecture notes.

"Sure, you'll have to slap some more paint on it," Bernie says. "Ellie, can you look through the shed to see if there's any leftover paint?"

"Won't it have gone off?" Marc asks.

Bernie wipes his mouth with the back of his hand and shrugs. "It's exterior paint."

"If you just take a chip off the side," Marc continues, "you can get them to match it at the Canadian Tire."

I notice Richard scrawling this down. Bernie waves Marc's suggestion away. "Not important now. We've got to pack the insulation in, get the drywall up and do something about the bathroom upstairs. I want to get as much done today as we can." He doesn't say it, but his other work's piling up. "Let's decide who can do what."

Marc nods. "Sure. I can start on the bathroom. I'll fix up the flooring and then tear down the rest of the tile and rotted wall."

"You know plumbing?"

"So-so."

"Don't finish the wall then, just leave it open and I'll come up afterwards."

"Luke can help you put things into garbage bags." Bernie picks Luke up and pulls him onto his lap. "What do you say?"

Luke nods, excited to be the first one asked.

"Richard, how are you at drywalling?" Marc asks.

"Might need a little supervision."

Bernie's not impressed. "The four of us can start on the insulation. Then I'll get you started on the drywall while I'll go out to get the fixtures for the bathroom."

The first thing Bernie does is get everyone fitted up with dust masks and gloves, taking extra time with the boys. Luke and Marc go upstairs and the banging starts right away, debris floating down from the hole in the ceiling.

Downstairs, we work in pairs, packing the pink fibreglass in and stapling plastic overtop. Bernie has to keep walking over to inspect Richard and Stephen's work and to give them a hand. Each time they get corrected, I see Stephen looking up at Richard, questioning. He's been promised his own bedroom and it's becoming more obvious that Richard doesn't have the skills to finish the basement.

Drywalling's the same ordeal. Bernie has to walk us through the whole process, gesturing with his hands and describing how to measure around the edges.

"Can I leave you to keep working on this?"

Richard nods.

When Bernie's left for New Minas, Richard keeps trying to get me aside to ask about the interview but Stephen is always within earshot. Despite his earlier nonchalance, I can tell that Richard is on edge about my applying.

The work goes much slower without Bernie, but we manage to get the regular-sized sheets finished, leaving a few areas that will need to be fitted around the windows. We try to measure out one of the notched pieces, Stephen and I holding the tape and Richard making a diagram, but once it's cut it doesn't fit. We have to ask Marc to come down to help.

"Easy mistake to make," Marc says, jovial. "You reversed it."

"Can't we put it on the other way?"

"The other wall doesn't have such a narrow clearance."

The one sheet is ruined. Marc helps us measure out the next piece and then leaves us. When we try again, Richard insists that we double-check all the measurements. "Are you sure?" he asks when we're on the last jag. He's just nervous but it comes out accusing.

"Yes," Stephen answers, exasperated.

Richard carefully tells us where to cut. When we hold the piece up, we get the same problem, it's a mirror image and won't fit.

"You measured wrong."

"You measure it then."

Richard takes the tape and checks each side against his note. "It's off a quarter-inch here."

Clearly that quarter-inch wasn't the problem.

Marc hears us fighting and pokes his head down through the hole in the ceiling. "You guys need help?"

"Please."

He looks at Richard's diagram then holds up the piece of drywall. "It's how you're cutting it. You're measuring it out opposite to how you should."

Richard looks over at us, as if to say, see.

Stephen glares back. "You told us how to cut it."

"It's okay," Marc says. "Give me the exacto knife." He manages to make a few adjustments and fit the piece in, then uses some scrap to fill in the gap.

"How's it going upstairs?"

"Almost there. Your son's a trooper."

It's getting late and Marc needs to head back. The boys are getting restless so I phone for pizza delivery, which in our area will take over an hour. It's a ridiculous wait, but we're glad for the break.

Bernie arrives shortly after the pizza gets there. He wants to unload before eating, while we still have the light. Once we've got everything in, including the one-piece shower unit that will become my mother's tub, he goes into the kitchen to inspect the drywall. Richard's nervous, but I can tell that he's also proud that we got it done. Bernie rubs his thumb over the gaps then stands back.

"Yeah, she's done," he says. "The seams are a problem, but I should be able to fix them with the plaster."

We eat in awkward silence. Richard offers to work on the taping but Bernie shakes his head. It's got to be done a certain way. He sends Richard upstairs with more garbage bags and a Shop-Vac to clear away the last of the garbage in the bathroom. I stay behind to help.

We work quickly together. The seams are taped before the vacuum comes on and then Bernie gets started on the plastering. He works on the more difficult seams and I cover the screw holes. I make two mugs of instant coffee with creamer and hand one to Bernie. He kisses the top of my head absent-mindedly. I look around to make sure no one has seen, but they're still upstairs and the vacuum drowns out all the noise.

When Richard and the boys finish, Bernie says they can take it easy for a while. Richard offers to take our sons to town for ice cream. It's a good chance to use the bathroom, just in case we don't get the toilet hooked up tonight.

The two of us get started on the upstairs plumbing. Bernie heats up some PVC tubing with a propane torch and slides it over a metal joint. I crouch next to him, apprehensive at being alone with him and try to make myself useful, handing over tools as they're needed.

"You're getting good at this," he says, grabbing the rubber mallet. He leans in to kiss me and I pull back after our lips touch. He shakes his head. "I'm not trying to get into your pants."

He launches back to work, his lips set in a thin line out of concentration or anger. My job is to put the flux on the copper piping before he starts soldering. It's uncomfortably hot cramped up here, both of us hunched over the iron.

I focus on the droplets of excess solder.

"Linda's a great woman," Bernie says, standing to unplug the extension cord. "In a couple years, we're thinking of putting in a hatchery for Max to run."

"Yeah?"

"She's still real young. Lindie and I could still start our own family."

Bernie kicks a piece of baseboard into alignment then grapples me over to him, so I'm braced against the window frame. The sill pinches my back. Bernie's mouth tastes of sweat and coffee whitener. I push him away, reflexive, but he keeps me pinned, his breath shallow and fast. He looks me straight in the eye. "I don't want to be left holding the short end of the stick."

He thinks I'm leaving Richard.

The car turns in the drive and there's no time to explain.

We sleep indoors for the first time, the boys in their sleeping bags and Richard and I in my mother's room. There's still no toilet or sink, but the bathtub wall unit is hooked up to running water. Before he left, Bernie gave explicit instructions for sanding the plaster before priming. "At this point it should be pretty foolproof," he said, condescending as all hell.

Lying there, his sleeping bag unzipped because of the heat, Richard tells me he's counting down the days until we're back in our own home. He tucks his knees up, curving his back. Richard's lost weight this summer and in this position his spine is super-articulated. Sometimes I forget how much older he is than me, than Marc, than Bernie. He isn't used to people outshining him. These renovations are driving him crazy. My fingers trace his spine and ribs.

"That feels nice," he murmurs. He shifts onto his back so I can rest my head on his collarbone. "I'm sorry about the drywall."

"It's new for all of us."

"No, I was being a crank. It's just—how much does a sheet of drywall cost? The way Bernie reacted, you'd think I'd have to sell a kidney to replace it."

I roll on top of him, resting my weight on my elbows. "After the plumber comes tomorrow, we can do the rest ourselves."

He tugs my shirt up so our bellies are pressed skin against skin. He asks for a blow-by-blow of the job interview. The day's been so long, it feels like it happened yesterday.

"Is this something you'd want?" he asks. "Something in government?" It's hard to read where it's coming from, if he's disappointed.

Nothing about Richard's working life, from his early tenure to his field of research, has prepared him to seek out change. What excites geochronologists about rock is its stasis. Unchanged, it's a glimpse into the way things were. The less altered the rock, the more it spreads open like a mineral history of our planet.

Soil science is a different kind of endurance sport. It wouldn't exist if rock never changed, if the parent material never weathered into soil, into a medium for life.

"We were fighting when I applied," I start to explain.

He motions for me to blink so he can brush a lash out of my eye crease.

"If I make it to the next round I can withdraw."

Richard shushes me. "What I was thinking is that for the next sabbatical—I know it's not for another year—but if you need to move somewhere for a contract job, I can arrange things around it."

Without anything to rage against, all I can see is his tenderness.

9

WE MOVE MY MOTHER'S THINGS the next afternoon. It's only a carload—a bottle-green ceramic table lamp, some doilies from the basement, a few books, three framed family photos from her bedside and seven changes of clothes. My mother's jumpy about having personal items in the new room—she's equated making it more homey with making the move permanent. I lay out the doilies on the side table and window ledge, place her toiletries in the drawers and buy her a proper box of Kleenex and a bag of hard candy. With so few mementos, the place looks like a soft prison.

Thursday I drive her and the menagerie of plants she's collected from hospital visitors over to the nursing home. I wheel her into the room and she surveys it, then wheels herself over to the ledge with the photos. She shakes her head and rearranges them, angling them away from the light. The task irritates her, as though she's righting a prized possession upset by a rough houseguest.

There's a big lawn out front and I ask if she'd like to have a coffee outside with me before I go. She glares at the mention of it, a warning that she won't be easily appeased. She thinks I've betrayed her leaving her there but sooner or later she's got to realize that she's going to need assistance. She's got to understand that I'm only trying to protect her.

Protect her from herself. I sound just like Richard did earlier this summer. It isn't the same, I say, trying to justify the difference, but it nags me for the rest of the day.

Friday night there's a double bill of pirate movies at the New
Minas theatre and Linda's asked if Stephen and Luke want to
go with her kids. It's also karaoke at Legends Bar in Coldbrook
and Bernie calls early Friday morning to extend the invitation,
his voice flat as a dental receptionist confirming a six-month
checkup. I can't decide if it's because he's still angry about the
other night or if Linda's in the room.

Luke's hanging between Richard's arms, using his father's
shoulders as a jungle gym. When I ask about karaoke, Richard
swings our son into a somersault and shakes his head, pass.

I tell Bernie we're happy to take the kids to the movies.

Stephen pauses his video game and groans when he hears
this, disappointed about being chaperoned. It's his first kids-
only event this summer. Richard catches our son's frustration
and tells me to firm it up with Bernie after all. "It'll be fine," he
says as Luke flips over again. "Give us a chance to relax."

We give Stephen forty dollars to treat everyone to popcorn and
candy. He carefully folds the bills into the utility pocket of his
jeans and I notice him checking it periodically on the drive
over. Sometimes I forget how young he is, that forty dollars is
the most money he's ever had on him.

Bernie and Linda don't make a fuss with goodbyes like we
do. They stand by the double doors, impatient, as we give the
boys one last hug. Linda's wearing a flowery dress with spaghetti
straps that gives as much coverage on top as a triangle bikini.
Next to her, in my unlaundered tank and shorts, I look like a
bookish kid sister.

"You got your CDs?" Bernie asks her.

She hits him on the shoulder. "Christ, Bernie, stop pester-
ing about the CDs."

He gooses her rump and she swats him away. In the tussle, her breast slips precariously close to the seam. Linda looks up, laughing. "Bernie's making fun of me because I like to bring my own music."

"The host only brings his own five thousand songs."

"I don't always want to sing the oldies." Linda knocks on the car window to get Bernie to open up faster. It's the first time I've seen the two of them flirting like this. "A person likes to practice, too."

Richard hums as we continue towards our own car. "Hardcore karaoke."

Legends is the Pulpit minus the university students. I guide Richard into the parking lot and he tilts his head at the cheesy backlit sign. *Here? Really?* There's no lineup, but the bouncer's already at the front door, solid as ham hock.

The karaoke host, Bobby Vince, is at the back of the raised dance floor, setting up for the night. He's a short man, probably about Richard's age, but paunchier and dressed like he's judging the twist at a sock hop—black shirt, black pants, checkered suspenders and bowtie. He's busy plugging in AV cords and chatting with a few of the regulars who've also brought their own backup CDs.

Pretty soon, the place starts filling up. The few students are easy to spot. They sit on the far side of the room—the girls in terry cloth shorts and tube-tops, the boys in jeans and ironic T-shirts. Except for an old-timer sinking five-dollar bills into the video gambling machines, we're the oldest people here.

Richard and I half-heartedly flip through the request book.

He leans closer so no one hears. "Do you notice anything different?"

I scan the crowd but don't see anything out of the ordinary.

He tilts his head. "Twelve o'clock." Lined up at the bar, there's a group of about eight black men. It's the first time since he's arrived in Nova Scotia that it's been anything other than Wonderbread.

Bernie interrupts our conversation to line up twelve plastic cups in front of us. The beer is cheap and pale, a queue of urine samples. His brother, Jason, squeezes in next to Richard and distributes the draft. Richard doesn't want any, so that leaves four for the rest of us. I'll be lucky to get through two.

Linda calls over from the next booth. "Bernie, Gail wants you to do *Summer Nights* with her."

"Lindie, you know I don't sing."

"I'll do it with the big handsome guy then," Gail drawls.

"She means you, Richard," Linda says. "It's from *Grease*. You ever seen it?"

He ducks his head and waves off the suggestion but Linda wags her finger at him. "I'm putting your name down."

Bobby opens the night at nine-thirty with his own rendition of *Rambling Rose*. Then it's Linda's turn and the sounds of Britney Spears' *Hit Me Baby One More Time* blare out from the speakers. Her voice isn't terrible. Performing, Linda's totally unselfconscious, like an indulged child. She gyrates through the chorus and deftly swishes the mic cord from side to side. During the bridge she purrs, "This song's dedicated to all the good lookin' men I see out there tonight."

Jason howls back, "Quit talkin' about me!"

Bobby starts the applause as soon as the percussion dies. Linda walks back, triumphant.

It's a group of students next. Three guys rotate through *So Whatcha Want* by the Beastie Boys. The university girls rush up to the front to dance for them, grinding their asses into each other.

Gail leans over the booth, the exertion pushing her breasts farther up and out of her V-neck so we can see the fuchsia lace trim of her bra. "We're up soon, buddy."

Richard shoots me a look. He's decided he wants a beer after all. Something in a bottle. The bar is packed and I have to jostle to get to the front. I order a Coors Light because it's the only thing I can think of when the bartender takes the order. I also get four more draft beers. The bartender is a young guy, second year maybe. When I pay for the drinks he smiles and asks if I'm going to need help taking them back to the table.

"You got a tray?" I hear my accent slipping back in.

The bartender waves to his buddy. "Give her a hand."

A hulking guy comes over and grabs all four drafts in one hand. "Where are you sitting?"

The kid gives me a wink when I thank him.

"It's about to get awfully hot in here," the host bellows on the mic. "Because we've got some *Summer Lovin'*."

Gail props Richard over by the left mic, takes hers off the stand and slides over to him. She's exceptionally breathy when she sings—Olivia Newton-John with a tracheotomy. At first Richard's terrified, but he plays along once he picks up the tune. When the line about getting so damp comes, Gail dips down, the wire between her legs and barely resists grabbing her crotch. Richard swings his arm around her, leaning in like an old crooner as they hit the final high notes.

Even the university kids cheer. Gail waves us away as we keep whooping then announces that she's going to the can. If I don't go now too, I'll have to crawl over Richard again.

The women's washroom is filthy, graffiti everywhere, the taps running, paper towels scattered across the floor. Only one of the doors locks and there's someone in it. "Come on," Gail says. "You hold the door for me and I'll hold it for you." She goes into the far cubicle and I'm stuck trying to keep the door closed, which is hard when you're short as I am. There's a big gap between the edges of the cubicle and I tilt my head so I won't catch a glimpse inside. She pisses loudly, in a great big stream that goes on forever.

"Your hubbie's got a good voice." There's the rip of a pad off the wrapper. "How long you been married?"

"Fifteen years."

"Christ, I'm lucky if I can keep it together with a guy for three months." She flushes and comes out of the stall. "I like variety."

My turn. I get shy once I'm on the toilet.

"You need to take a dump or something?"

"Nervous bladder."

"Please, Linda's the same way. Just break the seal already."

It takes almost another minute.

"So," she says while I'm mid-flow. "Is Richard as big as his voice?"

"What do you mean?"

"You know," she titters. "Black cock."

The right thing to do would be to shut this down with a quip about racial stereotypes. I just say I don't know, he's the only black guy I've been with.

"But you didn't save yourself or anything?" Gail asks, horrified.

"No."

"I forgot—you and Chuck."

"What do you know about that?"

"Everyone knows you two fucked around."

I zip up my pants and come out of the stall. "Well, Richard's a lot bigger than Chuck." It's so stupid. I don't know why I say it. But Gail starts to laugh and then we both laugh and she holds her hands out about a foot and I hold mine out double. "Oh honey," she says. "That would come out your nose."

When we get to the table, Linda's nuzzling into Bernie and holding one of my draft beers. He's supporting the back of her head, her bleached hair pouring through his splayed fingers. They don't notice when I slide onto the bench. Bernie and I haven't talked all night and watching him so into Linda brings a mixture of relief and feeling left out. I down the remainder of my drink, letting it slide over my tongue quickly so I don't have to taste it.

Richard's ordered himself a gin and tonic.

"Am I driving?"

He shakes his head. "I'm just sipping this one. It's courtesy of them." He waves over to the group of black men we saw earlier and nods his head in thanks. "They've invited us to a part-ay next week," he says, putting on a Jamaican accent. "Apparently they know a guy from Trini, but he didn't come out tonight. They're trying to reach him on his cell."

"How did they know your dad's Trini?"

"They kept asking where I was really from."

"Are they seasonal workers?"

"Yeah. You never told me about that."

"Well, we get seasonal workers."

"We?"

I wave my hands to signify the bar, the town, the province.

"They wanted to know why I talk so funny."

Gail leans over the booth to whisper in Linda's ear. A moment later, the two of them drag me up to the bar to do shots. Someone is singing *Sweet Caroline*. The bartender pumps the peach schnapps in the air for the chorus "bah, bah, bah." It goes down sickly sweet as Dimetapp.

Linda orders the next round.

"Same thing?"

"No," Linda says. "Screaming orgasm. Ellie here needs a screaming orgasm."

Gail starts giggling. "We all need a screaming orgasm."

The bartender's seen it all before. He pours out something layered and says, "Happy to help, ladies," his voice flat.

"Sounds funny when you say it," Linda says to me.

"Say what?"

"Orgasm."

I pull out a twenty and motion to the bartender. "Another round. Your choice." This one's second cousin to Pepto-Bismol.

Linda looks back and forth between me and Gail, smirking. "When I first met you, I thought you'd be one of them frigid city bitches."

I don't know what to say to this.

"Then I heard a few rumours about you in high school." Linda stacks her cup into the empty one in Gail's hand. It's high school again—Charla giving me a hard time on the way to Martock. Any girl-to-girl camaraderie has vanished. I turn to walk away but Linda grabs my arm and spins me back. "Heard you nailed two guys at the same time. Chuck told me."

"Chuck still screwing everything in sight?"

"Bernie told me you and Chuck couldn't keep out of each other's pants."

"Come off it, Linda," Gail says. "Chuck brags that he nailed all the tail in his class, doesn't make it true."

"No, it is," I say. "When I was eighteen I was stupid."

"Aw," Gail says. "We all screwed him too."

Linda slaps her shoulder, but Gail continues. "Come on, Lindie, you said you blew him at Apple Blossom."

Linda scratches at the corner of her mouth, ready to lunge.

"That was before Bernie, of course," Gail says, oblivious to what Linda's really getting at.

"Maybe we should ask Bernie," Linda snarls, "if he knows about you, Chuck and Jason."

I don't know if it's the drink that's making her mean or if she's been storing it all up since we met. "Jason?" My mumbled denial's interrupted by Bobby Vince calling Linda's name.

Richard doesn't have to ask as I collapse in the booth. We both know I'm blitzed. He gets up to grab me some water. When he's gone I reach for the last beer. I'd like to get this night over with. Bernie slides in next to me and kisses my cheek. When I react, it's less a double take then the slow pan of a flashlight over a crime scene. He laughs and holds his hands up, pretending to back off.

"Where's Linda?"

"She's off with Gail. She pissed off with you or something?"

"You tell me."

"Yeah, she's pissed with you."

"She asked if I ever had a threesome with Chuck and your brother." More beer. Bernie and I have still never spoken about that night. Most likely, he saw it for what it was, a betrayal.

"You know I didn't tell anyone." Bernie puts his hand on my leg and rubs his thumb over my knee. He whispers, "This is only hard because we're sneaking around."

Richard comes back to the booth before I can answer. Bernie's hand is still on my thigh. My husband hands me two glasses of water and Bernie backs right off. Richard's got one eyebrow cocked as he watches him slide out of the booth in search of Linda.

"Drink this then we'll go pick up the kids."

I need to pee again.

Richard gets out of the booth instead of letting me scoot over him. It's ten-thirty now and there's a lineup for the girls' bathroom. The guys laugh as they go past. One of them looks me up and down and says to his buddy, "Cougar time." It's loud enough for everyone to hear. I wait a moment and then twist behind me, hoping to see someone else—Gail maybe. It's all young co-eds. Twenty years on and it's still the same. I'm eighteen, trashed after the ski trip, hating that all they can see is townie.

There isn't enough distance between Coldbrook and New Minas to get sober. I lower the windows, press my wrist to the cold metal exterior and try counting back from 100. We pass all manner of neon lights—motels, fast food, gas stations—and I strain to decipher the lettering, my success a barometer of sobriety. Richard drives in silence, abandoning me to quackery.

It's just the two of us picking up the kids. Linda still had songs in the queue, so she and Bernie suggested we all meet up at Traders Restaurant in Wolfville. Richard was happy enough with the arrangement. Food's my last hope of getting up in the morning and he can't hide the tension in his voice as he says it. Richard's a knot of concentration but the alcohol's left me in slow melt. With each breath, I sink deeper into the upholstery. We're only two feet apart but we're on opposite sides of a single process—Richard the contraction, me the release.

In the end I decide that the best thing will be to say as little as possible. Our kids haven't seen enough inebriated people to recognize the subtler signs of shit-faced.

Traders is one of the few places in town that hasn't changed. Same cheesy movie posters, same forest green paint, same salted potatoes on a plate. We order six baskets of potato skins, two sundaes and a full complement of fountain pop.

Richard asks how the kids liked the movies.

Stephen and Max look down at their plates and Lisa starts to well up. Max gives her a pleading look but it's too late. She wiggles her way onto my lap and I have no choice but to hold her against me as she cries. It's late and she's probably over-tired.

"It was scarier than we thought it would be," Stephen explains.

Luke looks at his brother, then his father and doesn't say anything.

Max mouths "baby" at his sister and she chucks a sugar packet at him.

She wants to know when her mom is coming.

It takes an hour for Linda and Bernie to arrive, long after we've finished the chips and ice cream. Even with the greasy food, I'm still feeling tipsy. Linda, however, is ripped. She sways and stabilizes herself on the back of Lisa's chair. Bernie's drunk, but he's holding it together. He pats Linda on the back. "You should have seen her close the place down with *I Will Always Love You*."

Max smirks and Linda calls him on it. "What?"

"That song blows."

Stephen almost loses it.

Bernie breaks it up by asking Richard what he owes him for the food.

"Don't worry, you've been taking care of us."

"Nah, come on, let me pay for the kids' food."

"No, no, it's on me."

"Save the money for gas, Bernie," Linda says and hiccups. People are looking over at the table.

"Well, thanks," Bernie says, and motions to the kids.

Richard stands with them and puts his hand on Bernie's shoulder. "Can I give you guys a ride?"

"Nah, got the truck. Plenty of room."

"Come on, I'll drop you home, you can get the truck in the morning. The last thing you want is to get stuck in one of those RIDE programs."

The two of them stare at each other, deadlocked. The rest of us hover around the table, unsure of what to do, like players in a game of musical chairs waiting for the music to start.

"Ellie, you know Bernie can drive," Linda says. "He drove your drunk be-hind home enough times in high school."

"That was 1984." Pregnant women were still smoking in 1984.

Bernie pulls out his keys. He forces a chuckle and waves away Richard's concern. "Christ, we're all adults here."

Stephen has his arm around Luke and both of them are looking at the floor.

The waitress asks us to leave.

Once outside, Bernie starts walking away and doesn't look back. Linda shepherds the kids behind him.

"Am I going to have to chase after him?" Richard asks.

Stephen looks up at his dad, pleading for him not to embarrass him in front of his friend.

I go running off down the street. Bernie stops when he sees it's me.

"What is it?"

"Richard just wants," I pant.

Linda looks at me, filled with contempt. "Honey, back off." She stumbles towards me but Bernie holds her back by putting his arm out. She turns on him, swatting him with her purse. "What the fuck?"

"Don't be like that, Linda."

"You've been screwing her, haven't you?" Linda screams down the street. "It was you and Chuck in high school wasn't it?"

It breaks my heart that the boys have to witness this.

Bernie relaxes his grip on Linda. She totters on her mules and props herself up against the lamppost. Bernie takes a step towards me, into the pool of light. His face is an open target. For a moment all I can see is him at seventeen. "What do you think, Ellie?"

"Why don't you just take a cab?"

He grabs my forearms hard and leans into my ear. "It's always the short end of the stick." He lets go and stumbles backwards.

"I'm trying to do the right thing."

"Is that what you've been trying to do?"

Richard calls out from behind, "Ellie, just let them go."

We're halfway up the hill to Canning when we see the blinking lights of a cruiser coming from behind. The first thing I think is, *I hope the kids were wearing seat belts.* Then I realize how ridiculous that is. Even if they'd had an accident, there's no way a cop would be coming to inform us. I don't know if they've phoned our plates in out of revenge or if this is a legitimate spot check. The cop shines a flashlight in the open window, the beam washing over the boys, terrified in the back seat. I don't recognize the officer at all.

"Licence and registration."

Richard hands everything over, very calm.

"I'm going to have to ask you to step out of the car."

The officer asks him if he's been drinking tonight.

"Two drinks several hours ago."

The cop makes Richard walk in a straight line and explains that there's been a report of a car matching our description swerving dangerously. Richard is released back into the driver's seat. I roll down my window and haul myself half out of the car, leaning on the roof. "Did Linda set you up to this?"

"Ma'am, I'm going to have to ask you to lower your voice." The cop shines his light full force on my face, blinding me. "Ellie Lucan, right?"

"Ellie Bascom."

"Grant Jenkins. You remember me?"

I've got no recollection of the name.

He sets his flashlight on the roof and makes a few notes in his pad.

"Linda set you up to this, didn't she?"

"Settle down."

My leg is being tugged back into the car—Richard's forcing me into the seat. I relent and sink back against the headrest.

The officer nods at Richard, then taps on the car. "Go ahead."

In the driveway, in the dark, the house looks like the flat front of a film set. It's not the same house we left this evening. I'm sure that if we walked around the back, all there'd be is timber bracing.

Richard tells Stephen to take his brother inside and get ready for bed.

Stephen helps Luke out of his seat belt. No one says anything. I press my cheek against the window to cool its flush. Richard leaves the headlights on until the boys are inside. There's enough reflected light from the moon to see Richard's profile, but when he turns to me, it's all in shadow.

He unbuckles his seat belt and releases the seat to give himself more legroom. He's planning to be here for some time. "I want to say this where the boys can't hear me—have you been screwing around with him?"

I jerk myself upright. "No."

Richard's hands seem to glow blue in the moonlight, as if outlined with pastel. He grips the wheel and repeats his question.

"Bernie's an old friend."

He releases the wheel and props his head up with his hands, letting out a long exhale. "You've been leaving me all summer, haven't you? Cancelling the flights, the Kentville job, Bernie—I should have added it up a lot sooner. I'd thought it was Marc I had to be worried about." He rubs the pad of his thumb over his cheekbone and across the bridge of his nose. It's like the arc of a snail, the same wet trail in its wake. "What I don't understand is how you can build your whole life in one direction and then...."

We've been hurtling all summer towards this conclusion but now that I'm confronted with it, I'd make any bargain for us to reconcile. If I denied everything, if I offered to leave tomorrow, he'd relent, I know he would. But for better or worse, Richard's got the right to make his own decision based on all the facts.

"It happened the night before you got here."

Richard clenches his fist and bangs it against the dashboard so hard that the whole unit shudders. He slaps his open palm down in the same spot. Dust stirs up with each hit.

"Don't." I reach over to stop him. "The airbag."

He leans back in his seat, breathing hard and shallow, pressing the exhale out between his lips. The whole of his body is humming with rage. "With him?" he asks. "Him? What the fuck does *he* give you?"

Anything I say will roll away cold and hard like a marble.

"Do you think I haven't had opportunities to cheat? I've always respected you." He rubs his hands across his head. "I don't even know if you used a condom."

"It's never happened before," I say. Not even close.

"How could you after the fire?"

"I didn't want to after that first time."

"So what does that make you?"

The guilt is a hollow along my sternum, the scrape of a plow over bedrock.

Richard shakes his head. "You want to act like a teenager, go ahead. But I sure as hell don't want my sons being raised by one."

He grabs hold of the wheel and lets out a deep, wounded groan and I realize how decent he was to tell the boys to go inside. Even a yell at that volume would barely make it out of the car.

10

THE FIRST THING I do is leave a message on the Kentville Agricultural Centre's voicemail, withdrawing my name from the competition. Richard's still prone when I open the door to tell him. The sleeping bag is low on his chest and he's got one arm behind his head, the other draped off the mattress. It's the same pose he always has in the early morning. I stand in the doorway, wishing I were lying next to him, the whole flank of my body draped over his. It doesn't seem possible for that kind of intimacy to be finished between us.

Richard catches me looking at him and reaches for his shirt. "The boys up?"

I shake my head. He pulls his jeans on under the sheets and motions for me to sit on the corner of the mattress. "Did you sleep?"

Not really. Neither of us did.

"I think the best thing would be for me to drive back with the boys tomorrow. You've got your hands full with your mother."

"Are we really doing this?"

"I can't stay here."

"What if I went with you?" I tell him about my phone call.

"You can't ask me to accept this right away." He lowers his voice to a whisper, the calm so incongruous with what he's saying.

He wants to talk to the boys right away. I don't ask him to, but he promises not to tell them about the affair. "But," he warns, "I'm not going to lie if they hear it from someone else."

We choose the living room because it's the only place with enough seats. Richard's on a chair from my mother's room, the boys on the loveseat Bernie brought up from the basement. I'm on an upturned milk crate and the plastic hatching digs into my legs. Luke wants to sit on my lap, which I don't allow because we want to keep this as neutral as possible. Stephen hasn't spoken to me at all this morning. Both of the boys are on edge—they've never really seen us fighting before and they know something's off.

I start the conversation. "Your father and I are sorry about the fight last night. You shouldn't have had to see that."

Stephen rolls his eyes. "Can you guys talk to Bernie and Linda before I have to see Max again?"

Richard gives him a stern look and he slumps back into the cushion, propelling a cloud of dust. The couch came from the house's previous owners. Dad always meant to re-cover it.

"We've decided to go home," Richard continues. "We'll be leaving tomorrow. Your mom's going to stay for a while to take care of your grandmother."

Luke wants to know when I'll be home.

"There's a lot that still needs looking after here."

"That's crap," Stephen says. "You're separating, aren't you? Because of Bernie."

Richard stares Stephen head-on, waiting for the explanation. My instinct is to pull Luke outside, but if Stephen knows, Luke will find out.

"Because Bernie's an asshole but Mom's friends with him." For all of Stephen's maturity in understanding the argument's implications, he's still got a child's perspective.

"We're not separating," Richard says.

Luke doesn't know what the word means.

Stephen leans towards his brother. "Divorce."

"Stephen."

"Well it is. Parents separate and then they get divorced."

"We're trying to take this one step at a time." There's nothing to say that doesn't sound like a TV special.

"We want you to know that we both love you."

"Whatever. I'm not leaving before the soccer tournament."

"That's not until next weekend."

"I'm not missing the only good games this team will play all summer because you and Mom had a fight." He kicks his feet up onto the bookshelf that's doubling as a table. Dirt flakes off his sneakers onto the veneer.

Richard's firm. This isn't negotiable.

"You're the one who's supposed to know what this means to me."

Richard still doesn't budge.

"This is bullshit."

"Stephen, go to your room."

"This fucking sucks." Stephen stomps off towards the stairs. "I'm glad you guys are splitting—two times the presents at Christmas."

Luke is now sobbing. I scoop him onto my lap, rocking him back and forth.

Stephen watches me from the stairs and scowls. "Why do you always go over to him?"

"I don't always. . . ."

"Yeah," he says. "You do. It's okay. Luke's just a big baby."

"Your room, right now," Richard bellows.

I put my hand on the top of Luke's head and whisper, "It's okay, it's okay."

Richard tries to give him a hug too, but Luke won't let go of me. Richard leaves by the side door, the slam quickly followed by the car's engine revving.

Luke and I sit until he exhausts himself crying and falls asleep against my chest. I should go upstairs to release Stephen, but can't let go of this closeness with Luke, this last chance to be a good mother before they leave tomorrow.

I think about the collection of receipts in my wallet from earlier this summer—BeaverTails in Halifax, admission to Grand Pré, overpriced apple juice from Peggy's Cove—the last remnants of my naivety that coming here would be good for the boys. I'm forced to confront the fact that because of me, this is the worst summer my sons will ever experience.

Richard comes back an hour later and announces that he's willing to stay until after the tournament. I don't know for sure, but I suspect he spoke with Terrence. He expects the boys to behave, despite the circumstances.

Richard turns to me when they've gone upstairs.

"This doesn't change anything."

*   *   *

"Everyone knows he only got hired because he's the son-in-law of the mayor's sister."

When I open the door to my mother's room, there's a woman seated in the armchair, knee-deep in conversation. She's a heavy-set woman in a fuchsia boat-neck, sweat beading up on her collarbone. She doesn't pause for breath as I come in, just keeps barrelling through her news and swatting the air as if she's waving away a gnat. "Turns out them carnies never got permits and one of the cages flew off the monkey ride."

"Anyone hurt?" my mother asks.

The woman shakes her head, jangling her tiered earrings. "Hit a parked car ten feet away. You could hear the alarm going off for half an hour." She must be talking about the annual mini-carnival in the County Fair Mall parking lot. There was an article about it in one of the Kentville Advertisers my mom had lying around.

I walk over to give my mother a kiss on the cheek, which she coldly accepts.

Her visitor does a double take. "No. It's not," she stutters. "There's no way this is our Ellie." She pries herself out of the chair and grapples me towards her. "You look like you haven't aged a day. Of course, you've got some of them eye lines— what's the word for that Lynne?—crow's feet." She shakes her head in disbelief. "Who'd have thought I'd live to see the day that Ellie Lucan has crow's feet? Thought you were the orderly—you remember me, don't you?"

It takes a moment, and then I do. Fat Mary.

"Your Mom's kept me up with all your news over the years," she says. "Sounds like you've done well for yourself out in Toronto."

I squat on one of the footstools, my back against the base of the bed. "You're still at the co-op?"

"God knows I'm going to be there until I buy the farm. I was just telling your mom how my kids haven't done so well—all over forty and still asking me for money. When it's not them, it's the grandbabies." She crosses herself. "Of course, they all live close by, so that's a blessing." She glances at me, then looks down at her hands folded in her lap.

I feel about as tall as the footstool, crow's feet and all.

My mother's buoyed by the conversation. She laps up Mary's gossip, which must be what it was like at co-op. When there's a break in the chatter, I hand over the tin of photos I've brought. My mother opens it and digs through the pictures to find one of her wedding reception. There's one of her and Dad standing in his parents' backyard; she's wearing a knee-length wedding dress and Dad's making bunny ears above her pillbox hat. On the back, there's a scrawled line "Horsing around, June 7, 1965."

"None of the Lucan women had elegant weddings," my mother says and hands the picture over. "I always wanted to go shopping for Ellie to get one of those princess trains."

"You got hitched at city hall, no?" Mary asks.

"Didn't want to spend the money."

Mary nods. "Costs a fortune now—when my Maureen got married she wanted the whole lace and satin number. We paid over two thousand on it. Looked a picture though." She hands around a wallet-sized portrait and my mother nods approvingly.

Mary stays for another half-hour.

When she leaves, she says, "Got to go visit you-know-who," and winks.

At first I think it's a euphemism for the bathroom.

"My mother-in-law's two doors down. Sugar before the pill."

As soon as Mary leaves, the room falls quiet. My mother goes back to rustling through the photos. There's nothing warm in her face—the earlier joy trailed out with Mary's exit. She asks when she's going to see the boys and Richard again.

"I need to tell you something," I say. "We've had a fight."

My mother sets the family photos aside. "Don't worry, I've heard all about the noise you were making down Main Street."

Fat Mary.

"You just can't go around telling people what to do. Well, it's backfired now and you're going to have to make it up to Linda and Bernie."

"He shouldn't have been driving home, especially not with the kids."

"Things aren't the same out here with that kind of thing. Besides, you don't go telling another woman's man what not to do." She unwraps one of the caramels that I bought her, the plastic crinkling noisily. "And now you're going to tell me that you're going home, aren't you, before you've even got the place fixed up?"

"All of us are staying until after the tournament."

"And after that?"

"The boys will be going back with their father." The fight with Richard is too raw to talk about. "I might stay on to take care of you."

My mother purses her lips. "I don't need to be taken care of. Especially now that you've got me in here." That's what this is all about, the diatribe about minding my own business. She's still livid about the discharge meeting. "Mary drove by the house. She said the power's back on. You got water?"

"Yes."

"Good. The faster it's done, the faster I can come home." She curls back into herself, a giant mollusc settling in for the night.

I'm the only family she has left. She's got to forgive me sometime.

*   *   *

Richard wants nothing to do with me, my mother or this province. He's holed himself up in the boys' room, using the phone jack to dial into the U of T Internet. Late Sunday night he was on the phone to the UK, begging *BBC Science* to reaccept his pitch. They'd already assigned a replacement story to someone else but agreed to accept his article on spec. Once they get it, they'll decide if it's worth bumping the other feature.

Stephen's spent most of the time in the same room as his Dad, playing video games. The two of them don't talk. The only signs of life filter out of the room in the electronic pings and zaps when Richard reconnects the modem or Stephen explodes an enemy target. Luke and I have kept busy priming the walls and going to the lake. Meals are the only time we are all together but after ten minutes of stilted small talk, Richard usually puts his food on a paper towel and goes back up to the computer.

Thursday, Stephen has a soccer game and it's up to me to take him. I don't argue. I want the alone time with him because there aren't many days left to make things right between us.

On some level, he must know the real problem with Bernie. As badly as I feel about cheating on Richard, I feel worse about the repercussions for the boys. Everything is going to change for them and they've had no choice in it, just as I had no choice when my father died. Stephen hasn't spoken to me since the fight so I'm not sure if he's had a chance to talk things over with Richard or his granddad. I want to tell him that he should confide in whoever he feels comfortable with. Maybe he's already figured that out.

There's a bit of drizzle—just enough to have to put the intermittent wipers on. I ask if he thinks they'll cancel and he stares me down, cutting. He springs out of the car as soon as I park. By the time I lock the door he's already hit the field.

There aren't as many parents out today and I wonder if they're waiting for the big tournament, banking their hours. I climb up to the top of the bleachers and try to get comfortable, hunched over a paperback, my feet up on the seat in front of me. I notice that Max and Stephen aren't talking, but they're standing fairly close together. If Max knows about the affair, Stephen's going to find out tonight.

Out of the corner of my eye, I see Linda and Bernie arrive with Lisa and I flip through my book again, a sci-fi thriller that my mother bought years ago from the co-op. I'm too tense to read but I still flip the pages every few minutes, glancing up only occasionally.

Stephen doesn't get the ball for a long time—the other team keeps passing it back and forth in our end, but can't make a play. Finally, he manages to steal the ball and get it over the halfway line before passing back to Max. There's no goal, but Max gets a shot in and the boys high-five all the same. It's the greatest relief seeing this small gesture between them.

With all the motion on the field, it's hard to keep up the pretence of reading. I drop the book to my knees to watch a corner kick and end up staring straight at Linda. She's climbing up the bleachers towards me. Bernie and Lisa are nowhere to be seen.

In high school, I never got in physical fights but I saw a few. The worst was out behind the Cornwallis dumpster. Before they both fell, Denise Round pulled a clump of hair out of Carly Atkins' ponytail and Carly pummelled her with a right hook that broke two ribs. The playground was paved with coarse gravel asphalt. It looked like the two of them had been in a motorcycle accident, Denise's cheekbone bruised to egg-plant. There must have been fifty of us watching but no one stepped in.

When Linda reaches me, however, she doesn't lunge.

"Bernie's some pissed with you." She drops down beside me and pulls out her cigarettes. I don't know what to say because she deserves the chance to tear a strip off me. She's still wear-ing the manicure from Bernie's party but one of the palm tree decals has chipped off.

She doesn't bat away her exhale when it drifts into my face. "I told Max the fight had nothing to do with him and Stephen." She takes another drag, her fingers thin as chalk. "It's not your kid's fault."

Linda shrugs when I thank her. I wonder if she's warming up to confront me about Bernie.

"Ellie," she says. "Sometimes you've got your head so far up your ass you can't see right in front of you."

Here we go.

"Christ, I've got to spell it out for you?" She wiggles the fin-gers on her left hand, showing off a small gold band with a pear-cut diamond. "He popped the question the day after karaoke. Dropped the kids off at my mother's, took me for dinner over at Peppercorns, got down on his knees when they brought dessert—did the whole thing right. Told me he'd been thinking over the summer, especially the past couple of days. He wants to start our own family." She taps on the diamond. "It's a full karat."

"It's beautiful."

"Soon as I said yes, he drove over to the mall, told me to pick out whatever I wanted."

"Congratulations."

"At first, I just picked a little bitty diamond. I figured, you know, don't press your luck." She pulls out another cigarette and lights it from her own, then hands it to me. I take it, grateful to have a prop. "I know we haven't gotten along this summer— I thought you were a stuck-up bitch come sniffing around." She tilts her head and laughs wryly. "But I've been waiting for Bernie to propose for a long time. Whatever you told him this summer's made up his mind." She holds out her hand and I have no choice but to take it. "I'm hoping we can start over."

At least at the end of a scrap, there's the relief of being punished.

"So when are you getting married?"

"Honey, I want to get down the aisle fast. You know what I'm saying—run don't walk. But I also want to do it right. We're thinking New Year's or next summer."

"Bernie's mom must be happy."

"Clarence even offered to pay for a honeymoon. Bernie just wants to go up to Cape Breton for a weekend but I want to go south, one of those all-inclusive places with piña colada. Maybe your man can set us up somewhere in Trinidad."

"Sure."

"You and Richard will be back in Ontario, but you guys should come to the wedding. Bernie's angry now, but it'll calm down quick." Her optimism is as overwhelming as her reasoning is flawed. "I'd like to ask your mom to come to my shower."

After spending all summer disliking Linda, I realize that of all of us, she's the one with the most integrity.

Growing up, becoming someone like her was my biggest fear. I didn't want to end up knocked up and dependent on someone like Chuck, someone who'd be screwing around on me before the kid's first birthday. With a kid, it didn't seem possible that I'd finish school, that my life would be anything more than spending forty years at the co-op with my mother, scanning food through parallel cash registers.

In some ways, Linda's the daughter my mother would've had if I'd stuck around. The difference is that in the bleak picture I'd envisioned, Linda's thriving. Right now, being Linda doesn't seem so bad at all.

She asks how my mother's doing in the home.

"She's pretty mad at me for putting her there."

"She'll come around," Linda says. "You'll get the house sorted out, then she can move back."

"They think she might need ongoing care."

"Like a nurse?"

"Maybe. At least someone to help look after the housekeeping, run errands."

"If that's all, she's got Bernie and me for that." Linda says it like it's nothing at all.

We sit for a minute watching the game. Stephen's hassling his opponent, trying to crowd him out so he can't pass.

"Your boy sure knows sport," Linda says.

"Max is a great player too."

Linda turns to me, beaming. "That's the other thing Bernie said—he's putting money aside for Max's college. Once we get back from the honeymoon, Clarence's going to fix it up so Max's name is on the farm too."

When the soccer game finishes, I don't even know who's ahead. Linda scoots over to give me a hug, warm and full, without malice or reservation. I sink to the back of myself, ashamed.

Stephen's waiting for me at the car. We don't talk on the way home. As soon as we get in, Stephen announces, "Mom's been smoking," then goes off upstairs. Richard's playing with Luke in the living room and I can't deny it when he walks over and smells it on me.

Irene McInnes calls my cell early Wednesday morning because Clarence is in a state. There's a new agent at the bank who's demanding some environmental form along with the usual line of credit paperwork. She's got a brochure, but she'd like me to come over to see if I can make sense of it. I'd offered to help Clarence with the operation before the fight and don't want to renege. Even if he's there, Bernie's not going to make a scene after his parents invited me, no matter how livid he is.

Stephen is still giving me the silent treatment but Luke decides he'd like to go to the farm with me. In the car, he starts asking questions. Are we going to Bernie's? Are we going home after? Are we going to soccer? He knows the answers to all of them but I can see his mind at work, trying to reconcile everything. With so much up in the air at home, he needs reassurance on the minutiae. When I tucked him in last night, he went through every member of our family, asking where they lived.

I park out back by the old shed where Clarence worked on his cars. Luke holds my hand as we walk towards the barn. It's an old structure, maybe a hundred and fifty years old, painted red before I was born. The paint's peeling off quite badly now and I'm sure it's lead based. I'm sure Clarence knows that too, so I decide against mentioning it. This barn was used mostly for farm equipment when we were growing up. They'd already built the newer barns for the chickens and livestock on the other property.

Luke is fascinated by the building, but also scared. He shifts closer towards me, as if he's worried it's a house out of a story-book—the kind with witches who eat small children. Clarence and Irene are inside, standing by a crude desk under the old hayloft. There's no sign of Bernie.

Irene makes a bit of a fuss over Luke, telling him how handsome he is, how much he looks like me. Luke relaxes enough to let go of my hand, but doesn't speak.

The brochure from the bank doesn't explain much. It seems to be a free service to farmers to assess whether they are meeting current environmental regulations. There's a few farm visits and the end result is an environmental plan for the operation.

It reminds me of the stroke brochures, the colours supersaturated and the content oversimplified. I can understand why Clarence would be concerned that there's something more sinister lurking underneath.

Irene asks if this is something they need to be worried about.

"I don't think so."

"It's interference," Clarence says. He's leaning up against a thick, square support beam, the rafters above whitewashed with pigeon shit. "This guy at the bank's just transferred in from Halifax, never worked with farmers before. Now he's saying EFP this EFP that, as if Irene needs any more paperwork."

"It looks like they'll take care of all that," I say, trying to reassure him. "They'll send a consultant out and take a tour round and talk to you about the op. You'll get a report you can give the bank. You might not have to change anything."

Clarence shakes his head. "It's like sending your car to the mechanic when it ain't broke. Sure it don't cost for them to take a look," he says. "But it will. It will."

He swipes his hands to the side to show he thinks it's so much hogwash. He grabs some keys from the desk drawer. It's an overcast day but the light streams into the barn from the spaces between the slats. From outside the whole thing looks solid, but in here, it's propped up by so many toothpicks.

"The big thing they'll want to know is what fertilizers and pesticides you're using. Are they draining into open water— that kind of thing. If you've got an hour, we can have a quick go-over."

The McInneses have property spread all throughout Gaspereau, Canning and out to Grand Pré, cobbled together by family mergers, deaths and the occasional outright purchase. We decide to start at the field from the dig.

Irene offers to take Luke back to the house for a snack but he's too shy.

"He can come along," Clarence says. "Won't be long." He points to Luke. "You want to ride the tractor?"

Luke wants to ride the tractor. It's a mid-50s Massey-Ferguson, red body and blue accents, rigged with front- and back-end loaders. There's no cab, and just one seat, which Clarence takes. He motions for me to lift my son onto his lap then asks, "You remember how to ride on the side?"

Bernie used to take me out on this machine sometimes. There's just enough of a grip to hook my heels in and lean back along the guard next to the wheel well.

We back out of the barn and then head for the road, driving mostly on the shoulder. The tires are massive and it's a bumpy ride. We can't be going more than 40km/hr but it feels like we're at full tilt. I hold on nervously to the few grips the frame affords. A few cars pass us and I feel momentarily ridiculous, but then I grin, despite everything. It's a beautiful feeling, the lurches of the machine and the summer wind. When we reach the field, Clarence lets Luke take the wheel and I think of my Dad, get one of those rare flashes of his face. He once took me for a ride on a neighbour's cow. It was just supposed to be me riding it, but I'd been too scared, so Dad sat up on the cow too, as close to its rear end as he could stay without falling off. We walked maybe a hundred yards. I remember looking back at him, seeing him smiling at me, the two of us propelled forward on the lumbering animal. I wonder if Luke will ever remember this day thirty years from now and if it will be Clarence who he sees, or me hanging onto the side.

We park at the crest of the field and take a walk around. The corn's shoulder-high on me now. To Luke it's a maze and I explain how he needs to be careful of the crop as he walks, but then set him loose to explore the rows.

I point to the creek that divides the fields. "They're going to want to take some samples there, check for contamination. You using the poultry litter?"

"It goes out in the fall before we till. We spray in the spring."

"Still plowing after harvest, discing in spring?"

He acts like I've asked him if he's still swallowing after he chews. "Ellie, I farm the way my father farmed."

"You considered conservation plowing?"

"Is this guy going to give me a fine if I don't?"

I lead him over to the patch we dug. "You remember how thin the topsoil was up here? How much soil do you think you're losing each year?

He shrugs, tracing his cigarette over the slope of the field. "I get a bit of blowing, spring and fall."

"It wouldn't take much to get a soil conservation plan in place."

Clarence just frowns. I hold his arm horizontal and pull the sleeve back on his plaid shirt. "Think of your skin as the top soil. If you're always rubbing it, like with a plow, you're going to lose the top layers, right? Eventually, you'll get calluses. If you cut the callous off or start rubbing again, it's going to get raw and start bleeding.

"You could get a chisel plow and then you'd only be breaking smaller lines in the skin—think of it like a cat scratch—then it's doing less damage. It leaves a lot of plant residue on the top." I pull his sleeve over his skin. "It's going to protect from wind and rain erosion and leaves more organic matter to decompose and fertilize."

When I release him, Clarence stays rigid, his arm frozen in the same angle.

"What's that cat scratch going to cost me?"

"That's one route, the other's no-till." I grin, cajoling. "Then you drill into the stubble and plant in one go. More herbicide, but less runoff."

Clarence raises his eyebrows and looks out over the field. "I've got a barn full of equipment that's working fine."

"Think of the hours you're spending plowing. Factor in the fuel cost. If you used a third of the fuel because you only make one pass over the field, how much would that save?"

He unbuttons his front pocket and pulls out a cigarette. "Ask Irene."

"I could run through the numbers with her, build up a few scenarios. You have to do this consultation anyway, but I could help you with the other. We can look into better fertilizing and tilling practices. Put that together with the EFP—stacks of paperwork you can shove up the bank's ass."

Clarence laughs, despite himself. It makes him cough and he covers his mouth with his fist, doubled up, the blue smoke rippling over his face.

Irene is waiting by the door when we get back, nervous the delay means it didn't go well. She watches Clarence's approach from the barn and busies herself setting out a plate of wafers and microwaving the now-cold coffee.

"All straightened out?"

Clarence braces himself against the entryway, prying off one boot at a time. "Oh, she's got plenty of ways to keep you busy. I'm just glad she's not a doctor. Go in with a nick, come out with half a leg missing."

"I've got some ideas to streamline things."

Clarence hams up a grimace but Irene's got his number. "Thank you, Ellie," she says, pouring out some orange soda for Luke. He's busy forcing apart the neon-pink layers of wafer between his teeth and licking off the filling.

"So," Irene beams. "Linda said she told you the news."

I grab a wafer too, just to have something in my mouth.

"We're over the moon." She nips into the living room to pull out a bridal planner book. "Got this for five dollars over at the mall. Clearance."

"She's in a fuss," Clarence says, spooning volumes of sugar into his mug.

"Don't give me that. You just about cried when they told you." Irene hands the planner over. "It's just Jason never got married and I thought Bernie'd never ask Linda."

"Have they set a date?"

Luke asks what we're talking about.

"Bernie and Linda are getting married."

"They are married."

"No. But it's like they're married. They're common-law spouses." He won't understand the phrase, but it might steer him away from the topic.

"Is that what you and Daddy will be?"

Irene and Clarence look at me, confused. Irene jumps in before I can explain. "Your Mom and Dad have been married for a long time."

"Stephen said they're separating."

"We're not separating, honey." Luke looks down at his glass. The pop has already gone flat; only a few tiny carbon bubbles cling to the edges. I hadn't wanted it to come up but now there's no choice except to elaborate. "We're having an argument but nothing's been decided."

Irene puts the bridal book away. Clarence takes his mug to the sink and leaves it noisily in the basin. He refuses to look at me. I don't see why he, of all people, should be angry.

I reach for Luke's hand.

"Please, stay," Irene says.

"We should get back. Thanks for the coffee." Luke and I retreat to the door. As I'm starting up the car, Irene rushes out of the house, waving for us to stop. I slip out to see what she wants.

"Thanks for coming over, Ellie. Clarence is. . . ." Her voice trails off. "Clarence's always been fond of you. He just didn't want to say anything in front of your boy. We want you to come to us if you need help." Irene grips my shoulders, pulling me to face her. "If you've got those boys and your mother to look after alone. Don't be too proud."

"Nothing's been decided," I repeat. "Richard's taking the boys home after the tournament. I'm going to stay for a bit to help my mother while we figure things out."

It's clear that Irene hadn't considered the possibility that Richard would take the boys. She releases my shoulders and hugs me tight as Luke stares at us through the gap between the front seats.

*   *   *

Three a.m. and no sign of sleep, same as every night since the fight, but at least the visit's given me something else to fixate on. I wish I'd brought my computer so I could start a spreadsheet for Irene to plug in the existing figures. Still, I start running through different variables and formulas. At Guelph, they were experimenting with ribbons of no-till corn next to strips of bare soil and I make a note to email a former colleague about her research. Corn doesn't do well with competition early on in the growing process, so it doesn't always respond well to no-till. Conservation tillage or an undercrop might work better.

There's something in the calculations beyond the simple distraction from the tension in the house. Being out in the field today, I realized that the only things I liked about being a professor were teaching and research, which is like eating only the strawberry in the Neapolitan. The job's also committee meetings, grant proposals, administrative politics and answering a daily shitstorm of email. Until this summer, I didn't realize how much I've missed agricultural land. It felt good to be out there today. For the first time since losing my job, it's felt promising to be changing course.

Thursday morning, before our appointment at the bank, my mother insists on wheeling herself to the car door. She's been walking a bit with a cane, but it's short distances—halfway across a room at most. The nurses instructed me to stand next to her and assist her into the car, but my mother huffs and interprets it as interference. She's forgotten to fix the brake on the chair, however, and it rolls back as she pushes up on the armrest. It means she has to sink back down, apply the brake, and try again. She stands by herself and I open the door for her, but we've misjudged the distance and she needs to take a few steps to reach the seat. I offer her my arm but she's determined to do this herself. She thuds into the car, caught and righted by the bucket seat.

Next week they're starting exercises in the pool, which they say can help significantly with regaining muscle. We're still deep in the land of conditional optimism. It's impossible to make plans, never knowing if we're still climbing towards greater rehabilitation or if this is the peak.

. "They say they can jimmy the steering wheel for people like me," my mother says as I start the car. "Even if I don't get the leg back. You think Jason could rig that for me, or do I have to get it done special?"

I can't picture her driving again, but don't want to discourage her. "Maybe get it done special."

"How much do you think that would run me?"

No idea.

"It's one of the things I'll be asking at the bank." She settles herself into the vehicle, adjusting the belt strap and moving the visor.

We pass by the farmers' markets and she swivels to catch the line of families loading the first bushels of apples into the trunks of their cars. The berries have all gone back up in price now that the glut of high season's passed. It doesn't seem possible that so much time has lapsed since we came out here.

"You got errands to run?" my mother asks as we pull into the lot.

"I thought we'd go in together."

She puffs up like a startled bird. "You're being nosy."

"I'm fixing the house up and there are some things I need to know."

She flips the door lock on and off, unable to figure out which way's which. She cracks the door open and pushes it with the strength of both arms, almost dinging the car next to us. Still, the effort's not enough. The door swings back with the weight and latches closed. She tries one more time, wedging her elbow to prevent it from closing, wincing as the door pinches her against the car frame. She pauses like that for a while before pulling her arm free. Even if she gets out of the car, she'll need me to get the wheelchair from the trunk.

"You're trying to meddle," she snaps, covering her face with her hand. "You just want to know if there's enough to keep me in that place." After a moment, she has to drop her arm, unable to sustain the exertion.

It would have been better if I'd told her the extent of the damage as soon as she was stable. I was wrong to blindside her at the meeting. I start the conversation by apologising, by explaining that the fire and the stroke shook me so much I've been overprotective. I walk her through the expenses of the restoration company, the appliances that will need replacing, the estimate of cosmetic repairs.

She's still swivelled towards the window, stubbornly avoiding me.

"I'm sorry," I say. "I'm sorry that I left you alone for so many years."

My mother finally turns to face me. "Even if I can't live there, I need to fix up that house. Your father put so much work into it, I can't walk away until it looks the way he left it."

The financial advisor is young and freshly ironed out of business school. I wonder if it's the same one Clarence spoke with. He advises us to get my mother on early CPP, despite the penalty. The co-op pension will cover the cost of the nursing home but there's nothing to spare. With the damage to the house, it won't be worth over a hundred thousand. Apart from that, she has sixty-five thousand in savings—enough to modestly pad the rest of her life at this level of care. But if serious medical expenses come up, it'll burn through in a heartbeat.

We leave with a certified cheque for ten thousand made out to the restoration company. Richard and I will cover the rest. The last order of business my mother brings up herself, instructing the advisor to add my name on all her accounts.

She wants to swing by the co-op before she goes home. As soon as we get in the door, word gets around and I can't roll her two feet forward without another person rushing over to ask how she's doing—employees and customers alike. I stand behind the wheelchair, mute as a wallflower watching my mother greet everyone like the reigning Apple Blossom Queen.

The manager, who's worked with Mom for almost two decades, swoops down to give her a kiss on the cheek. "You're looking good as new, Lynne," he says. "Paula's called in sick— you want to fill in at the deli for us?"

"I'll get my arm in the slicer," she says, holding her bad one up and letting it drop into her lap.

"We'll mark it down special," he chuckles. "Lucan Lunch-meats. Got a ring to it."

He pulls an envelope out of his apron pocket and hands it to her. "Open it later. We all chipped in."

Fat Mary waddles over and announces that she's on coffee break. "You got any shopping to do, Ellie?" She takes the wheelchair handles and carts my mother off before I can answer.

I should pick up some groceries anyway—more juice tins and bottled water at least. I take my time walking through the aisles, grabbing breakfast supplies, fresh fruit and some snacks for the tournament. Dinners are harder to plan because we still don't have a fridge. It takes a good twenty minutes before I've been rung through but Mary's still chatting away, unconcerned about starting work again.

As I get closer, I realize they're talking about Linda and Bernie's engagement. "Never thought the McInnes boys were the romantic types," Mary crows. "But I've seen front teeth smaller than that diamond." She catches her tongue as soon as she sees me.

My mother wheels around, loaded down with so many sundries that I can barely see her in the chair. I ask if she wants me to pay while she finishes her visit but Mary waves away my suggestion. "On the house," she says then lowers her voice. "We're supposed to throw them out tomorrow anyway."

Fat Mary's turned my mother into a hospitality basket. As I propel her out of the store, I count three jars of honey-roasted peanuts, liquorice allsorts, four boxes of Ritz crackers, a bunch of bananas and several tins of her favourite shortbread cookies.

In the car, my mother gives me the envelope from the manager. Inside is a cheque for almost four thousand dollars, the result of a two-week drive with tins at the registers.

Richard hasn't said much about it, but I can tell that the article isn't going well. Last night there was another long call to the UK. His chief research partner is on vacation so he hasn't had anyone to run his drafts past. I'd hoped that today's news of my mother's savings and the co-op contribution would be some consolation, but it's barely acknowledged.

I've been trying to give him as much space as he needs, but tomorrow's the first day of the tournament and we won't be able to avoid each other. I catch him alone after supper and ask how it's going to be tomorrow.

"I thought we decided to go as a family." He's irritated by my question. "But I'm not sitting anywhere in the vicinity of that fucking redneck."

I nod my consent.

"We should get up by seven," he continues. "Do you want to help pack up Stephen's gear or do you want me to?"

I can do it. "Do you mind getting Luke ready for bed?"

It's so alien making these overly polite requests. When something needed doing in the past, one of us would get in there and do it, none of this fussing through each detail. Mostly, I'd like to ask if we're going to have time to talk before he goes but don't want him to think I'm pushing him into making a decision.

Linda's name shows up on my cell call display after the boys have gone to bed. I take the phone outside to Dad's tool shed, nervous that Linda's talked to Irene and has put two and two together.

Sure enough, she launches into a bluster of concern. She strings her questions together so fast I don't have time to answer—Why didn't you tell us? Do you need a place to stay? Is Richard really taking the boys? Do I want to talk about it?

"I'm fine," I say. "It's civil."

"You really aren't going back to the city with them?"

"We're still trying to work the details out."

"If you don't want to talk about it, just tell me to lay off," Linda says, but steamrollers ahead without giving me room to do it. "If it's about your mom's place, you know Bernie'd help with that. When he heard he felt as bad as I did."

I doubt Bernie feels remotely the same.

It isn't until Linda mentions how Max never took to Lisa's daddy but that he'd be wrecked if she and Bernie split that I realize what the phone call is about.

"Is your mom the only reason you're staying?" she asks.

I'd been worried she was going to ask for an out and out denial of the affair. All she wants to know is that I've got no designs on her fiancé.

"You know Bernie'd do anything for your mom—you're practically his sister."

I'm not that either.

Satisfied or not, Linda changes the subject. "You guys going to watch the tournament tomorrow?"

"Yeah."

"Do you want us to save you seats?"

"I don't think that's a good idea."

"Richard's still. . . ?"

"We just want to keep it together for the boys."

After she hangs up, I sit in the shed a little while longer. There are details I hadn't noticed the last time I was out here— little scraps of card stock stuck in the door frame with carpentry plans on them. The paper is yellowed, but the pencil's still legible. There are the measurements for a side table, a birdhouse and what I believe is the bookshelf up in my old bedroom. It makes me wonder how many plans my father got through before he died, how much he left unfinished. It makes me wonder what he'd say now, if he was witness to our family's unravelling.

11

$\mathcal{B}$ Y THE TIME Luke and I get to the tournament, the place is so packed that the lots are closed and we have to park up on the trail out of the complex. We find Richard in the stands just before the ref blows the starting whistle. There isn't nearly enough room and the woman next to him scowls as I pry my hips in between them.

Twelve teams are competing today in three divisions. The formula for advancing is based on number of wins and points scored. If Stephen's team wins all three of its games today, they automatically go through to tomorrow's semifinals. If they lose one, they can still get a wild-card spot with enough goals. Lose two and the boys will be on the road back to Toronto first thing tomorrow morning. We're playing Berwick first and I rack my brain, trying to remember the outcome of our earlier game.

At halftime, the other families get up and stretch, but Richard and I stay rooted in place. We sit in silence, Luke between us, watching a tournament volunteer dole out Dixie cups of Gatorade. All of our earlier games were in the evening. Now that they're playing in the heat of the day, the boys are slick with sweat. They wilt in a line while the coach parades past, barking orders. When his back's turned, Max waves to someone in the stands. Bernie and Linda must be farther down the pitch on the next set of bleachers.

The teams are too evenly matched. They volley back and forth, frequently intercepting passes and charging into the opposing end, only to have a quick reverse. Ten minutes left and there's still no score. Richard sits with his arm level on his knees, his watch in full view. One of our players fumbles a shot on goal. It rebounds out of the crease and Berwick's defence braces to kick it out. Stephen launches himself feet first to scoop the ball away. He times it so exactly that the ball shoots free, but his opponent has already started the arc of his kick and his cleat connects with Stephen's back thigh. For a second, everyone is too stunned to react. I'm up and on my feet, ready to scramble over to Stephen. The ref reaches for his whistle as one of our players makes a shot on goal. It goes in as the whistle sounds.

Richard holds my waist as I crawl across him and points out to the field. Stephen's up and walking but he's obviously favouring his left side. Both coaches are in a heated conference. "He's okay," Richard says, suddenly tensing. I slide back into my own seat. "He's okay."

The call comes down—no penalty but the goal stands. Canning 1, Berwick 0. Stephen is benched for the rest of the game, but the team holds onto the lead. The next game isn't until one, so at least he has a couple of hours to rest.

Stephen ambles over to us, an ice pack wrapped around his thigh. He doesn't complain, but I'm worried that he's really hurt.

"You've got to stretch it out," Richard says. He motions for Stephen to lift the hem of his shorts. There's a fist-sized bruise blooming on his upper thigh with dark purple rounds where the cleats hit. "Yep, that's a war wound." He massages the area and directs Stephen into a series of bends to keep the blood moving and the swelling down.

Stephen doesn't say much as he eats lunch, but Richard talks almost continuously. "You've just got to shackle their players. I watched Kentville for a bit this morning and they're weak in defence." He glides a tomato slice and a pickle across the wax paper wrapper, demonstrating the way Stephen can cut off their striker. At first I'm worried that it's overwhelming him, but Richard's tips have a hypnotic effect. Instead of making Stephen nervous, it relaxes him. I do my best to entertain Luke so that the two of them can make the most of the time.

As the game against Kentville approaches, I keep an eye out for Brad and his father. Before Richard found out about the affair, I fantasized about what it would be like having my husband here and watching Brad's father squirm. But now I just want to make it through the day without incident. We've all had enough confrontation.

When the boys line up, Brad isn't on the pitch and I wonder if his father pulled him off the team or if the coach couldn't cope with the ongoing vitriol. Regardless, the team's doing better without them—Kentville scores early in the game and we have a hard time keeping the ball in the offensive zone. Knowing how important this game is, it's impossible to follow its progress calmly, especially now that Stephen's hurt. I hold my breath each time he intercepts the ball, my pulse barrelling.

I don't want to leave before the end of the game, but the water has gone through me too quickly. The washrooms are off behind the other pitch, so it's a hike to reach them. All over the fields, the bleachers are packed, filled with families supporting their under-eighteen soccer enthusiasts. Seeing them reminds me that even if our team makes the finals, tomorrow is the last day that we'll be together as a family. The thought makes me start to panic. It'll be fine, I think with each step, it'll be fine. I reach my hand under the back of my tank top and find the channel of my spine is soaked.

I make it to the bathroom and lock myself in a stall, dabbing the sweat with wads of toilet paper. Sitting brings down the anxiety but gearing up to leave the bathroom is slow and painstaking. I numb my wrists under the cold tap trying to calm down.

When I leave, Bernie's waiting by the concession stand and there's no way to avoid him. He flags me over and I watch him juggle four smokies underneath the ketchup nozzle.

"You guys avoiding us?" he asks.

"I thought it would be easier for Richard."

"He still in a twist about the bar?"

There are too many people around to talk comfortably so we wander ten feet off, into the shade of a maple tree. I keep an eye on the field, nervous that Richard's going to see us.

"Heard you were over at the farm."

"Clarence's got nothing to worry about with that inspection."

"Said you were launching into one of your own." The cardboard hot-dog sleeves are already glistening with dripped grease. I can't read Bernie's expression, whether he's grateful or thinks I'm interfering.

"Linda mentioned you're staying."

"For a while at least."

He stops shuffling the drinks and snacks and catches my eye. "Were you hoping?"

I shake my head, no.

Again, I can't determine his reaction.

"Your mom's so excited about the wedding," I say. "Congratulations."

There's a long line forming at the concession stand and I recognize some of the people from our section, which means the game's over. I've missed it. I start to walk away, desperate to know who won, but Bernie keeps abreast of me. After a few paces, I stop him. "Do you mind if I go ahead? Richard's promised not to fight, but I don't want him to have to see us."

Bernie whips his head around to make sure no one's standing close enough to hear. "You didn't say anything to him did you?"

"He's not going to tell Linda."

"Christ, Ellie, why'd you do that?"

In high school, Bernie was the only person who didn't always register as a separate entity. Being with him, I sometimes felt the same communion I got walking out on the dykes, facing across the shore towards the Blomidon look-off. There's no stretch of land more beautiful than those few kilometres of clay and marsh grass.

The landscape shifts, however, on the walk back. Instead of ocean and fields, it's the town you see, Crowell Tower rising up in a thick, brick block. The path hasn't changed but the journey's entirely different. Now when I look at Bernie, it's like I've got reoriented.

No, that's not it at all. Bernie is Bernie. I've just been blindsided, looking at him all one way or all the other. This is the truth I've been running away from my whole life, trying to connect with the place while distancing myself from its inhabitants. There's a word for that kind of person and it's just as ugly as the word townie. In the very place I was born, what I've become is a tourist.

Richard eyes me suspiciously when I get back to the pitch. "They lost two to three. You missed Stephen's goal."

On the rankings board, there isn't much hope for our team to make the wild-card slot. There's an hour's rest, then they play again. The coach doesn't release the players. We leave our stuff spread out on our seats and take Luke to the park entrance to kick the ball around. I want to ask Richard what the team's prospects are, what would have to happen to meet the formula, but he's focused on our son.

He flicks the ball up with the top of his shoe and bounces it on his knee like I've seen Stephen do countless times. I don't know why it never occurred to me before, but Richard must have taught him the trick. Watching him play with Luke, it feels like we're back in Toronto at one of Stephen's games down at Christie Pitts. All we're missing is Terrence.

I'm startled by the ball hitting my calf and look up to see Luke grinning at me.

"Pay attention," he teases. He and Richard fan into a triangle to include me in the game. We pass back and forth a few times then Richard seizes the ball and starts juggling it with different parts of his body. He counts off five head-butts followed by three toe bounces and eight alternate knee kicks.

"Show off." I shove into him to knock him off balance and he catches the ball in his hands.

"Penalty."

"You're not supposed to touch it."

Richard lets me pin his arms back long enough for Luke to rush in and steal the ball. As soon as he has it, Richard shakes me free. Luke circles the two of us, dribbling the ball and we freeze in the centre, embarrassed by the contact.

The last game is against Halifax East, a team they've never played. The other team must have better funding, because their gear is flashier—technical soccer shirts and matching cleats. If they have that much to spend on uniforms, I'm worried about how much more experienced the coaching must be. It's also the only ethnically diverse team we've played all summer.

Our coach has switched the formation from 4, 4, 2 to 4, 3, 2, 1. Stephen's striker. All the boys look like they're channelling their best William Wallace, raising their fists to cheer when they win the coin toss. The whistle blows and Stephen charges ahead with the ball, weaving his way in between the other players. Max sprints ahead to make the pass but he's cut off.

Stephen's on it. Again, he gets the ball out past the centre line, deep into the end. This time he doesn't pass to Max, just runs until he's trapped by another player. He tilts to the left and rolls the ball under his foot. The opponent leans to match him. In a kind of hop, Stephen switches onto his other foot and kicks out from underneath so the ball flies sideways. Max stops it in front of the net and slices it in.

The boys don't have time to celebrate. There's still twenty minutes left in the first half. Not much happens for a while— a few skirmishes but the play stays in the middle of the field. Finally, with five minutes on the clock, our team gets the ball past the midfielders. Our left winger drives it into the net for a two-point lead.

After the break, the other team gets a goal right out of the gate. Our coach sends in two subs. Richard sucks air through his teeth in disapproval. The new kids aren't as tired, but they're less aggressive.

We just need to hold onto the lead.

Richard shakes his head when I say it. To make it through, we need at least another goal.

Max and Stephen make a neat series of zigzag passes through the other team's defensive line until they're stopped by the centre-backs. Stephen's got no choice but to try a long shot. It arcs straight towards the goalie. Richard exhales, anticipating the miss, but it spins in off the keeper's glove. We win three to one.

By the time Stephen reaches us, most of the other parents have cleared out for the supper break. His clothes are completely drenched and he's visibly exhausted, but he wants to stay for the Kentville game at six. Richard's so proud of his son, he agrees without hesitation.

"Did you see that first goal?" Stephen asks, still out of breath, but Richard's distracted by Max walking past with Bernie and Linda.

"Yes," I say, trying to skate over the awkwardness. "You dangled it."

Stephen raises his eyebrows at my stilted lingo and Richard recovers his attention. He runs his fingers along the round of Stephen's head, fluffing his hair up out of his headband. "You dangled it."

The echo cracks Stephen up.

Sydney's the clear winner in the blue division, having dominated all three games. None of the other teams have enough goals to be in contention for the wild card. Kentville's the favourite in our division, with two banked wins going into tonight's match with Berwick. The yellow division is anyone's call. I get a sinking feeling, sure that Stephen's tournament will end tonight.

As the evening games start up, Luke and I are dispatched to the other fields to keep an eye on the scores. After each report, Richard and Stephen trade the numbers back and forth like bookies. Even if Kentville loses with fewer than two goals, everything still depends on the yellow game. At last check, the underdogs were winning three to two, which would put them at two wins, ten goals and their opponents at two wins, nine. They'd both advance to the final.

We sit the games out. Kentville clinches the division and we file down the bleachers, grabbing our belongings and sprinting over to the other game. It's gone into sudden-death overtime, three–three. The cheers go up before we make it. We stop running, deflated.

When we see the scoreboard, however, the other team's won. That's three wins for them, one a piece for their opponents. Our team is in.

After the boys have gone to bed, I stand under the showerhead for a long time, watching my body turn pink with heat and scrubbing away the dead skin with an old, bleached cloth. It reminds me of our towels at home, which have the same sickly yellow burns from the peroxide in Stephen's acne cream. I picture Richard back home in a few days, sorting through the closet, piling my belongings to the side, catching stray hairpins in the corner of the shower stall. I picture the house without me in it.

We haven't thought this through, this untangling of our family life. As soon as I get dried off, I tap on Richard's door, hoping he's still awake. He's reading in bed, the same battered sci-fi paperback that I was looking through the other day. He nods, making space for me on the mattress and I sit propped up against the wall, hugging my knees. He still smells of soap from his shower, of the jasmine sandalwood bar he brought from home.

"Stephen's lucky he wasn't facing the other way," he says. "A hand-width up and he'd be in the hospital with testicles the size of cantaloupes."

"He played really well, didn't he?"

He lays the book down on the sleeping bag and stares at the cover, composing himself. "Do you have any idea how hard it was for me to keep it together?"

He rubs his forehead, straining to relax. There isn't a single square inch of our skin touching but I'm hyper-aware of our proximity. It's a struggle to keep our arms parallel, to not force an intersection. "The kicker is that I keep forgetting. That's what's making it so hard. Each time I look at you, I get this real visceral rush, this gut knowing—how much I love you. Then it's you and Bernie in a fifteen second porn clip. All I can do is fixate on the mechanics. Stupid, irrelevant details like wondering if you spent the whole time biting your lip."

"I'm worried that when you leave there won't be any way back."

He surprises me by putting his arm around me and very gently pulling my head into the crook of his neck, resting his chin on my temple. "Sometimes I can't decide if it would have been better not to know."

The room is dark except for a three-foot cone of yellow spilling out from the reading lamp. With the door closed, with no other witnesses, each breath is an apology. I'm sorry. I'm sorry. I'm sorry. The tears come but I don't reach up, nervous that any motion will break this closeness.

After it's over, the only thing we can talk about is minutiae, the minor incidents that have collected while we've been fighting. They're ripping up the streetcar tracks again. A squirrel was nesting in the crawlspace above the garage. We've got a trial subscription to *Wired*.

His article's fifteen hundred words over the limit and he's finding it a struggle to cut. I assure him that they'll edit it down, but he shakes his head. They want text that's ready to drag and drop into layout.

I talk to him about Clarence's farm. My current dilemma is which fertilizer configuration to suggest—composting the poultry litter first or sending it solid through the box spreader in the spring. The details are a way to work up to explaining why I won't be seeking another tenure-track position.

He sighs and slides his hands behind his head. "Did you think that's why I was with you?"

We've sunk horizontal into the bed, looking up at the ceiling like we're preparing for twin CT scans.

"Can't we start again?" I ask.

"What happened isn't going to change in a few days." Richard's face softens, his bottom lip falling away from the top, showing its full colour gradient of dusk to blush. "These plans—the farm, fixing the house—you're getting into something that's going to take months, at best. If I asked you to drive home with us on Monday, would you?"

"When we were in Toronto, I left my mother alone for a very long time."

Richard throws up his hands in frustration.

"What if I flew home every few weekends to be with you and the boys? Just until this is all over."

"What's happening between us, what's happening with our family—this is a crisis. It's not something that can be fixed with every other weekend." He catches himself raising his voice and swallows hard before continuing. "Every other weekend is what happens after a divorce."

The cell rings first thing in the morning as I'm hunting down Luke's headphones.

"Good news."

Marc. I'd been meaning to phone to thank him for coming over.

"I've gotten word from the department that I can make you a formal offer—an adjunct position for the winter term. Earth Science 415, special topics in agroecology."

January? I don't want to still be here by January.

The figure's only enough to cover utilities and a big-ticket appliance or two. It's much less than what I'd have made teaching Prescott's courses. Still, if Richard and I can't reconcile, I'm going to need money. I get a vision of myself asking Linda if she can pull some strings for me at the Superstore, imagine working as a cashier in the bakery while Ray commiserates about going through the divorce.

I only give a conditional acceptance, but Marc reacts like he's signing a star quarterback for the playoffs. "We'll have you over to celebrate—Richard and the boys'll be around for another week or so?"

"Stephen's got the soccer tournament today and then they're heading back tomorrow." I try to keep my voice calm and steady, not wanting to go into the separation. "School will be starting. I'm staying on to look after my mother."

"Come by whenever you need company. Do you play three-handed euchre?" he asks, genial as ever. "Margie's keen on three-handed euchre."

Luke's the only one who tries to talk on the drive over.

"Do you get a medal if you win?"

"It's not the Olympics."

Luke sticks his tongue out at his brother then asks me the same question.

"I don't know. Maybe a trophy?"

"Is the other team good?"

Stephen shrugs.

Richard makes eye contact with Luke in the rear-view. We haven't spoken all morning except through the kids. "No one's as good as your brother."

"Max is good too."

"Yes," Richard says. "Max's good too."

We're up first against Yarmouth, at the same time as the other semifinal. Then it's the consolation match at two and the final at four. There's still a fair crowd of parents and supporters out in the stands but it's going to be harder to avoid Bernie. We run into Linda right away—she's laying out a line of jackets and folded towels on the bleachers. She catches me looking at them. "I don't know about you, but my butt just about fell off yesterday. You want one?"

"That's okay," I stammer. "We'll probably sit farther up."

Richard stays ten feet back with the boys.

"Thanks, though."

Linda doesn't make a big deal about it, just goes back to setting up. Lisa, however, wants Luke to sit with her. Luke's already drifted over to his friend and the two of them take turns catapulting off the first bleacher.

"Just leave him," Linda says. "It's no trouble."

Richard climbs to the top row. Without Luke between us, there's no need to keep up the pretence, so we fall silent, the excitement of yesterday gone.

Today's game is more formal—the ref's older and is dressed in traditional black shirt and shorts, knee-high socks topped with bold black and white bands. The friction between Richard and me eases slightly as the teams line up in single file and someone calls out the boys' names over the PA system. I can't help beaming when "Stephen Bascom, Number 22" crackles out of the speakers.

The other team's centre-forward is a very tall, shaggy haired kid who bowls right past Max. He dribbles ten feet ahead then passes to another player who's less cocksure but a faster runner. This team's better oiled than our boys, the players more aware of their teammates' positions.

Stephen manages to pry the ball away from an advancing player, but a little wiry kid lunges in from the side, slicing his leg in so closely that it catches Stephen off guard, and he has to hop to keep his balance. That's all it takes for the kid to tap the ball off to his teammate.

"Is that allowed?" I ask.

"He made contact with the ball, not Stephen."

"But it was a trip."

Richard shakes his head. "Only if he'd aimed for Stephen's legs. Haven't you seen enough FIFA games to know?"

"I've always been with the cousins in the kitchen." Of the four World Cup viewing parties that Terrence has hosted since Richard and I have been together, I've always managed to avoid watching the game by helping to cook the dumplings, curries and other food that we feast on afterwards.

"Bumping's okay but you can't cause bodily injury. That's why they gave Zidane the red card." He sees the blank look on my face. "You remember the head-butt, don't you? From the final?"

"We were out here already."

"Didn't you see it on the news? What about the foot stop in '98?"

"In '98 your auntie was teaching me to make currant rolls."

The second half isn't much different from the first. Yarmouth has an easy time keeping the ball in our end. Time after time, our goalie has to throw himself on the ball and punt it out. It looks like it should crush the air out of him, the way he slams his body down. It's only by corralling all our players into defence that the regular game time elapses without any goals scored.

Richard's as nervous as the boys as it goes into the second five-minute overtime. He unclasps his watch and lays it on his knee, counting down the time and mouthing plays. He taps on the watch face as the whistle blows. "Penalty kicks."

While the coach is deciding which five to put in, our keeper doesn't stop moving, alternating between deep knee stretches and slow motion jumping jacks. If his face didn't look so grim, I'd think he was leading the crowd in a cheer. *Give me an A*. It's not fair to either goalie that the game comes down to them.

On Yarmouth's team, it's the shaggy-headed kid up first. He makes the goal look effortless. Our keeper shakes his hair free and repositions his headband, then claps a few times, preparing for the next attempt.

Max is up first for our team. He shoots on a wide angle towards the upper right of the goal post. From where we're sitting it looks good, but Yarmouth's keeper deflects it with his glove. The next three shots are misses—two for them, one for us. We just need one goal to stay in the game.

Our next player sinks it right to the back of the net and we all cheer. One all. As the fourth Yarmouth player steps up, Stephen waits his turn at the side, rolling a ball under his left cleat.

Richard stares straight ahead, hands clenched. Stephen takes his time jogging into position. He leans to the right, preparing to side-foot it, then quickly shifts to his left and slams the ball in the opposite direction. The keeper lunges, misses. Yarmouth fails to catch us on their last attempt.

Everyone on our side of the bleachers cheers. All around us, parents are hugging and turning to the people next to them. Richard and I stay planted in our separate celebration.

We meet Stephen a few feet away from where Max is standing with Linda and Bernie. Richard grabs Stephen close and pats his back, but then releases him to me. "You were amazing," I say, holding him tight. "You were amazing." Stephen's embarrassed by the praise, but he grins totally unselfconscious, the sweat pouring down his hairline.

Richard walks straight over to shake Max's hand. "You did great out there."

Max hasn't seen Richard since the fight and isn't sure how to act. "I missed that shot."

"No, you nailed the rest of the game. I saw you yesterday too. Great job."

They're heading over to New Minas for lunch and Max wants to know if Stephen can come with them. Once Luke hears this, he wants to go as well.

"You can all come," Linda says.

Richard accepts before I can decline. "It will be good for the boys," he whispers, but I can hear the grind in his voice.

We're seated in the back of the restaurant, at the only table where we can squeeze my mother's wheelchair in comfortably. We've picked her up to join us for the final game and she's happy to have this visit with Linda. I take one of the table ends and Richard sits to my right so he doesn't have to stare at Bernie, who's across from me. The kids are a buffer in between.

There's an easy business at first, deciding what we want to order—how many pizzas, what toppings, do we need any salads. When the waitress comes, we list off a vast quantity of food.

"How do you want me to divide up the bill?" she asks, glancing back and forth between me and Bernie, unsure which kids belong to whom. She's probably still in high school, her ponytail secured by one of those elastics with bits of fake hair poking out.

As soon as she leaves, Bernie leans towards Max. "What do you think of her?"

Max breaks out in bright red splotches.

"He likes her," Luke says, smiling at Bernie for approval. "She's going to be Max's girlfriend."

Lisa finds this equally funny and starts to join in, the two of them repeating it until Stephen kicks Luke under the table. Bernie raises his eyebrows up and down and pokes Max. I cringe at the pantomime. Just sitting through the meal is going to be hard enough for Richard, he doesn't need to watch Bernie hamming it up.

I raise my voice to interrupt them. "Max, how far did you guys get in the tournament last year?"

"We only got to play the first day."

"Who won?"

"Dartmouth. They always win."

"Are you going to play soccer next year, Lisa?"

She nods. "I want to do gymnastics too."

"As long as you don't want to play hockey," Linda says. "That's the one bankrupts you."

The conversation soon breaks down the middle of the table, with Richard and the kids on one side and Bernie, Linda and my mother on the other. It's hard not to eavesdrop as my mother asks question after question about the wedding. Lisa is going to be their flower girl; Jason is best man; and Gail's maid of honour. Red flowers if it's a winter wedding, pink if it's summer. Reception at either the King's Arms or Clarence and Irene's. Linda's got a gentle touch with my mother, just like my father did. She knows when to needle her to keep talking.

We have more pizza than mouths. The cheese slides off the tomato base and oil pools in the pepperoni slices.

Richard warns Stephen not to eat too much.

"Is it like swimming?" Max asks.

It's a question that Richard likes answering. It launches them into a discussion about the origins of old wives' tales. For a brief few minutes, the meal feels comfortable.

When the waitress brings the bills, she's made a mistake and put one of our orders on Bernie's. Richard asks her to bring a new set of cheques.

"It's fine," Bernie says. "May as well just pay it."

"No, I'll give you the cash," Richard insists. The rest of us clam up, nervous.

The two of them lock eyes and I expect Richard to push the issue. Instead, he leans back in his chair and puts his arm around Stephen. "Thanks then."

"Thanks," I repeat.

Now that we've eaten together, it would be strange to sit apart for the game, especially with my mother there. We find her a folding chair so she can have a break from the wheelchair and Linda steadies the seat while I help my mother make the transfer. For the first time, she doesn't put up a fuss with the assistance.

Stephen favours his left leg as he warms up. He's not limping exactly, but he must have hurt his ankle. The coach notices too but Stephen refuses to sit down. He cycles through all the same drills as the rest of the players. Still, every so often I catch him shaking his leg, trying to loosen the joint.

"Who are they playing?" I ask Richard. The other semi-final finished after we left and I can't read the scoreboard.

"Dartmouth."

Even though they're undefeated three years running, we're still hoping for a win after the excitement of the morning's game. We get steamrollered, five–nothing.

I expect the boys to be released, but there's an end-of-tournament assembly. All four final teams line up on the pitch and an official struts out to meet them, followed by three assistants. Someone whispers that he's the MLA. Starting with the fourth place team, he shakes each player's hand and hangs a medal around their neck. As he reaches the third place team, music blares over the speakers, a bombastic classical score that's being butchered by the scratchy PA. In the crowd, a kid howls like Chewbacca at the end of *Star Wars*.

After the medals are distributed, the MLA invites the coaches up to present the MVP awards. I'm not surprised when the shaggy-haired centre forward is called up by the Yarmouth coach. He accepts his trophy and stands there for a minute while the photographer snaps him shaking hands with the officials.

"Do you think?" I ask Richard.

He shakes his head. "Max's been on the team longer."

He's right—Stephen didn't even play the whole season.

Our coach gives the usual speech about how it was a strong team, how difficult it was to pick just one player. "This year," he says, looking out over the line of expectant thirteen-year-olds, "the Canning MVP is going to most valuable pair. Max McInnes and Stephen Bascom, come on up."

My body launches into ecstatic choreography, drum-rolling my arms and jerking my legs into hop-kicks. Richard hoists Luke onto his shoulders, the two of them screaming "MVP, MVP." Bernie's already out on the field snapping pictures. Linda's hugging everyone. Even my mother's beaming, clapping her hand against her leg.

I'm so happy for them I start to cry, laughing as I wipe away the tears. By the time Stephen reaches us, Richard looks close to tears himself.

"See," Luke says, "it was like the Olympics."

Stephen loops the medal over his brother's neck.

We should be getting back so the boys can pack for tomorrow. As I gather our stuff together, Linda walks over with the trophy. "There's only one."

Stephen doesn't care. He's already said Max can hang onto it.

"They can share," she insists. She promises to bring over a set of the pictures from Bernie's camera. "I can print them off at the Superstore, no problem."

When they say goodbye, Luke and Lisa don't really know what to do. Stephen and Max bump fists and Stephen promises to talk to him soon on IM. It doesn't take long. Then we're left standing there, awkward. Linda pulls me into a hug and tells me to call her if I need anything. She smells like apricot lip gloss.

As I grip the handlebars on my mother's wheelchair, Bernie looks at me sidelong. It makes him seem wounded, and I get that same pang I got years ago, surprising him in the cab of the truck. I wave goodbye to avoid any physical contact. "See you soon."

"Yep," he says. "See you."

Richard leads the charge when we get in, reminding the boys to check if they've left anything in the bathroom, bedroom, living room. I busy myself making dinner, frying onions on the new electric pan. Stephen thuds downstairs. "Dad wants to know if you have a tensor bandage."

I head up to the linen cupboard to see if there are any left and if they're usable. Packed away at the back shelf, I find two old ones. Despite the fire, they still smell of sweat and elastic. We go into the bedroom and I get Stephen to sit on the mattress and prop his leg up on my lap. I pull off his sock and find the ankle's quite swollen. I prod different spots to see what hurts. It's sore, but he's still got a lot of extension and can point and flex without wincing.

"Did it hurt the whole game?"

"No."

"Was it when the kid tripped you?"

Stephen looks up at me as if he's nervous he's going to get in trouble. Richard comes in with a plastic bag and packs Stephen's sneakers in them. "Your ankle's worse than a pregnant woman's," he says.

"I'm impressed you kept playing on it." I hold the end of the tensor with my thumb and start winding it around the arch. "This too tight?"

Stephen shakes his head.

"The games were pretty exciting this weekend."

"You don't have to lie," he says, poking at another bruise on his leg. "I know you don't like soccer."

"I really enjoyed watching you play."

Richard looks over my shoulder at the bandage. "Your mom was ready to ream the ref out for calling offside in that second game. If I hadn't told her that he had a bad angle, she'd have gotten the team a red card."

Stephen laughs, despite himself.

There's only one hook for the bandage—the other one must have gone missing years ago. I rummage through the bedside drawer for a safety pin and carefully thread it through instead. "Keep your foot on the dashboard for the drive."

I say it to Stephen, but it's Richard who nods.

It hasn't seemed real until now. They'll drive away tomorrow and I'll stay behind. I wish there was something profound I could say, something to bind us all together as a family. Nothing comes. Richard works right up until we eat and by then we're all so tired that we scarf down the eggs, not paying attention.

The boys want to talk to their grandfather before going to bed. Richard agrees on the condition they keep it short—he's waking them up at six-thirty to get on the road by eight. While the boys chat, Richard and I wait downstairs on opposite sides of the couch, each pretending to flip through a newspaper. Terrence and I haven't spoken since the karaoke fight and I'm not sure how much Richard's told him. I lower my paper to ask, only able to get out the words, "Does Terrence?" before my throat constricts.

Yes, Terrence knows.

After a few minutes, Stephen calls down that they're ready for bed. I get up to tuck him in, but Luke's still on the phone. He asks his grandfather if he'd like to say goodnight to me too. My heart's thudding as he holds his arm out for me to take the receiver. I make a quick exit to my mother's room before answering, shutting the door and sinking down to the floor.

It's difficult to get out a simple hello. Everything's gone numb except for the parts of my body touching the phone— the folds of my ear pinched against the hard plastic, the slight vibration of speech through the receiver, my shoulder pinning the mouthpiece to my chin.

"Stephen tells me you're staying."

I mumble out an apology for the way Luke set the conversation up.

We're quiet for a long time. There's nothing that I can think of to say to him. I've never felt more sick over something I've done.

"I'd noticed that things have been strained between the two of you all summer," Terrence says. "It's a difficult position. As a father, I'm angry. I'm very sad for my family." He pauses to take a swallow of something and I get a picture of him sipping a Carib by his condo window, the Kensington hipsters drinking on the patio across the street. "But a marriage is its own ecosystem. It's hard for someone looking in to understand."

In the background, there's music playing—an opera I can't place. I'm concentrating so hard on it, hoping it'll carry me through this moment, that at first I don't realize that my crying is audible. My breath escapes in short gasps.

"Richard doesn't know this and I'm not planning on telling him," Terrence says. "When he was in college, there was a woman I worked with, a young teacher—twenty-four, twenty-five. She was born here, but her parents had come over from St. Lucia. It lasted the better part of the school year until her father found out. One night, he and his friends jumped me outside the school. I had to explain to Evelyn why I wouldn't be pressing charges."

He takes another sip of his beer. In the other room, I can hear Richard saying goodnight to the boys.

I ask Terrence why it happened.

"Things had gone flat—there was tension about money." He sighs as if hashing out an old excuse. "But mostly, it didn't feel like I was doing it to Evelyn. That insight didn't come until afterwards. In the end, I had to convince her that what happened was the anomaly, not the pattern."

"Will Richard?"

"I don't know," Terrence says, his voice falling. "I hope so."

This is what it would be like, I think, to still have a father. This is what it's like.

When I hang up, the boys are asleep. I kiss them goodnight anyway because I'm not sure when I'll get to do that again. For a long time I sit watching them, the way I did when they were babies.

I think about my mother, alone in her new home. After all these years, it seems impossible that I was once inside her, that she carried me for nine months just as I carried the boys. It makes me think about the umbilical cord that attaches mother to child, child to mother. It makes me question in which direction the bond is stronger. Thirty years from now, I'm not convinced that Stephen and Luke would choose to stay with me. I'm not convinced I'd want them to.

When a soil is removed from its environment and lands as effluvium or alluvium, it becomes part of the new soil. Subjected to new weathering and secondary processes, it slowly becomes unrecognizable from the original. That's why it wouldn't have worked with Bernie, why I'll never again be my mother's one and only. I made my choice a long time ago and it's too late to change my mind.

I hover outside Richard's closed door, the light long since turned out, straining for any indication he's still awake. Nothing. Downstairs, his laptop case is propped against the door, ready for tomorrow. I open it up and plug it in. At first I consider typing him a letter, using Terrence's words to plead my case. Then I open the file with his article, save as copy, and cut it down to the guideline.

The sound of water in the pipes wakes me up. It's already seven-thirty and Richard's busy organizing the exodus, trying to wrangle the boys and their belongings. Catching him alone is going to be difficult. I go back downstairs, still in my pajamas, and start mixing up pancake batter. It's from a box, just add water, but it's the closest I can get to giving them a send-off.

I thought we'd all sit down together, but in the end we eat in shifts. I'm the only constant in the kitchen, doling out pancakes from the fry pan. Richard eats his leaning up against the wall while the boys are doing a last sweep through the house.

He forces a grin before I can speak. "At least you'll get the bed tonight."

"Will you call me when you get in? Just to let me know you arrived safely?"

He's eating in massive bites, spearing his fork through three layers of pancake, shovelling it in. "I'll probably pick up another cell so you can call the boys or they can call you when they want."

"Can't I call the house?"

"We'll figure it out later."

He's dangerously close to finishing his food, the window for conversation closing.

"Can I make you another?"

"No." He rests his fork on his plate and pats his belly. "This is plenty."

Even if Terrence is right, Richard doesn't want to talk now.

I tell him that I love him but Luke bounds in with his suitcase, almost knocking his father over. All of Richard's attention switches to our youngest.

Upstairs, I check on Stephen's ankle and re-bandage the tensor. "You can get some ice on it tonight from the motel."

"It's fine, Mom."

"Get your Dad to check on it, just in case."

"It's fine."

At ten o'clock Richard grabs the last bag from the house. The boys stand outside by the car and wait for his okay. The time has gotten away on me. I'm not sure what I expected— tears from Luke, maybe. There's nothing. The boys each give me a hug. Richard puts his hand briefly on my shoulder. "We might call tonight, depending on cell service in Quebec."

It feels less like our family is falling apart than that they're leaving for a day trip to Halifax. Richard backs the car out of the driveway and the three of them wave when they reach the road. I wave. They wave. The car lurches forward, past the tree break and out of sight.

* * *

I start with the bathroom. The chalk blue's pretty, but the paint bubbles up in sections and it takes a while to figure out how to apply it evenly. I forget to put down a tarp and have to pause several times to wipe a drip off the tub. As I work, I keep listening for the thud of Stephen's soccer ball against the outside wall. It feels like he and Luke are going to rush in at any moment, bickering as usual, wanting me to mediate. Instead, the house stays quiet, the only sounds coming from the squeak of the paint roller and the jiggle of the ladder. There are only enough trays to work with one colour at a time. I finish the bathroom, but there's no point washing up because it'll need a second coat.

I look over my notes for Clarence, but I'm going to need a computer before I can get much further. I make a note on the back of my hand to ask Richard to ship out my laptop. There are a few changes Clarence could implement as soon as next spring, but the bigger ones will require significant investment. Until this year's harvest receipts come in, we're not going to know if he can raise that kind of capital. The smartest thing to do would be to twin the proposal with the Acadia course, get the students involved as a pilot project.

There's nothing else I can get started on around the house without outside help. There's nothing I couldn't be doing at a distance.

* * *

I visit my mother in the late afternoon, but Mary's there with another friend from the co-op. They're watching reruns of *Wheel of Fourtune* and *Jeopardy!* The answers to the final puzzles are "Spelling Bee Hive" and "What is the Chrysler Building?" My mother and I barely speak.

I've bought a cheap microwave and I heat up a Jamaican patty for dinner because I don't feel like cooking. The pastry goes soggy in the microwave and a tongue of ground beef and oil spills out from the seam. I set it down on the milk crate and grab a rag to wipe up the splatter in the oven. In the end I don't feel like eating.

The phone only rings once.

It's Irene, calling to invite me to Linda's bridal shower.

*   *   *

First thing in the morning, I go to Evangeline Beach because I have to get out of the house. It's drizzling as I drive over the bridge from Port Williams and it's hard to tell the grey of the clouds from the grey of the water. The campground is quiet except for a few gulls cawing and a thumping sound in the distance like a wooden spoon in a metal bowl. There aren't any other cars in the visitor lot.

I walk back through the forest trail that Bernie and I walked down years ago. I sneak past a cottage where the path ends and scurry down to the beach. The shore isn't private, but I don't want to have to talk to an angry property owner about using his access point. The tide is going out and there's still a slick over the sand. Water pools in my footprints. I wander out towards the red cliffs—pocked sandstone that will one day be the clay beach. There are bird nests in the tops, fist-sized cubbyholes.

I wonder where the boys are now. I check my watch again—seven-twenty. They've been gone eighteen hours. They didn't call last night so Richard might have driven straight through, which would put them approaching Cornwall—four more hours to go. More likely, he stopped late, probably before Montreal. It's possible that they didn't have phone reception. I try not to think of the other, darker possibility that my family is functioning just fine without me. The boys have been on sleep-overs, but never even to summer camp. In ten hours, this will be the longest we've ever been apart.

All over the beach, little bubbles are sprouting in the surface from the tiny mud shrimp that burrow in the sand. The sand-pipers have begun to flock, soaring over and landing on the beach to feed. They walk without knees, their funny bodies like the molecule models Stephen and I used to make for science fair, Styrofoam globes on pipe cleaner legs. They eat noisily, chattering and scuttling across the beach like it's some merry all-you-can-eat buffet. I'd like to take a picture to send to the boys but I don't have my camera.

The birds lift off, hundreds of them rising up on some unknown cue, the whole group swarming above me. In flight, the flock squishes and stretches, fans out across the water then curves back over the waves. It's hard to fathom how so many separate beings can operate as one, their movements so per-fectly synchronized that there's an audible snap as they switch directions, crisp as a flag in the wind.

That's how we should be, I realize—me, Richard, the boys. That's how we're meant to move through the world—seamless and attached, buoyed and cresting on the same current.

If I flew out today, we would arrive home at the same time.

Acknowledgments

This book would not be in your hands without the support of the following people.

Brianna Brash-Nyberg, Michael Christie, Jamella Hagen, Kellee Ngan, Ria Voros, Sheryda Warrener, Michael Wheeler and the rest of my cohort at UBC—you set the bar so high with your own talent that you push me to be a better writer. Thanks to the faculty at UBC, especially Keith Maillard and Linda Svendsen. And to others who've helped along the way: Iris Turcott, Bonnie Green, Emil Sher, Kim Jernigan, Cady Allen, Megan McDowell and Amy Stuart. Huge thanks for the support of my lifelong friends Catherine Livingstone and Lisa Harrison.

Since I have no background in soil science or medicine, I had to ask a lot of nosy questions to a lot of busy people. Thank you to Joanna Bernat and Dr. Shannon Venance for medical advice; Dr. Maja Krzic for letting me sit in on her soil science lectures; Fire Captains Gabe Roder, Rick Meisner, Tim MacLeod and James Wheeler; Renata Ali for her insight into Trini culture; and to Jon Regan for all those drives through Canning.

Thank you to Dan Wells and the team at Biblioasis for the care you've put into publishing this book, and to John Metcalf for his early enthusiasm and thoughtful edits.

My very deepest love and thanks to both the Tacon and Lopez families. Special thanks to my parents for their longstanding belief in my writing and to my brother Carl and sister-in-law Lyn, whose talents always inspire me. I'm grateful for my grandmother's firm belief in the importance of libraries and for both families' enthusiasm for reading.

Finally, to Julio. For sharing the highs and lows, for all the laughter over the past 9 years, for the depth of your love, this book is as much yours as it is mine.

ERIN SAMUELL

Claire Tacon's writing has been short-listed for the Bronwen Wallace Award, the CBC Literary Awards and the Playboy College Fiction Contest, and has appeared in *The New Quarterly*, *sub-TERRAIN* and *Room*. She has an MFA in Creative Writing from the University of British Columbia, is a past fiction editor of PRISM international, and the winner of the 2010 Metcalf-Rooke Award. *In the Field* is her first novel.